Stolen Destiny

STOLEN DESTINY

Tormented by his past, former police officer Varek Leale merely exists now since he lost his wife and daughter, barely alive in Nil when the Aeveren Council summons him to catch a serial murderer in New Hope, New York. Little does he know in exchange for his freedom, he'll be given a gift he was sure he'd never have again in his life, but if he isn't careful, it may slip right through his hands.

Callia Reynolds has spent seven of her fifty Aeveren lifetimes without a destined one and wants nothing more than the happiness of love she sees all around her, but she's resigned herself to yet another lifetime alone. Her world will be turned upside down by the killings of her fellow Aeveren and the two men fate brings to her.

In the Aeveren world, few are more powerful than Amon Kalins. Born with his powers, he can travel through time and manipulate it like no other of his kind. But with great power comes temptation, and when Amon has the chance to use his gifts for good to help catch the New Hope serial killer, the desire to have what he shouldn't may prove his undoing for while Varek possesses no powers, he isn't going to let anyone take away his second chance at happiness.

Not even one of the most powerful beings in the Aeveren world.

STOLEN DESTINY

(DESTINED ONES #1)

K.M. SCOTT

WRITING AS GABRIELLE BISSET

CHAPTER ONE

N IL. AEVEREN PRISON AND WORK camp. But for anyone who'd ever been sentenced to even a year in Nil, it was hell.

Varek Leale stood against a stone wall in the yard and looked up at the tiny glimmer of light barely piercing the grey that forever bathed every part of Nil. Each day of his time here had been grey, and any sunlight was a welcome change. Warmth and light were strangers to Nil, even to the upper regions where he stood now. Deep below in the cells there was nothing but darkness. Like a medieval prison, each level had long corridors of cells on one side, each looking out into the shadows of nothing that seemed to go on forever, the only light flickering from the small fixtures positioned outside of each cell not for the prisoners' benefit but for the guards'.

The yard was like any other prison yard but without the barbed wire fence. No one left without consent, so no barbed wire was necessary. Surrounded by stone walls, the area was designed like a place where animals were herded to before slaughter. Concrete lined the ground, adding to the hardness of the place. Nothing grew here, even if the sun did manage to reach this place.

Anger coiled inside Varek like a snake waiting to strike as he watched the vicious scene unfold in front of him. Time and again in his existence in Nil he'd seen the weak as they were preyed upon, as he'd been in his first days there. He'd survived, but not without becoming like the predators he now watched from the side of the work camp yard. But he still had something left of what he'd been before being left to rot for lifetimes in this hell hole, something that made his gut clench when he watched prisoners attack the new inmates who were unable to defend themselves, no matter how violent they'd been in the outside world. He wasn't completely lost to the savagery that the place brought out in them.

Varek eyed the young, blond prisoner they planned on attacking. *He should know better by now than to let himself be found alone,* he thought callously. But if his first reaction had been apathy, it quickly gave way to a need to defend a soul he saw couldn't do so himself. He moved toward them after the fourth fist hit the prisoner, and in seconds he had his hands on the next attacker, restraining his arm in a twist hold behind his back.

"Get the fuck off me!" the man bellowed as he struggled to turn around to see who had grabbed him.

Varek remained silent, forcing his forearm further up toward his neck as he pushed him down toward the ground. Never taking his eyes off the rest of the gang around him, he subdued the man quickly amid his shrieks of pain. The prisoner's friends instinctively took a step back as they watched.

"You're gonna break my fucking arm, motherfucker!"

Looking around for a guard, Varek saw he was free to impose his own brand of punishment on the man who kneeled in front of him with his arm twisted behind him. It would be nothing to snap his arm or any other of the smaller man's body parts, but that would make him truly like them.

"Drake, I warned you about this last week," he said in a deep, flat tone.

"What the fuck do you care?" Drake wailed. "You know how it is. You're either one of us or one of them in here. Why do you act like their fucking guardian angel?"

Varek pushed the man's wrist down against the back of his neck as Drake let out another howl of pain. In front of him stood the blond prisoner who watched in horror as if waiting for Varek to take over where the other men had left off. Just for a moment, his eyes met the blond's blue eyes, and in them Varek saw the fear he knew his own eyes had held all those days ago. As Varek got lost for just a moment in the thought of how much he'd changed since his first days in Nil, his focus slipped from the others around him, and in seconds he himself was under attack. With the first blow to his face, he released Drake's arm and fell to the ground.

Although he'd been surprised, his survival instinct kicked in, and he swung violently at the nearest body. Again and again, his fists savagely battered the men's faces, leaving them bloody and swollen. His own head dripped with blood from the beating, but he was relentless in defending himself and the young prisoner. It didn't take long for the guards to decide they'd been entertained enough, and three of them pulled Varek off the last of the men.

He said nothing as they led him away, the young prisoner in tow, as Drake and his gang hollered words of bravado of the recently defeated. He knew what would happen next. The punishment for any kind of misbehavior in Nil was always painful, but he'd be spared the brand for this act of defending another. This day he'd spend in solitary, but to Varek, the justification was clear. He couldn't save all of them, but the beating and the punishment was worth it if the blond knew there was still good left in some of the men he found in Nil.

THE NEW HOPE ORPHANAGE SUFFERED from overcrowding, a fact obvious to the dozens of children who resided there. Aeveren took excellent care of orphans, and New Hope Orphanage was no different, but recent events in New Hope, New York had caused the number of children who needed a place to live to dramatically rise in the last four months alone. Five Aeveren families had been torn apart by a serial killer targeting parents, and fourteen resulting orphans had found care at the orphanage, with five others being luckier and having extended family to take them in.

To Aeveren, every other member of the race was considered like family, and the bond between Aeveren was strong. As with all races, though, there were those who chose a destructive path, not only to themselves but to the entire race, and disregarded the laws and customs of Aeveren. For those souls, future lifetimes promised nothing but time in Nil, whether it was imprisonment for one lifetime or ten or eternity. Aeveren justice would be swift and severe when the murderer was caught.

New Hope's humans had been shocked by the murders, but the targets were all Aeveren. Since most humans in New Hope, and everywhere else for that matter, didn't even know Aeveren existed, the townspeople didn't know they were as safe as they'd ever been. Aeveren in New Hope understood all too well the danger they faced with a murderer in their midst, though.

Callia Reynolds's heart went out to the children at New Hope Orphanage. She had lost her parents in a car accident when she was just six but had been fortunate to have her grandmother to take care of her. But she knew the pain of losing both parents and understood the children she spent time with at the orphanage better than anyone else.

She volunteered during the week, helping them with their studies and running the library the orphanage had on site after working at her job as a veterinarian tech. Sometimes she brought animals people left for others to adopt at the vet's to visit with the children. They loved the visits and repeatedly asked Callia to bring more kittens, bunnies, and hamsters.

As she walked toward the orphanage, Callia made sure to be careful on this dark February afternoon. Winter afternoons slipped into night so early, and no one was really safe while there was a murderer on the loose, even if he or she seemed to be only preying upon parents.

The big, grey stone building that housed the orphanage came into her view. In a small town like New Hope, such a building stood out. It had a presence that made it seem like the town had been built around it. It sat at the end of First Street, almost like a final destination of sorts. Behind it stretched woods that seemed like an odd fit in the town. During spring and summer months, the area provided the children additional space to explore outside the sizeable grounds that surrounded the orphanage, but in the fall and winter the wooded area seemed like a specter that lay frighteningly beyond the grounds.

It was five-thirty when Callia reached the steps of the orphanage, and she hurried up them to escape the frigid weather. Snow had begun to fall at midafternoon, and it was beginning to accumulate on the grass and roads now. Callia planned to visit the children until a little after seven and then take the walk to her apartment eight blocks away.

As she entered the building, she was ambushed by children calling her name, thrilled to see her.

"Callia! We thought you might not come to see us tonight because of the snow!" the children yelled.

"Are you kidding? Wild horses couldn't keep me from my favorite people on the whole Earth," she said with a smile as she hung up her coat on a hook near the front door and knocked the snow from the ridges on the bottom of her boots.

"When will you be able to bring the animals again?" a little girl with strawberry blond hair and big green eyes asked as she tugged at the bottom of Callia's wool sweater.

"I think we may have to wait until it's a little warmer, honey. But I promise I will bring them as soon as I can." She took the girl's tiny hand in hers and began to lead the children toward the library.

"Who needs help with their homework?" she asked of the crowd around her. Every child shot a hand up in the air. It was going to be a busy night.

More than two and a half hours later, Callia stood at the front door dressing for the cold walk home. As she put her coat and gloves on, one of the orphanage's administrators came out of her office.

"Callia, you stayed late again?" Jessica Anders asked.

"You know how it is. I can't say no to them."

"Dear, you know we love what you do, but when do you spend time doing things young women do?"

Callia knew where she was going with this, so she just smiled and shrugged.

"You might meet someone if you spent just a few hours out."

"Good night, Jessica," Callia said with a grin.

The walk home was cold and crunchy, her boots chewing up the snow with each step. She walked quickly, her shoulders up near her ears, and thought about Jessica's idea of meeting someone. Callia knew that Aeveren were biologically drawn to their mates, and once an Aeveren met their destined one, their true love, they would be theirs in future lifetimes until it was time to move on. She was in her seventh lifetime and had never had a true love. Each lifetime she waited and hoped as others around her met their destinies, but each time she ended up alone. She seemed particularly alone in this lifetime, unlike in her previous six, because she was an only child and had lost her parents so early. Sometimes she wondered if something was wrong with her. She was pretty, she believed, with long chestnut brown hair and hazel eyes, but she still wondered why she remained alone.

She made it home safely and curled up on her living room couch in front of the fireplace with a steaming cup of tea, still thinking about when she would meet "him," the one for her.

IN A PLACE FAR AWAY from New Hope, Varek Leale stood in wrist shackles and leg irons in front of the Aeveren Council in Nil. His jet black hair was cut close to his scalp, and his eyes, dark as pitch, stared straight ahead. He was dressed as a prisoner, with black work pants and a black T-shirt that showed the effect of three lifetimes in prison on his now muscular body.

He watched the Council members speak to one another, not knowing why he had been summoned to appear in front of them as there was no chance for parole from Nil before his full sentence was served. After a few minutes, the head of the Council turned to him and spoke.

"Mr. Leale, you are being released early from your imprisonment. You will be returning to the lifetime you left as you are right now with no rebirth. You will assist this Council in capturing a murderer. Failure to do so will result in eternity in Nil, and not just the work camp. Do you understand?"

Varek understood just fine. Whatever reason he was being released from the hell of the past three lifetimes didn't matter. He was being released. That's all that mattered to him. But he was curious why he'd been chosen.

"Why me?"

"Because you're expendable. We don't want to take a free Aeveren from his duties on the outside when we can use you."

"Where am I being sent?"

He was pretty sure he could handle himself virtually anywhere after the three lifetimes he'd just spent, but he didn't want to be dropped into the Middle East or in the middle of somewhere equally as fucked-up without some serious firepower, which he was fairly sure the Council wasn't going to supply.

"New Hope, New York."

Varek had no idea where that was and didn't care. He'd be back home in the States and free.

"Take care of the gifts we've given you. Your future will be yours if you are successful in catching this murderer."

Gifts? he thought. *What else are they giving me?*

Before he had a chance to even form the words, he was in New Hope in the middle of a snowstorm with just his work camp clothes on but thankfully without the shackles and leg irons. Immediately freezing, he jammed his hands into his pockets and found a wad of money in the right one.

Another gift. Thanks, guys. At least I won't freeze to death tonight.

Feeling something behind him, he reached around and pulled out a gun from the back of his pants.

"Nice gift," he mumbled.

He looked up and down First Street for anywhere to spend the night. The snow fell harder as he made his way to the only motel in New Hope, the Town Inn. The snow turned to water on his warm skin and the cold air stung as it entered his nose. It had been so long since he'd felt any sensations other than painful ones that even these felt good. They meant he was in the land of the living again.

After convincing the clerk at the Town Inn to give him a room, despite the fact that the man thought he was a homeless person since he had no coat in the middle of winter, Varek lay down on the bed in Room 14 and let his body rejoice in the feel of the mattress against his back. Lifetimes sleeping on a stone floor in a cell slowly slipped away as his body celebrated the newfound freedom. Tomorrow he'd think about the murderer. Tonight he'd just enjoy the feeling of life again.

CALLIA AWOKE IN THE MIDDLE of the night and sat upright in bed. A feeling she had never experienced in any lifetime washed over her and alarmed her. Her skin burned like it was on fire and her head spun. She stumbled out of bed and walked drowsily to the bathroom. As she stood looking at her reflection in the mirror, she wondered if she had caught the flu. *Whatever this is*, Callia thought, *I definitely don't feel okay.*

Back in bed, she tried to get back to sleep but only tossed and turned. She began to feel like she was hallucinating and swore she heard someone say something to her in her mind. Over and over she heard the same words but wasn't able to make them out. On the verge of tears, she silently asked her parents to keep her safe and help her get well, as she had done ever since she was a small child and was scared. Moments later, as she quietly lay in bed watching the snow fall outside her window, she heard the voice again, but this time she understood the words clearly.

"Go to him. He is here."

VAREK FELT ILL AS HE lay in his bed in the Town Inn, but he knew exactly what it meant the moment the feeling came over him.

No. Not this. Not now. The words echoed in his head over and over.

He couldn't believe he was going to have to go through this again. Any chance of being with a destined one had been stripped from him when he was convicted and sent to Nil. He wondered why they would do this to him again. He cursed them for it, hoping they heard him.

His mind replayed what it hadn't thought of for almost three lifetimes. The crime that sent him away. The murder of his last destined one and her lover.

The memories came over him with excruciating pain that

shot through his chest like a knife being plunged into his heart. He saw her with him, smelled the scent of her perfume all over him, tasted the bile just as he had that day when he saw her naked body writhe under another man in the bed he slept in every night next to her. He felt the rage that had overcome him as the actual act repeated in slow motion in his mind.

The feeling of betrayal that sent a signal to his brain to take out his gun.

The gun in his hands, pointed at them as they moved together in sex, not knowing he was standing there watching them.

The tears that blurred his vision as he aimed the gun in his shaking hands.

His finger pulling the trigger once. Twice. A third time. Blood all over the bed. Both bodies silent and still. Him slumped on the floor unable to move, unable to take his eyes off the two souls he had just killed.

Why would they do this to him? For him?

BEFORE SHE WENT TO WORK the next morning, Callia visited her grandmother for breakfast, as she often did. She lived only a few blocks away from her and loved the visits from her only grandchild.

After a breakfast of store-bought muffins and tea, they discussed the killings, both unable to understand why anyone would do such terrible things.

"Grandma, do you think it's one of our kind doing this?"

Callia didn't want to believe a fellow Aeveren would kill another of their own kind.

"I don't think it can be a human, unless they have help from an Aeveren. How would he know who to kill?

"You think it's a man?"

"Oh yes, dear. A woman wouldn't do such a thing."

Callia smiled. "Grandma, that may have been true when you were young, but nowadays...and what about Lizzie Borden? She murdered both her parents."

Her grandmother sniffed in disgust as she poured them more tea. "That's different."

They sat silently for a few minutes, both sipping their morning tea, until Callia spoke again, needing answers about what had happened to her in bed last night.

"Grandma, something strange happened."

"What, sweetie? Are you okay?"

"I don't know. I woke up last night feeling sick and then..." She hesitated, knowing what she was about to say sounded crazy. "Then I heard a voice say something to me."

Callia looked away from the older woman's gaze, sure she was thinking her granddaughter had lost her mind. When she turned back, she saw her grandmother looking at her sweetly like she always did.

"What did the voice say?"

Callia hesitated again to make sure she said the words exactly as she'd heard them. "Go to him. He is here."

The smile that came across her grandmother's face surprised her, and she nervously blurted out, "I know. It's crazy, right? I must have been having a nightmare." She began to fidget, like she always did when she was uncomfortable.

"You're not crazy, Callia," she said, taking her granddaughter's hands in hers to calm them. "Sweetie, your destined one has finally come."

Callia wasn't sure what to say. Her destined one was here. But where was he?

"How will I find him? What do I do?" She heard herself and thought she sounded much younger and far more innocent than she was.

"Don't worry. It will happen naturally. When you least expect it, there he'll be, right where you're supposed to find him."

"Do you think he heard the same voice telling him I'm here?"

What if he doesn't know I'm his?

"He might have, but maybe not. Both mates are drawn to one another sometimes, but not always. Other times only one is drawn."

Callia sat silently, thinking about what he might be like and if he'd like her.

As if she were reading her mind, her grandmother lifted Callia's chin with her forefinger and looked into her eyes. "He will love you from the moment he sets eyes on you, and when he meets you, he'll see the wonderful person I see."

FIVE FAMILIES. THAT WAS JUST the start. Who was going to

stop him? *New Hope Police department? I don't fucking think so. The Aeveren who live in New Hope? No. The human police have a better chance.*

Derrick James sat in his apartment a few miles outside of town feeling very satisfied with himself as he cut out the latest article about the murders from the *Albany Times Union*. They had started to call him the New Hope Slayer, a name he thought was good on a number of levels.

CHAPTER TWO

V AREK LAY IN BED UNTIL the housekeeper had knocked twice, the second time quite impatiently. The curtains in Room 14 blocked out the day outside, so he had no real sense of what time it was, nor did he care. He'd get to what he needed to do about the murderer later. Now he wanted to shut everything out, especially the feeling he'd gotten during the night.

Why would they do this? He groaned as he thought about it. What could he offer any female after what he'd been through?

The hands on his back pushed him roughly to the concrete floor, his ribs splintering on contact. Before he was able to attempt to get up, his face was smashed into the ground. The pain in his left cheek sent out stabs of more pain radiating through his forehead and temple. Shards of glass, broken bits of stone, and splinters of metal ground into the skin on his face, dangerously close to his eye.

Panic raced through him, and his voice screamed in his head. A hand pushed his head as a man's weight settled down in a rush on the small of his back. A body kneeled in front of his head, and hands pressed his shoulders forcefully into the hard ground. He waited in terror, knowing what was to come next. The sadistic click of the switchblade made him freeze in fear as it touched the skin on his back. He screamed into the cold stone beneath him as each cut was made. He didn't know how long the knife carved into him, but when they were done, his shoulders and back were numb, and a dull ache held him to the ground.

Varek ran his hand over his right shoulder and felt the scar his fellow inmates had given him that night lifetimes ago. What kind of female would want him with that pain seared into him?

He closed his eyes and cursed. He'd been foolish to think they would let him out without expecting him to pay. They called it a gift.

Called her a gift.

As he drew a deep breath, he swore silently that he wouldn't let this one do what the last one had done. He'd suffered enough for this one to be different.

He showered and dressed in his work camp clothes again. When he hit the cold winter air, he realized he would have to get a coat if he were to find a murderer.

The February sun shone on the five inches of snow that had fallen overnight. Nothing melted, but the day seemed bright and cheery. Varek set out toward the first clothing store he could find. It was hard enough blending in being six-foot-four and built like someone who had just spent almost three lifetimes fighting to make sure his first prison tattoo was his last. Looking like he was dressed for sometime in May when everyone else was dressed like Nanook of the North made it worse.

Two hundred and fifty dollars later Varek was dressed for the weather in a black leather jacket. He walked out into the streets of New Hope to find his fellow Aeveren and the one he was sent to capture.

Finding one of his kind wouldn't be difficult. Although humans couldn't see the difference between themselves and Aeveren, it was impossible to miss for someone of the race. Aeveren looked different—an aura surrounded each of them. All he'd have to do was walk down the street and watch for them.

His mind drifted back to the message his body had given him about her. *Her*. Varek knew, as every Aeveren old enough to have a destined one knew, there would be no avoiding her. Biology was involved, and once an Aeveren's body sensed a mate, nothing on Earth could change what would happen, what must happen.

But he was stronger than most males, thanks to almost three lifetimes in Nil. He wouldn't be able to truly fight his biology, but he could exert some control over how fast his body led him. He wouldn't surrender as easily as last time. He'd make sure of that.

He walked down First Street and saw the orphanage. A quick glance at the workers shoveling snow from the sidewalks told him he'd find his kind there. As he approached the imposing building, the maintenance workers clearing the snow saw him. Their expressions told him they instinctively knew that while he was a fellow Aeveren, he was different from them. The lifetimes spent in Nil covered him like a cloak that his kind easily sensed, but since it was rare for murderers or others convicted of similarly heinous crimes to be released from Nil, the workers would know that while he may be fearsome-looking, he was still one of them.

"What can we do for you, sir?" one of the men asked him as he stopped shoveling and looked up to face him.

"I'd like to speak to the person who runs this place," Varek said, looking over the man's head to a window on the first floor where a small child's face stared out at him.

"Go up those stairs, and as soon as you enter the building, there's an office to the right. She's in there."

Varek walked away without saying a word, but after a few steps he realized he should thank the man. He wasn't in Nil anymore. He had to remember that.

"Thanks," he said to the man, who gave him a quick smile, almost as if to signal that he realized he was dealing with someone who wasn't quite used to interacting with others in any normal way.

Varek took the stairs two at a time without stretching his legs, and another stride took him inside the building. As he turned to step to the right toward the administrator's office, he felt something latch onto his left hand. When he looked down, he saw the child who had been watching him through the window looking up at him. Her green eyes startled him, and for a moment, he stood motionless, staring back at her.

"Who are you?" she asked in a voice as small as she was.

"Varek," he said as she gripped his forefinger in her tiny hand.

"Do you want a little girl or a little boy?"

He was silent, unable to think of how to answer her. For a moment, he thought of the daughter he had left without a mother or father lifetimes ago. Before he could think of what to say, a woman walked out of the administrator's office and picked up the little girl.

"Tia, who's your new friend?" The woman adjusted the girl in her arms, but she continued to hold Varek's finger. Tia leaned into her ear and whispered his name.

"Well, sweetheart, I need you to run along and find the other children. It's almost time for lunch. Say goodbye to Mr. Varek."

Tia let go of his hand as she was placed on the floor and looked up at Varek. "Goodbye."

As the little girl ran away, Jessica Anders introduced herself and led him to her office, offering him the hook by the front door to hang his coat on.

The moment his hand touched the hook, he was overcome by a sensation that rolled across his skin. *She's been here.* He looked around but saw no one. Shaking his head as if to get himself back to reality, he entered Jessica Anders's office.

"What can I do for you, Mr. Varek?" she asked as she gestured for him to take a seat on the old wooden chair in front of her desk. As he sat, the chair creaked as if it were groaning under the bulk of the person on it.

"It's just Varek. I need some information about the person murdering the children's parents." His voice was deep and made everything sound like a command, another trait that had been useful to him in the place he'd been but now was as startling as the rest of him.

"Do you have any identification? Are you working with the police?"

The Council hadn't stuffed any ID or explanation letter about what he was doing in New Hope into his pants, and Varek knew Jessica Anders wasn't going to help him without them.

"I'm working with the Council," he said, offering nothing to support his claim.

"Well, I'm going to have to check out your story before I tell you anything else. If you come back tonight at six, I should have an answer from the Council by then."

"Six then." He stood up and looked down at her to see her hand extended. She shook his hand, and as he stepped out of her office, once again he remembered where he was and turned around to say thank you. The administrator gave him the same smile the man outside had, and Varek stepped out into the cold and zipped up his coat to his neck.

AT FIVE O'CLOCK CALLIA WALKED into Jessica's office, hoping to ask her a few questions before the children found out she was there. She had left work early, her body and mind directing her to the orphanage. As soon as she entered the building, the feeling she had experienced in bed the night before came over her again.

Was he here?

Jessica was on the phone, so Callia nervously stood in her doorway until she finished. Jessica completed her notes she was taking on the conversation and hung up the phone.

"Callia, are you okay? You don't look good."

In an effort to not let Jessica know she was a nervous wreck, Callia attempted a smile and answered as calmly as possible, "Anything new?"

"No, the same. Oh, wait! Yes! We had a visitor today. Somebody working for the Council on the murders. He's coming back at six. You should see him, Callia. Tall, dark, handsome, and huge, like a giant." Jessica's eyes sparkled. "I think you'll like him," she said in a singsong voice.

You have no idea.

Callia struggled to remain outwardly calm as her insides turned to shaking Jell-O. *Huge. Like a giant.* That didn't sound like someone she'd think of for herself. She had always envisioned her destined one as smart, strong, but well, more like her and less like a giant.

Turning to find the children, she smiled and shrugged at Jessica and hurried off toward the library room. When she got there, she was thankful they were still at dinner and she would have some time to get her head together before they came in. She looked down at her hands, which shook at the thought that after almost seven lifetimes she was finally going to have a mate.

I'm going to meet my destiny.

The words repeated in her head a second, third, and fourth time, interrupted only by the noise of the children running down the hall toward the library.

"Callia!" the children screamed as they flooded into the room.

Instantly, her focus changed to them. They had questions about homework, stories to tell about their time outside in the snow earlier in the day, and complaints about mandarin oranges for dessert. Before long, she had forgotten about destiny and her mate, and they all settled down to work on their schoolwork.

VAREK RETURNED TO THE ORPHANAGE at six o'clock and sensed instantly as he turned the doorknob on the orphanage's front door that she was there. He closed his eyes, steadied himself, and entered the building, darting his eyes left and right to look for her.

Jessica Anders greeted him and took him into her office, closing the door behind her. "Please sit down. Now that I know you are working for the Council, I'm happy to help."

Taking a seat, Varek began. "Has anyone spoken to the children before they arrived here? Maybe Family Services?"

"Family Services? Just how long have you been in Nil, Varek?"

He sat stonily as she reminded him of the reality of the

Aeveren and human worlds.

"It's been a very long time since we Aeveren had to deal with human governmental agencies. We may not have an Aeveren in the White House yet or one of us in the state house currently, but we have people in power and always have. Family Services is a human entity."

"I guess that explains how an orphanage can exist in this day and age."

"Exactly. Whether they know we exist or not, they see this place as somewhere that's always been here, always been a place for children who had nowhere else to go. It's been my experience that humans don't spend a great deal of time on things that don't seem to concern them. And even if they did ask, the mayor and other important people in New Hope are Aeveren."

"Others? Any police? That would be a huge help."

"No, unfortunately, none of the police are Aeveren, but the coroner is, a man named Gene Dizer. He should be able to give you some information."

"Is there anything else you can tell me?"

Jessica handed him a folder he saw contained the addresses of the families the murderer had attacked.

"These may help you. I wish I had more."

As Varek stood to leave, Jessica stopped him. "Please do all that you can to stop this madman. I know why you were sent to Nil, but I also know you were a policeman before."

Varek simply nodded and said good-bye as he quickly flung open her office door to see Tia standing there, her green eyes wide and staring up at him. She reached up to grab his finger again and smiled as she said his name.

In an instant the forces of Aeveren biology took over and presented him with his destiny.

"Tia? Where are you, sweetheart?" a female voice called down the hall. In just five words, Varek's life changed.

Tia tugged on his finger and answered, "I'm here."

Varek's will to fight his nature melted away, and he waited to see the woman who possessed the voice that had just touched his heart.

Callia turned the corner and stepped into the old building's spacious foyer, seeing him instantly. How could she miss him? He was a giant, but he didn't seem like what she had imagined him to be earlier. He was huge, standing there holding Tia's hand. Her head barely reached the bottom of his jacket, but he looked kinder than she imagined from Jessica's description.

Tia pulled Varek toward Callia. "This is Varek. He's my friend," she said looking up at him.

Callia smiled and took Tia's hand. As her hand briefly grazed his fingers, a jolt like an electric shock ran through her.

"It's nice to meet you."

Everything else in the room seemed to have vanished but the man standing in front of her. She looked up at him, his black hair, his eyes that seemed darker than any she'd seen before, and his enormous frame that dwarfed everyone and everything else in the room.

Varek replied that it was nice to meet her also, but it was

almost as if he had simply mimicked her words because his mind was focused on things other than manners. He took in the sight of her. Her long, brown hair that looked like the sun had kissed strands to warm it, her hazel eyes that made him feel like he was experiencing a color nature had created just for him. He let his gaze drift down to where her hair fell across her breasts and then lower to her small waist and toned legs.

As he stood in front of her, feeling himself begin to fall no matter what he'd promised himself, something deep in his mind reminded him of what he was. He held on to that thought and said good-bye gruffly before he quickly strode out the door. He hit the frigid, night air and inhaled deeply, as if he had held his breath from the moment he met her and now, finally alone, could resume breathing.

Callia stood in the foyer looking at the closed front door. Her heart sunk as she thought about how he had reacted. Her grandmother had been wrong.

He didn't love me the moment he saw me. He didn't even like what he saw.

She felt like her feet were made of lead and she couldn't leave where she stood. Her only destined one in seven lifetimes and he'd rejected her. Her chest felt tight. All she wanted to do was cry, but she couldn't while she stood in the orphanage's foyer with Jessica and Tia.

Callia forced herself to act as if nothing had happened and turned to take Tia back to the library for a story before she left for the night. She heard Jessica comment that he had acted strangely, but Callia kept walking without answering.

Varek stood on the orphanage's steps, feeling like shit. Even a thick, old wooden door couldn't block the feelings of hurt and rejection coming from Callia. She had been drawn to him as he had been to her. She knew how he was supposed to act, how she was supposed to feel now. He listened to the voice that repeated what he was, what he could never be for her, and he worked hard to convince himself that he'd done her the biggest favor of her current lifetime.

When Callia had finished reading to Tia and helping the other children with their homework, she wished them all a good night and walked toward the front door, hoping to not have to talk to Jessica, who would surely want to discuss how oddly Varek had acted. Thankfully, she had been called down to the cafeteria and Callia could leave without having her feelings of humiliation overcome her and cause her to break down. She found her coat and gloves on the hook next to the door and braced herself for the cold walk home.

She stepped outside and turned to pull the front door closed. Out of the corner of her eye she caught the figure standing on the porch with her. She turned her body to face him, to make him face her and explain what made him deny their destiny.

CHAPTER THREE

V AREK STOOD LOOKING DOWN, HER hurt coming in waves toward him. He wanted to take her in his arms, hold her body to his, and kiss her pain away, taking it into him. But he didn't because he knew he would only cause her more pain in the end.

She seemed so small standing in front of him. Her head would rest on his chest just over his heart if he pulled her to him. His mind wandered, and he thought about his hands stroking her long hair as he held her to him. The thought caused him to reflexively breathe in deeply, and before he could stop himself, he sighed as he exhaled.

Callia watched him silently and told herself to just walk away, but something possessed her to ask him why he'd acted like he had.

"Why do you reject me as your destined one?"

The words were like knives that cut him but didn't leave him numb. Her pain stabbed at him, causing his chest to tighten and ache.

"You don't want me. Trust me," he warned her before

taking another deep breath of cold air.

Callia couldn't believe she had opened herself up for more humiliation. She felt angry at him and now herself.

"I guess I have no say in this. Great. Seven lifetimes with no destined one and when I'm finally given one, he doesn't want me and blames me, saying I won't want him."

Tears began to well up in her eyes like they always did when she was furious. She turned on her heel and walked away as fast as she could without looking like she was anything but angry. She was angry, but more than that, she was hurt and disappointed.

Varek watched her walk away and fought for control over his body, which wanted to run after her. *Finally given one? Why would the universe do this to her—make me her first?*

As he walked behind her, instinctively protecting her, he told himself he was doing the right thing by not being with her. He wasn't the type of male she needed. She should have someone kind and gentle, who knew nothing of the horrors he'd experienced, someone who didn't carry the scars of something wrong in him where she could see.

For every reason he told himself he shouldn't be with her, his body answered in making his legs move faster to catch up with her. He was losing this battle.

Callia realized about halfway home that he was following her. She considered turning around to ask him why and to demand he stop, but she didn't want to give him another chance to hurt her. She considered running, but knew that any man with legs that long and a body that well-built was in good shape and would catch up to her in no time.

She reached her apartment and turned to see if he was still behind her. He was, and he was coming toward her. Suddenly, she was frightened. Had she angered him? Was that why he was following her? She quickly reached into her coat pocket for her keys and nervously fumbled with them as she tried to put the correct key in the lock. She stopped dead and sensed him standing on the sidewalk behind her, staring at her as she stood too afraid to move.

Varek knew he had frightened her. She stood stiffly, as if readying herself for an attack.

"I'm sorry," he said, unsure why he began like that.

Callia turned around and stared down at him. The kindness she had seen when she'd first met him had returned. She decided to open herself up one more time.

"Would you like to come in?"

Varek knew what could happen if he went in with her. He could touch her soft hair, kiss her beautiful lips, and feel her next to him. He knew he shouldn't let any of those things happen, but biological yearning won out over fear and anger.

He nodded. "Yes."

He walked up the stairs and followed her into the apartment. As he closed the door behind him, he scanned the rooms in front of him. Her home was warm and open. It felt like a real *home*. The neutral colors on the walls helped showcase the knickknacks and pictures that decorated the space. Nothing seemed to be out of place, but it all seemed relaxed. Her home seemed to welcome him in.

"Sit down, if you'd like," Callia said to him as she passed by on her way to the closet to hang her coat.

Varek sat down on the living room couch, immediately wishing he had chosen one of the chairs instead. His body already knew what his mind continued to deny. She was his destined one, the female for him, and she wanted him. Lost in thought, he blankly looked up to see her standing in front of him with an expression on her face like she expected him to answer a question.

Callia repeated the question she had asked. "Would you like to take your coat off?"

She watched him with wide eyes as he handed her his coat. His black T-shirt stretched across hard muscle on his chest and arms. Without his coat, he seemed much bigger. As her gaze glided over his torso, she noticed a scar that barely peeked out of his shirt near his strong, muscular neck. It looked like it had been left over from a serious injury. She blushed when her eyes traveled up to meet his and she realized he saw she was staring at his body.

Varek adjusted his collar to hide the scar when he saw she was staring at it. Knowing it was visible reminded him of all the reasons why he shouldn't be there with her. As she stood holding his coat, he jumped up from the couch, nearly knocking her over, and grabbed it out of her hand on his way to the door, only stopping when she spoke.

"Why don't you want me?"

Callia silently chastised herself for sounding so pathetic, but she wanted to know what would make him go against their nature.

Why did she keep asking that?

He spun around and took two steps toward her, causing her to back up toward the far wall. He had a choice to make. He could either scare her or tell her the truth. Either way, he had to make her understand *he* wasn't the one *she* wanted. As he stood in front of her, looking into her wide eyes, he decided to tell her the truth, but then his body made its own decision.

Callia stood frightened, and then, in a split second, her emotions jumped from fear to desire. His mouth was on hers, his lips tender and soft but kissing her eagerly. She slid her tongue into his mouth and lightly glided it over his and the roof of his mouth. His hands moved from the wall next to her head to her hair, and he gently but passionately dug his hand into her hair and tugged.

Her tongue teasing his caused his already rock-hard erection to push more against his belly, straining to get free and find that place of warmth and wetness in her that it needed. He pushed his hips into her body, wanting to release at least some of the tension that was building in him. She arched her back and ran her hands up under his shirt, caressing his back with her soft fingertips. Lost in desire, it took him a minute to realize where her hands were. When he did, he suddenly released her and backed away from her as his decision minutes earlier came surging back into his consciousness.

"No, you don't want this. Me." When she began to protest, he stopped her with a cold look and continued to speak. "I murdered my last destined one and spent three lifetimes in Nil as punishment. I'd still be there if they didn't need my help to catch the parents' murderer. I'm not the one for you."

"I can't help what is destined, Varek. I may not like that my destined one is a murderer, but we are Aeveren. We must accept that this is meant to be."

"You have free will. Use it. You deserve someone else."

When he finished, he walked to the door and left without another word. Callia stood in stunned silence thinking about what he'd said. She felt exhausted, her emotions out of control, and confused. His kiss stayed on her lips, and the feel of him remained with her even later as she climbed into bed.

As she drifted off to sleep, she replayed in her mind what had happened. She had never felt anything like she did with Varek. She wanted to feel him next to her, but she wanted to run away from him. She could do neither because he didn't want her, and she couldn't deny her destined one.

VAREK LAY IN HIS BED at the Town Inn, tormented by his time with Callia. Kissing her, her body pressed up against his, had brought all the old, familiar needs back with a vengeance. Feelings he hadn't had in lifetimes tortured him, reminding him of a past he so desperately didn't want to remember. Every feeling, every memory he fought to banish from his mind, but they were stronger than he was and took over his thoughts.

His hands felt their way in the dark, not needing light as they knew every inch of her body. She was his, the only one who had ever made him feel complete. His hands found what they had searched for, and he cupped her firm breasts as he straddled her hips. Her hands pressed into the small of his back, urging him to her. His cock brushed her sex as he slid up her body to rest on top of her.

He held her face in his hands, kissing her with the passion of a male totally devoted to his female. As she tilted her hips and ground into him looking for relief from the ache of desire, he whispered into her mouth, "Neera," the word sounding more like a plea than her name.

She filled his days and nights, and he was a man lost without her. He desired her more than anyone or anything else, and she took full advantage of this fact. But he didn't mind any of the demands she made. He'd give his life to make her happy.

The feelings she brought out in him made him love her even more. He craved her, needed her. When he was with her like this, everything else in the world ceased to matter.

He lifted up from her and slid himself inside her body, feeling her surround him. Her hands pushed him in until they were joined skin to skin. Her moans let him know she wanted him as he wanted her—totally and completely. Her body arched to bring him closer.

She was hot and wet around his cock. He loved being inside her. When they made love, all the fighting and yelling disappeared, and all that remained was what they had been when they were called to one another.

A need only the other could fill, unlike anything else he had ever experienced with any other woman.

He felt her come apart beneath him, felt her nails drag down his back. She tightened around him, bringing him to the edge and then over it as he released into her, his groans of relief sounding into the air around them.

Hours later, as she lay in his arms, he watched her as she slept, her pale blonde hair tousled and covering part of her face. She was as fair as he was dark, his opposite in so many ways, ways that threatened to tear them apart if they couldn't remember the way they felt when they were naked in one another's arms.

Varek covered his eyes with his right arm and felt the pain of what he and Neera had become by the end take him over. He had loved her so completely that he had never seen who she really was. He knew they were toxic together at times, but he loved her, and after the baby, he couldn't leave even if he had wanted to. Neera was his destined one, and their daughter deserved to have a father.

He never saw her betrayal until it was too late. That she had chosen a human to betray him with, a man who could give her only this lifetime, was just salt in the wound. He had lost his mind when he finally saw the evidence of her betrayal that day as she fucked another man in the bed they shared. In seconds, he had killed the only one he'd ever truly loved, consigned himself to a future in Nil, and made his child an orphan. These things were never going to leave him. He was scarred, inside and out, and Callia deserved more.

She deserves more than me.

DERRICK JAMES ENJOYED LOOKING AT the wall-sized map of New Hope that hung on his living room wall. The address for each set of victims had a pushpin of a different color over it. The first murders on Meadow Drive had a red pushpin. Red seemed like the perfect color to show a murder. For the second murders across town on Browning Road, he considered keeping the red color since it was murder again, but decided on blue, his favorite color.

"Some asshole would probably think I should use brown for Browning," he mumbled to himself as he shifted his attention to his third crime's pushpin.

He had killed the parents of three small children for the third murders. Since he associated black with three for some reason he couldn't remember, number three got a black pushpin.

The last two sets of killings got green and purple. Green worked for four because of four leaf clovers, and purple just seemed good for number five.

The sixth murders would get yellow, but he hadn't decided who they'd be yet, so there was no yellow pushpin on the map. There would be, though.

CALLIA SAT AT HER GRANDMOTHER'S kitchen table, lost in thought about what had happened with Varek the night before. She really didn't want to discuss it with her grandmother, but she didn't have anyone else she could speak to about it. Most of her friends were humans, which explained why most of her romantic relationships had been with human men, so it would be impossible to tell them without telling them about her being Aeveren. The friends she had who were Aeveren were all with their destined ones, some happily, some not, but she'd found that once they were mated, they had little interest in discussing the trials and tribulations of those unlike themselves. That left Jessica at the orphanage and her grandmother. Callia quickly decided on her grandmother and considered the best way to broach the subject.

"Callia!" her grandmother said, her voice full of exasperation.

"I'm sorry, Grandma. I was a million miles away."

"I can tell. I asked you if you'd met him yet and you seemed to look right through me."

Callia breathed out in a huff and looked at her grandmother. "I met him."

The dejection in her voice was easy to hear. "Did something happen? You don't like him? He isn't cute? You know, I wasn't thrilled about your grandfather at first, but it didn't take long before I was crazy about him, and we were very happy in this lifetime, as we will be again in the next."

Callia looked away. "I liked him a great deal. It's he who doesn't want me."

Touching her hand, her grandmother said confidently, "Sometimes Aeveren biology seems mistaken, but it never is. You are meant to be his, and he is meant to be yours."

"Grandma, he told me I should exercise my free will.

Maybe he's right."

"Free will? It sounds like he's forgotten who we are."

"Even though we have destined ones, we have free will, Grandma."

"Let me tell you about free will. You and he have obviously forgotten the old stories. We're given the gift of destined ones from the Archangel Raziel, just like our other gifts of powers and reincarnation. And yes, that doesn't preclude us possessing free will. But there's not a case of an Aeveren fighting their destiny and being happy. Think of Josephine."

Callia smiled at her grandmother's reference to Napoleon and Josephine. It had always been her favorite story to tell when she'd first come to live with her after the death of her parents.

"I'm not Josephine, Grandma." Remembering what Varek looked like, she chuckled. "And he's definitely no Napoleon."

"Sweetheart, you're missing the point. When Napoleon was with his destined one, he was able to conquer the world. Nothing was out of his reach. When he chose to deny their destiny and marry another woman—out of free will—he lost everything. Choose to deny your destiny and you will be unhappy."

"Then what should I do?"

"Perhaps he just needs a little convincing."

Confused, Callia said, "What do you mean?"

"I'll explain sweetheart. Just trust me," her grandmother said with a smile and a wink.

CHAPTER FOUR

A FTER A DAY OF VISITING murder sites and figuring out connections between victims, Varek was happy to return to his room at the Town Inn. It was bland and slightly dingy, but he liked the solitude it offered. He threw his coat on the makeshift kitchen table, undressed, and climbed into bed. The fresh sheets felt cool against his skin.

Thank you, angry housekeeping lady.

He stretched his long legs and let the stress of the day ease out of him. His neck and back ached, a remnant of his days in Nil and a pretty good predictor of bad weather to come.

Maybe it will snow again, he thought to himself. As he relaxed, he let his mind go as blank as it could. He always seemed to be thinking but tried to make it about something mundane now.

A knock at the door roused him from his relaxation. He knew it wasn't housekeeping—it was far too late for that, and the knock was too soft. He slipped his pants on again over his bare skin. The desk clerk, who it most likely was, wasn't someone he'd put more clothes on for. Varek opened the door to find Callia standing outside the door of his temporary home.

Wondering first why she was outside his room and then how she knew he was there, he finally said, "Come in."

Callia walked into the dark room and made her way to the farthest wall from the door. Varek remained by the door, strangely feeling like a guest in his own room.

"How are you?" Callia said nervously.

Varek stood silently in his black pants and with no shirt on, instinctively remaining with his back to a wall. Suddenly uncomfortable, he pushed his hands into his pockets.

Callia wondered if she should continue. He hadn't answered even a basic question of how he was. Did he really dislike her this much? She began to get fidgety, but steeled herself to remain calm.

Please don't say no.

"So, I was thinking that you might want to stay at my apartment while you're here. You could work out of there—I'm never there during the day because I'm at the vet's, and then I visit the children at the orphanage every night after work. I usually don't get home until about seven or eight. I have an extra bedroom you could use. And I have a computer that might help you."

Callia knew she sounded like she was rambling, but she had practiced this speech a dozen times on the way over and wanted to make sure she got everything in.

Please say yes.

Varek stood looking at her in shock. He didn't want to say

no—well, his body didn't want to say no—but he sort of liked Room 14. She looked sweet, though, backed up against the farthest point in the room.

"Okay," he said, instantly wondering what had happened to all his resolve.

A wave of relief washed over Callia. Inside she felt the nervousness dissipate, and she realized she needed to sit. The bed was the closest to where she stood, so she sat down and leaned back to relax.

Varek felt like the room had shrunk to half the size it was before she entered. His eyes followed her legs, up over her hips, across her breasts, to her face as she lay on his bed. He stepped in front of her, hoping to take back control of the space and the situation, but as he looked down at her lying there with her eyes closed, he began to get hard.

"We need to have some rules if I'm to stay at your place."

"Fine. Like what?"

"Like my room will be private."

Callia opened her eyes and sat up, looking up at him and his half naked body. "I have no interest in what you do in your room. My only rule is that you bring no one to my home."

Varek sensed she was challenging him. "And what about you bringing someone to the house?"

She rose from the bed and stood no more than three inches away from him. She looked up at him and in a tone that told him she was definitely challenging him, she said, "Varek, it's my house. I'll bring whomever I want home."

He stood in front of her, looking down into eyes that

showed a strength her size didn't betray. He couldn't remember the last time another had faced him like this. In his time in Nil, he was used to so many others cowering in front of him, not staring into his eyes or facing off with him. He felt his body grow excited by her challenge.

She brushed past him and walked toward the door. "I'll be back in an hour. We'll go back to my house then, okay?"

He sensed she was enjoying this, but what had turned him on now changed to feelings of jealousy. Who would she bring to the house?

The reality was he had no business being jealous or even considering moving in to her spare bedroom. Nothing had changed about who he was. He was still a prisoner from Nil who had made a tragic mistake and deserved to pay for it for lifetimes to come, whether in Nil or out. But an even more important reality was his one-room lodgings at the motel were spartan at best, and he didn't even have access to a computer to help him in his investigation.

One hour later he checked out of the Town Inn and moved his meager belongings into Callia's spare bedroom. She seemed different than the woman he'd left standing in her living room after kissing her.

"Why are you doing this?" he finally asked.

"Because I want to help my people."

With that, she went into her room and closed the door.

Standing with her back to the door, Callia breathed hard and tried to control her emotions. She'd done what she'd set out to do, get him to her house. In addition, she had kept herself strong, which had been difficult when he was so close...and half naked in his motel room. The coming days would be difficult, though. Her Aeveren biology was making being around him as nothing more than an acquaintance almost impossible. Was it the same for him?

VAREK CLOSED HIS EYES AND took a deep breath. He listened to her breathing hard on the other side of her door. Was she angry?

A few minutes later, he was on his back on her spare bed, unable to get her out of his mind. He thought about the almost taunting way she'd told him what she'd do back in his motel room. The erection he had after she'd left him returned as he replayed the scene of her fearlessly standing so close to him. He had thought she was beautiful when they first met, but her change into someone who was strong too made denying his natural urges because she was his destined one much harder.

I do like a spirited woman.

As soon as he said this, memories of Neera rushed back into his head. But Neera had been more than spirited. She had been possessed by a rage at times that made life a living hell. Callia didn't seem like that.

Varek wondered how he was going to live in the same house with her without having her. But he liked that now she'd give him a little fight. They may have released him, but they couldn't erase what they had made him into over three lifetimes.

Maybe she was strong enough to handle him.

For the next week, Varek worked the case from Callia's apartment. It was nicer than the room at the Town Inn, and she'd been right. The computer was a great help, and she was rarely there. He came and went as he pleased, and even began to wish she were there more often.

On the following Saturday, he got his wish. She spent the day cleaning the apartment and even cooked dinner. He remained in his room working, and at five o'clock, she knocked at his door.

"I'm having someone over for dinner tonight." Implicit in the statement was a command. Don't get in the way.

Callia knew by the look on his face that he wasn't happy with her news. Maybe her grandmother was right, but Callia had also done something that she hadn't told her to do.

"I have something for you." She reached into a shopping bag she held in her left hand and pulled out two shirts.

"You can't go around in the same clothes. So I bought you these," she said as she handed him a dark blue dress shirt and a white dress shirt. She had particularly enjoyed fantasizing about him in the white one. "I didn't know your size, so I guessed."

Varek held the gifts and stood confused. Inside he was pleased, more than he liked. She was beginning to be someone he cared about.

"Thank you. You didn't have to…"

Before he could finish his sentence, Callia interrupted. "I know I don't have to, but I did. This is how good people are to one another." She pivoted away from him and walked down the hall as she said, "I have to get ready for my date."

Callia wished she could see the look on his face when he heard the word date.

Varek said nothing but felt a sting of hurt he couldn't place. He had told her she didn't want him, so her having someone for dinner shouldn't bother him, but it did.

Thinking it was better to leave before her guest arrived, he put on the new dark blue shirt with the things he already owned and checked himself out in the dresser mirror. She had nice taste and a good eye. The shirt fit perfectly. As he admired his new clothes, he ran his hand over his head. His hair had grown in a bit since he'd been released, and it needed something to make it look good.

He went into the bathroom they shared and found some gel among the seemingly endless array of bottles containing fluids dedicated to making Callia even more beautiful than she already was. Minutes later, he grabbed his coat and set off for the front door.

Callia saw him as he entered the living room and stopped fluffing the couch pillows, stunned. He was wearing one of the new shirts, and he looked incredible. And he was going out looking like that!

I hope you're right, Grandma.

Varek saw Callia dressed for her date and another pang of jealousy stabbed at him. She had a black sweater dress on and black heels, which made her legs look great. He had seen her in the T-shirt she wore to bed a few days before and had noticed she had great legs. He felt sick thinking of another male running his hands up those legs, but he told himself she didn't belong with the likes of him. He also considered sticking around to see what her date looked like.

Great. Now I'm jealous and overprotective.

"I don't know what time we'll be done, but please don't feel like you have to stay away. This is your home too." Callia saw how he looked at her and knew at the very least he was beginning to like something about her.

"That's okay. I needed a night out anyway. See you later."

VAREK FOUND HIS WAY TO the nearest bar and ordered a beer. With a plan to drink Callia with another man out of his mind, he quickly downed two beers and began drinking a third.

Jake's Tavern had a mix of Aeveren and humans, so after the third beer hadn't helped in the least to get his mind off Callia, her incredible legs, and whatever asshole was sitting with her thinking about getting between those legs, Varek decided to talk to some other Aeveren about the murders. Before he could move away from the bar, a petite blonde sidled up next to him, obviously seeing something she liked. She was also Aeveren, so Varek thought she might at least help pass the time for a bit.

"Hey, I've never seen you here before. What's your name?"

"Varek."

It didn't take long before he saw she had some serious interest in him. In no time, she had her hands on his thigh and was sliding them up toward his cock. If body language was any true indication, this blonde named Melissa was looking to get laid.

Varek listened as she talked and answered when she asked him questions, but his mind was still back at the apartment. He quickly decided against sleeping with Melissa or anyone other than Callia. The truth was that it wasn't just his body that yearned to be with her. More and more, over just the past week, he'd found himself thinking about her and how kind she'd been, about how maybe she could handle his past, about how maybe he wasn't the animal he'd convinced himself he was over three lifetimes. Each time he'd reminded himself of all the fucked-up shit that he'd gone through, the kind of shit that someone like Callia was too good to have touch her, but this was slowly but surely losing the argument inside him. He was falling in love with her.

Melissa got the hint that he wasn't interested and moved to another guy, which allowed Varek to try his hand at speaking to the locals. He spent the next two hours chatting up a group of male Aeveren in their forties and fifties, mentally noting any ideas they had about who could be the murderer and why he or she would be killing Aeveren parents. While most of what they said he'd either heard or thought of before, one idea stuck in his head. Perhaps this person had been seen by the children. He knew from the police that they had questioned each of the children after the murders, but they were likely human and the children would naturally not tell them much. From a very young age, Aeveren taught their children that humans were to be respected and could coexist with Aeveren, but anything important had to stay between

Aeveren. Varek wondered if any Aeveren had interviewed the children.

After three hours at Jake's, Varek couldn't keep himself away from Callia's any longer. He told himself he was tired, but the truth was that he was a mixture of curious and jealous about her date. He had to see who he was.

He considered knocking before he entered the apartment but knew that would give them warning he was back and he wanted to see them behaving naturally. He walked into the apartment and didn't see them at first. One thought ran through his mind.

They're in her room. In bed.

A noise caused him to look in the kitchen, and he found them drinking coffee at the counter. Varek assessed the situation, looking for how she related to the guy with body language but was instantly disgusted when he saw no aura around him.

The guy was human.

Speechless, he looked at her for just a moment and turned around to stalk back to his room. On his bed, he stretched out in the darkness and tried to think of anything but Callia with a human man. It didn't work. He couldn't think about anything else.

He wasn't a speciest or racist, or whatever. At least he didn't think he was. He had no problems with humans, overall. He recognized that Aeveren and human beings shared a similar physiology and knew by and large the differences between Aeveren and humans were mental since Aeveren were reincarnated and even gained extraordinary abilities later in their reincarnation cycle. He just didn't see why any female would choose to be with a human man for the few years of his only lifetime.

Varek knew he was like this because of Neera. He had never had a problem being with human females before she cheated on him with a human male. But now that he'd had three lifetimes to pay for what he did because of her affair with a human, he couldn't bear the idea of being with a human. And the idea that Callia might be in a few minutes just feet away from him tore him up.

He knew he was responsible for her even being on a date with another male, Aeveren or otherwise. He'd caused this because he'd been afraid to accept her as his destined one. As the minutes passed, his stomach twisted into knots over her with another man. Any other man.

Maybe it's time to stop fighting.

Varek got up and hoped he'd reach her before she did anything with the guy. He flung open his door, ready to go charging after *his* female. Before he took a step, there standing outside his bedroom door was Callia, just about to knock on his door. Before he could tell her he wanted her, that he had been mistaken all along, she began to speak and he immediately knew this scene wasn't going to play out as he had hoped it would.

"Why were you so rude when you came into the kitchen?" Her tone told him she was angry, but he would've known she was pissed at him even if he were deaf. Her scowl spoke volumes.

Instantly defensive, he answered, "I wasn't rude."

"Yes, you were. He was my guest, and you didn't even give me a chance to introduce you to him."

Varek listened but was more focused on scanning her body for any evidence of her being undressed at any time in the last few hours.

"I don't appreciate the fact that your rudeness made him want to leave."

Good. And even better would be him never coming back.

"I guess by your silence that you don't care that I think you were rude?"

Varek wasn't able to stop the words that came out of his mouth next. "If I were rude, I would have said something about you dating a human." He saw at once by the angry flash in her eyes that he'd said the wrong thing.

Callia's face became red and heated. She was furious, but for more reasons than he knew. It was bad enough that he seemed to be against Aeveren females being with human males. That was just discriminatory. Even worse was that the only reason he had any problem with her having a date was because he was human. He didn't care about her at all! Her grandmother had been wrong.

"Dating a human? What does that mean?"

"Nothing. Forget I said it. Forget I said anything."

Varek wished he was in another lifetime and had the power to teleport himself the hell out of her apartment. He'd planned to tell her how he felt about her and had fantasized about how they would spend an incredible night in each other's arms. Instead he'd made her think he was anti-human and had offended her.

Fuck.

"Forget it? Are you saying you had a problem with my date because he's human?" The exasperation in her voice made him feel like shit. This was getting worse instead of better.

Callia wished he would say something that would let her know he cared if she were with *any* male. She stared up into his black eyes, looking for any sign he cared for her the way she cared for him.

Varek wanted to say something to explain that he didn't hate humans, even human males. But that would require him to explain about Neera and her affair, which would then require him to explain how seeing Callia with a human man made him jealous. He didn't want to start into that conversation because at the rate the current one was going, he'd say things all wrong and she'd think he was comparing her to the woman who had cheated on him and whom he'd murdered in a crime of passion.

No, saying anything more was a bad plan. Silence was his only choice.

Varek looked into her beautiful hazel eyes and saw tears begin to well up in them. The sick feeling he'd felt when he'd seen a human male was her date had morphed into his insides all knotted up over her with anyone but him and now his whole body ached because he'd hurt her. Memories of Neera came back to him, and he waited for Callia to begin yelling and swinging.

Callia waited for him to answer her question but believed she already had his answer. He didn't care, and his standing there in his doorway like a statue proved it. Tears spilled onto her cheeks, and she put her head down and ran to her room so he wouldn't see her cry. He'd think it was because she was weak and wouldn't understand she was crying because of her anger at him and herself for believing he cared about her.

As he watched her bedroom door close, he knew she'd misunderstood, and he blamed himself. Just as when he'd left after meeting her for the first time at the orphanage and felt her pain as he stood outside, he sensed her sadness as he stood next to her door. And just as he'd then wanted to reach out to her but didn't, he now remained silent, wishing he hadn't made a mess of the night.

CHAPTER FIVE

V AREK AWOKE EARLY THE NEXT morning, hoping he could repair the damage he'd caused the night before. He hurried to get dressed to see Callia before she left for work, but found her gone when he got to the kitchen, her cup for the tea she had every morning upside down in the dish drainer. As he stood looking about the room, he muttered to himself, "I'm not good at this."

He stood lost in thought about what he would say when he finally got a hold of her. Before his time in Nil, he had possessed a softer side he had sometimes shown Neera, but three lifetimes had all but erased that from him. Just remembering basic manners was a struggle at times now. All that time in Nil he'd spent doing anything to first stay alive and later to stay on top had meant he was skilled in survival, hand-to-hand combat, but not in how to deal with others on any level other than life and death.

Now he was besieged with feelings, all thanks to having a destined one again. He was happy Callia was in his life, but he wondered what to do with the jealousy, how to handle the memories it caused within him again.

As he walked back to his room, he thought out loud, "I did this to myself. I should have known trying to fight nature was as useless as trying to hold the ocean back with a broom."

He knew what he had to do. He had to give in.

This was easier said than done, but Varek thought about all that life with Callia offered. She truly was a gift, just as the Council said. He thought about her beautiful eyes, so sexy and unique, looking up at him over and over in the weeks since he'd been sent back. Somehow without doing a thing, she'd found that spot inside him he'd convinced himself was gone forever. He'd let her in and had fallen in love with her.

After his shower, he made a promise to himself to fix what he'd done. And just as soon as he found New Hope's murderer, he and Callia would begin a life together.

The murderer was never far from his mind. He'd arranged with Jessica to speak to some of the orphanage children today in the hopes that what they hadn't told the human police they'd tell him. If they could give him a clue about the murderer's appearance, he might get the break in the case he needed.

Varek walked down First Street thinking about the children he would speak to when he remembered it was Sunday.

Callia doesn't work on Sunday.

Just as he became conscious of the fact that she wasn't at work, he saw her and a male walk into the town's only restaurant, Lily's Diner. Varek walked more quickly to get a closer look at her date, jealousy racing through his body.

If it's a human male...

Callia wore a light blue dress, and Varek saw the male hang her coat on the rack near the front door. They sat at a booth in front of a large window, and he studied the male as if he were prey and his next meal.

The man was Aeveren, but Varek quickly realized what he'd tried to convince himself of wasn't true. He'd told himself that he wouldn't mind as much if her date the night before was Aeveren because then at least he'd be dealing with someone who knew she wasn't for him and would understand Varek's right to be with her. But he'd lied to himself. He did mind her being with another Aeveren too. He minded a lot.

He stood on the sidewalk across the street from Lily's, unable to look away. She was his destined one—his—and for the second time in less than twenty-four hours, he had to see her with another male. He watched her smile and then laugh, his gut tightening from jealousy.

The guy must be funny.

She doesn't laugh like that with me.

The male was smaller than he, Varek noted. He didn't tower over her, and he looked like a nice guy.

Fucking nice guys. I thought they finished last.

They sat, talking about what Varek conjured in his mind and made him even more jealous. After standing there watching them for five minutes, he trudged off down the street toward the orphanage.

By the time he reached the end of First Street, his stomach

was in knots again and his imagination had sent his jealousy into overdrive and had brought on a nasty bout of self-loathing. Hours later, he went home, a man on a mission. He would tell Callia that she was his and his alone. And then he'd figure out how to be good enough for her. She was in her room when he arrived, and although he waited in the living room for hours to confront her with his feelings, she never came out.

Varek went to sleep with a plan to speak to her in the morning. He wasn't sure how much more of these feelings he could stand, though. But he knew he needed to do whatever he could if he were ever to deserve her.

He awoke to the sound of the front door closing and cursed out loud as he covered his eyes with his arm. She was avoiding him, damnit. Frustration grew inside him as he lay there planning what he'd do.

Today he'd find her and speak to her. She wouldn't avoid him any longer.

"WHO WOULD YOU LIKE TO speak to first?" Jessica Anders asked Varek.

He looked over the list of children's names and found those of the two children whose parents were murdered in the first attack. He read them off to Jessica, and she left to find them for him. As he waited, he examined the room he sat in. Off-white walls and deep brown carpeting on the floor were the most noteworthy aspects of the space. New Hope Orphanage may have done good work for Aeveren children, but this room made him feel sad for them.

He thought about his daughter, who had been just a baby when he'd last seen her. She'd have been put in a place like New Hope after he killed her mother.

Fuck. They release me to find a murderer in a town that has an orphanage like one my little girl went to after...The Council must really want me to keep paying for my crime.

He knew he'd never stop paying for his crime, even if the Council finished their torment of him. He'd never let himself stop paying.

Jessica interrupted his emotional self-mutilation when she entered the room with two small boys, each holding one of her hands.

"Trevor, Andrew, I need you to speak to this man. His name is Varek. He needs your help."

The two boys turned their faces from her and looked up at Varek's face. He saw the fear in their eyes as they craned their necks to look at him, and he looked around for someplace to sit to make this less frightening for them.

After he found a chair and sat down, he told Jessica he would let her know when he was finished and watched her leave with a glance back to see the children sitting down in front of him.

Varek began to ask his first question and stopped short as he heard what his voice sounded like. He reminded himself that these weren't inmates in Nil he needed to make sure knew his power. These were little boys. In a softer voice, he began again and right away saw the reward for his change.

"Boys, I need to ask you about what happened to your parents. Can you help me?"

The two little boys shifted their positions on the floor and looked down at their legs.

"I promise I'm going to find out who did it. You have my word."

Andrew continued to keep his eyes lowered, but his older brother quietly spoke up. "The man did it."

Varek continued cautiously, concerned that if he was too aggressive, he'd scare them.

"Can you tell me what the man looked like?"

The boy continued. "Like one of us."

"Do you mean he was Aeveren?"

"Yes."

"Do you remember anything else about him?"

"Yellow eyes."

Varek repeated what the child had said and asked, "Are you sure?"

The little boy nodded.

The younger brother never lifted his gaze from the floor, and when Varek finished speaking to them, he bent down and picked him up.

"You and your brother have been very good," he said as he walked with him in his left arm while Trevor held his right hand.

"Remember what I told you, boys. I promise."

After giving them to Jessica, Varek went back into the room to await the other children, but he now suspected what he was looking for. The only Aeveren who had yellow eyes were half-breeds. Most were part human, but a very few were mixed with other supernaturals. Whatever the other half his murderer was, he would be much easier to find now.

When he was done with his second day of interviews, his suspicion was confirmed. The killer was a half-breed. Varek wondered why there weren't more like this half-breed, angry and resentful. Many Aeveren were harsh on human-Aeveren children. They were shunned from the Aeveren world. Some Aeveren were kinder to them, but all official areas of his society treated them as pariahs. Often their parents were forced apart with the threat of the loss of lifetimes for those Aeveren who wanted to remain with their humans and half-breed offspring. It was hardest on Aeveren females who had the choice of either leaving the Aeveren world or leaving their children. He understood the need for controlling their world, but he sympathized with the half-breeds' fate as outcasts.

As he thought about these things, he heard Callia's voice as she entered the building. They hadn't spoken after what had happened two nights before, but he'd decided they would today, whether she wanted to or not.

He stepped out into the hallway just as she approached the room and forced her to stop as he blocked her path.

"We need to speak." Unlike when he'd spoken to the children, he allowed his voice to return to its natural, commanding tone.

Callia looked into his eyes and hoped hers communicated exactly what she thought of his idea, but she said nothing.

"You're not going to speak to me? Fine. But I have something to say to you." He pulled her into the room and closed the door.

Callia had to fight the urge to tell him to let her out at once. She was still angry about that night, but she liked that her grandmother's ideas seemed to be working.

Varek held the door shut and turned to face her. He had decided as he lay in bed the night before that there would be no more men and dates for her. If goddamned Aeveren biology said she was his, then she was his. Not another male's. She wanted him? Well, this was who he was.

Callia waited silently for him to speak, knowing her silence gave her the upper hand. If he thought he was going to lecture her on dating human men, he was in for a surprise. She'd break her silence to tell him where to stick his anti-human ideas.

He looked at her standing in front of him, full of pride and looking irritated at him. He had to fight the urge to push her up against the wall and kiss her deeply.

Maybe later back at home.

"I don't want you seeing anyone else."

The words hit Callia deep inside, and she instinctively took a step toward him, decreasing the space that separated them to just a few inches. Excitement coursed through her body. God, she wanted him!

But there was no way she'd make it easy for him.

"And just who do you think you are to tell me who I can and can't see? Or date?" Callia intentionally hesitated and then, choosing her words carefully, said, "Or do whatever I damn well please with them?"

Varek controlled his response to ensure she understood his point. He wasn't so much angry as he was jealous and possessive.

"I'm your destined one and if anyone is going to damn well please you, it's going to be me. And only me."

Callia silently congratulated herself and thanked her grandmother and then stepped up right next to him, her breasts grazing his ribs.

"Let me out." She wanted to say she didn't want anyone but him, but she also wanted to push him just a little more.

The blood rushed to between his legs. Damnit, she made him hard. He knew she wanted him as much as he did her, so why the power struggle? He felt himself begin to lose control. His body wanted to forego the verbal sparring his mind loved. With great effort, he tamped down his desire and leaned into her.

When he spoke, the words came out almost as a growl. "No one else."

Callia knew it was time to go in for the kill. She looked into his black eyes and whispered, her lips a mere breath away, "I'll think about it." Instantly, she understood that she wouldn't leave the room without knowing exactly how much he wanted her.

What had seconds earlier sounded very much like a growl turned into something far more animalistic. Varek grabbed both her wrists and pushed them above her head, holding them in his left hand. With his right hand he cupped her breast. His hips leaned into her body, and he pushed his hard cock up against the zipper on her jeans.

Callia wished she could have him inside her right there, her legs wrapped around his waist as he took her for his own. She knew other females might be afraid of a male acting like he was, but she loved it. There was nothing sexier than an Aeveren male claiming his mate.

Varek suppressed the overwhelming desire to take her right there in the room in the orphanage but couldn't stop himself from kissing her. His mouth covered hers as his hand moved up from her breast to hold her face to his. When her tongue plunged into his mouth to find his warm wetness, his hips pushed into her, grinding into her sex.

His mouth moved to her ear and he repeated his command once again. As he panted next to her ear, Callia thought she might orgasm right there. When she didn't acquiesce, he thrust his hips again and said, in a strained, hoarse voice, "No one, Callia. Do you understand?"

She watched as he stepped away from her and let her arms drop. His black eyes looked like shiny pieces of obsidian staring back at her. She knew he waited to hear her word of surrender, thinking he had persuaded her as a male to give up others in favor of only him. She knew better, though. She knew she had brought him to this point, exactly where she had wanted him from the moment she'd laid eyes on him.

Callia looked into those dark eyes so full of desire. Everything else she had said in that room she'd been forced to say to make him become who he was, her destined mate. Now she would say the one word to him that she didn't have to force.

"Yes."

A knock at the door thrust them back into the reality that they were still at the orphanage, but even as he answered the person on the other side of the door, he never moved his eyes from Callia's face.

"I'll be out in a minute, Jessica." His voice was deep, but not like how he had just spoken to her.

As Callia stared up at him, the sensation of having him gazing into her eyes as he spoke to someone else made her feel under his control, like he decided when she could stay and when she could go. She also felt like she was the most important thing in the world to him, his only focus.

Varek heard Jessica's footsteps as she walked down the wood floor hallway back toward her office. When he sensed she was out of earshot, he resumed what he'd been doing before she'd interrupted.

"Do we understand one another?" he said in a deep, husky voice.

"Why do you sound like that only when you speak to me?" As she spoke, her hands moved slowly up and down his torso from his waist to his chest, seemingly contradictorily since her question sounded like she was irritated by the way he spoke to her.

Varek felt Callia's hands brush lightly against the head of his erection just above his pants. He knew that even if she disapproved of the tone he took with her, on some level she liked it.

"Don't you like it?" he asked as he leaned his head next to her ear. When she didn't answer, he did. "Don't lie. You do. Your hands wouldn't be stroking my stomach if you didn't like it."

Callia didn't want to lie. She did like the way he was forceful and strong. It's how she had dreamed her destined one would be. She smiled at him and let her hands drift lower on his body as she said, "Don't get the idea that I think you should act like a Cro-Magnon man, Varek. I do like a strong and powerful man, but he needs to be smart too. Power without respect won't work."

Varek smiled a devilish grin and ran his hand up and down her neck. "Callia, if I were a Cro-Magnon, I would have thrown your date out of the house that night and then put you over my shoulder as I took you to my bed." His eyes shone as the words lazily left his mouth. He looked like power personified.

She felt her face grow warm as he spoke about taking her to his bed. If he was this sexy when he was telling her what he didn't want her to do, she could only imagine what he'd be like on top of her telling her what he wanted her to do. She felt herself get even wetter than she was before.

Varek sensed that he had frightened her with his reference to taking her to bed. He didn't want to scare her, knowing he was her first destined one.

"Don't worry. I promise I won't do that for your first

time," he said as he lightly stroked her cheek.

Callia smiled at him. "Varek, you're my first destined one, not my first lover. I'm not a virgin."

He dropped his hand from her face and released the door, and Callia saw the look of shock at her statement as she quickly turned and left the room. She knew he wanted to respond, but she didn't let him.

Varek struggled to keep his body and emotions in check as he watched her walk away from him. He had the strong feeling she'd been more in control of what had just happened than he'd even considered. He smiled as he chided himself for thinking such a beautiful and intelligent female hadn't been with anyone.

He had definitely underestimated her. Underneath that sweet exterior was a female who knew how to handle herself. She knew what she wanted and took it with both hands. He'd never had a chance once she decided destiny was right.

I was wrong. This is a female who can deal with my past and what it made me.

Now he wondered if he could handle her.

CALLIA LEFT THE ORPHANAGE AFTER she received a phone call, so when Varek left to go to the house, he expected to pick up where they'd left off at the orphanage earlier in the day, with her hands gliding over his body and his mouth on hers. By the time he walked the eight blocks, he'd thought about their encounter enough for him to be hard before he hit the front steps. The front door was locked, and when he walked into the house, he didn't hear any sounds that told him she was there. A piece of paper folded in half on the coffee table caught his eye, and noticing it had his name written on it, he picked it up.

Varek,

I needed to go with my grandmother to her sister's in New Jersey. I'll be back in a few days, and you can practice your caveman routine more when I get back.

Callia

He looked around the apartment as he stood with the letter in his hand. It felt empty, and he realized how much he missed her and how much he'd grown attached to her. It wasn't the color of the paint on the walls or the knickknacks she carefully placed around the house that made it feel like a home. It was her, her presence, her warmth that made it feel like a real home.

He undressed and lay in bed, going over the day. The information the children had provided gave him a much-needed lead he would pursue in the morning. It was unlikely the murderer would be leaving his eyes unaltered. Half-breeds knew as well as Aeveren that yellow eyes meant a mixture of blood. With colored contact lenses, it was easier to change eye color, but Varek knew the yellow would never fully be hidden. It bled through even the darkest color lenses and was noticeable if one was looking close enough. It was a mark that couldn't be escaped.

Varek ran his hands over his shoulders and down his sides, feeling his own marks. He thought about Callia's hands caressing his mutilated skin, her fingertips coming in contact with the evidence of what had been done to him and what he'd done. Would she turn away when he told her what he'd gone through in Nil? Or would she be able to handle a mate who was scarred inside and out?

He thought about the woman who'd stood in front of him hours earlier, challenging him to take control of her, of their relationship. She'd matched him in emotional strength then, pushing him to admit his feelings for her but never as other women might, with complaints and cajoling. No, she was smarter than that. Stronger.

As he thought of her beautiful eyes staring up at him and daring him to be in control over her, his cock thickened. His mind wandered over her body, lingering on her legs and then slowly traveling north until he saw himself touching her soft inner thighs with his fingertips. Her skin responded to him with a quiver, and he bent his head down to her thighs to replace his hands with his mouth.

As he thought of her body waiting for his, he slid his hand onto his erection and began slowly stroking his skin. While his hand performed, his mind continued to create the fantasy of making her his.

His lips gently sucked the skin of her inner thigh, slowly moving toward his ultimate goal. He rubbed his cheek against her leg, feeling her sex brush against his lips softly, delicately. His hands moved to her hips and his mouth took her in, the folds and swelling clitoris caressed by his warm, wet tongue. Her desire rising, he held her firmly against the bed as she rushed toward her climax, her hips bucking against his hold. She grabbed at the back of his head, straining to pull him closer as she slipped over the edge. When she was finished, the taste of her stayed on his tongue, his mouth glistening from her.

Varek began to breathe more heavily, the effect of his fantasy inching him closer to his own orgasm as he lay alone in Callia's house.

He rose from between her legs and held himself over her, his weight on his hands. She looked up at him, her eyes glazed and full of desire. She reached up and wrapped her arms around his neck to bring his chest to hers and arched her back to tell him she wanted him inside her. Her hands traveled over his back, her fingertips knowing the proof of his punishment. As he entered her and began thrusting into her, she kept her hands on his back, accepting both his body and his past.

She felt wet and hot around him as he filled her, sliding in and out, meeting her desire with his. As she came a second time, he pumped faster into her toward his own climax.

In the darkness of her house, Varek brought himself to the very point of release and imagined the feel of coming inside her, her legs wrapped around him begging him to be closer. As he came, it took with it some of the sadness he always carried with him and the pain of missing her, even if for just a brief time.

CHAPTER SIX

D ERRICK JAMES STARED AT THE *Albany Times Union* and angrily crumpled it into a ball before whipping it at the wall-sized map that showcased his killings. The newspaper hadn't run a story about him in days. His anger overflowed into a tirade as he paced around his house.

"Fucking newspaper! Like anyone fucking cares about the state budget or anything else those bastard politicians do."

His anger mixed with frustration over his inability to find his next victims. None of them were right. The mothers were too clingy, and the fathers were…the fathers were never right. Aeveren fathers were never right. They mistreated the females. Didn't care for their children, the ones *they* made.

Derrick James knew he needed to find number six. Aeveren wouldn't understand if he stopped now. They'd never understand how their world was an abomination if he stopped now.

He paced back and forth from the back door in the kitchen to the front door in the living room over carpet that was threadbare from so many passes. When he passed the mirror in the dining room, he watched himself walk by, looking at his hair, his eyes, his face and feeling sick to his stomach.

His mother had always told him he was the best of her and his father. She'd sit with him on the couch he still had in his living room and run her hands through his blond hair as she told him how much it looked like his father's. Then she'd turn his head toward hers and always say the same thing: "And your eyes remind me so much of your father's." When he got older, old enough to know that his eyes were a mark of shame for him and loss for her, he'd wonder how his yellow eyes looked like anyone's from a race of people that could have any eye color except yellow.

He'd ask her when he was feeling particularly sadistic, knowing it caused her great pain to think of him or his kind in anything but the best of terms. She excused his absence from their lives through self-delusion. He didn't have a choice. He loved her. He would come back to them. He wasn't to blame. But his eyes of any color other than yellow looked like his, her child by an Aeveren.

He had never known there was something wrong with him until she had attempted to find his father. Then they came into contact with many Aeveren, who almost to a man, woman, and child regarded him as an unwanted thing. His mother was at least human. They looked at her like she was different but not wrong. When they saw the telltale sign of his yellow eyes, they turned away from his gaze, or worse, said cruel things about his being a half-breed.

Yellow-eyed half-breed.

Their attempt to find his father was successful, but their attempt to gain his love was not. He could have sex with a human, profess love for her, irresponsibly impregnate her, but he couldn't love the yellow-eyed half-breed he'd helped to bring into the world.

His mother had excused his inability to show even the slightest kindness to his son through more rationalization that added to his pain. *They* kept him from them. *They* were always to blame.

His hatred grew each day he saw the ones who had an aura around them. He used to imagine them feeling as he felt, if humans could see how different they were. But they couldn't see that. They saw his yellow eyes, though. Humans didn't see him as unwanted or wrong. They saw him as angry, something he freely admitted to being.

He was full of hate. Full of hate for them. For Aeveren. He wasn't wrong. They were, for treating someone who was at least in part like them so cruelly.

Derrick stopped pacing and picked up a pushpin from the table. A yellow pushpin. The next ones would be soon.

He placed the yellow pushpin back into the clear, plastic box and closed the lid. It was time to go out. He walked to the bathroom and took out the deep blue contact lenses he wore outside his house.

He closed his eyes and tried to push the vision of his own eyes out of his mind, an exercise he did every day after putting his contacts in his eyes. When he opened them, he didn't see his yellow eyes, his father's eyes, or his mother's eyes. He saw dark blue eyes, the color that was most successful at hiding what made him wrong.

VAREK AWOKE EARLY, FEELING THE emptiness of Callia's house immediately. And before he could stop them, memories of another time of loneliness crashed into his mind and took over.

He lay on his stomach on the cold, hard ground. His ribs still sent stabs of sharp pain through his body whenever they touched anything. But the other choice was infinitely worse. His back still bore the cuts his fellow inmates had made on one of his first nights in Nil. The open wounds made standing or even sitting nearly impossible. The pain was excruciating and constant.

The pain did help to divert his thoughts from what he'd done. At least it did that. But the pain inside was worse, if that was possible, than the pain on the outside.

He was in Nil, alone from this point on. He'd had a true love, a destiny he adored, and a daughter he loved more and more each day, so much that he couldn't have asked for more in life. He'd had everything. And in a split second, he'd lost everything.

His nights in Nil so far had been all like this, full of self-loathing and regret. All except the night he'd been cut. That night was nothing but searing hot pain all over his body.

His days were hard labor with no time to feel anything. But nights were filled with terror, from within and without. They wouldn't try to cut him again, yet. He knew that from the conversations he heard as other inmates commented on how he'd withstood the attack.

He hadn't passed out. He hadn't cried. But he didn't know why. He didn't try to stop himself from doing either. He didn't know why he didn't die that night. He hadn't wanted to live even before then. He'd lost his will to live as he watched Neera vanish, as all Aeveren did when they died, leaving the human man she'd been on top of lying dead, covered in the blood from the gunshot wounds he'd inflicted on them, and a moment later the reality of Aeveren law flashed through his mind and he knew they'd taken his baby girl. He'd lost everything.

The emptiness of his existence—it couldn't be called a life— in Nil stretched out before him as a limitless vista of nothing. He would be alone forever. Alone with memories of how much he'd been blessed with before.

There were ways to die. He could pick a fight with another inmate. He knew inmates were murdered each night. One choice he could make here and the pain would be over. A stab to his heart and he'd be done. No more Nil. No more lives. He'd cease to exist. The strange Aeveren laws that considered the murder of even another murderer wrong but wouldn't allow them another chance at a lifetime would bring his existence to a final end.

He didn't know why, but he couldn't do it. He had no hope, but couldn't bring himself to die. So he continued to exist, to feel the pain in his body and his mind.

He slowly lifted himself from the stone floor that was his bed and stood in front of his cell's bars looking out into the darkness of Nil. He held on to the bars as his body sagged against them in pain and exhaustion. He couldn't think of what he'd lost anymore, but letting go of them was like losing them all over again.

He hung on to the bars as tears fell from his eyes. He didn't know if they were for the pain his body was in or the pain he felt inside knowing that since he'd chosen not to die, he'd have to let them go to exist. He closed his eyes and slowly began to let them go, hoping somehow his daughter heard him begging her for forgiveness and could find it in her heart someday to accept his pleas.

I'm sorry.

Good-bye.

A heaviness settled in his chest that was like a weight sitting on top of him. Three lifetimes of memories stayed in him, three lifetimes that had changed him into who he was.

He covered his eyes with his arm to shield them from the morning light. He thought about Callia, the first good thing he'd been allowed in lifetimes. He wanted to be what she needed, what she deserved.

For whatever reason, I've been given her, given the gift of someone who's strong and smart and wants me.

As these words sounded in his head, Varek rose from his bed and stood in front of the mirror. The man looking back at him looked stronger than ever before.

He leaned into the mirror, his weight on his hands, and looked into his eyes. Then he did something he hadn't done in lifetimes. He told his reflection today was going to be a good day, and he believed it. His days would be even better when Callia returned.

He knew his future happiness depended on his finding the person murdering Aeveren parents. If he wanted to stay with Callia and build a life with her in this lifetime and future ones, he had to succeed.

CHAPTER SEVEN

———— 〰 ————

CALLIA AWOKE AT HER GREAT-AUNT'S house to the smell of blueberry muffins and freshly brewed coffee. Her grandmother was a typical grandmother in that she doted on her and gave kindly advice, often unsolicited, but her sister had mastered the other arts of grandmothering, particularly baking.

She had loved going to her great-aunt's house when she was a child. An advanced Aeveren, close to her final lifetimes, Jean seemed to know everything about the world. Her stories stretched back to the beginning of the Aeveren world and included everything from ancient times to the present. Her gift, as she called it, the power she had received as she aged in her reincarnation cycle, was precognition. But she couldn't see everything about the future. She could only see things associated with people close to her. Her usual joke was that she had been given this gift instead of the gift of telepathy or mind control because the universe knew she'd be up to no good with those abilities.

Callia rolled over and stretched, knowing she had to get up

because her grandmother and great-aunt wanted to speak to her about a vision she'd had in the last week. But she wanted instead to just lay there and think about Varek.

She missed him. Even though they had never slept together, she felt like her bed now was missing his presence. She wanted to roll over and feel his body lying next to hers. She wanted to look into his eyes, so dark that they sometimes seemed to reflect her image, and see what she'd seen the day before—the desire, the need he felt for her. She wondered what he was doing. Was he in the bed in her spare bedroom? Was he eating breakfast in the kitchen? Was he in her shower?

Callia knew she wouldn't get out of bed if she continued daydreaming about Varek, so she promised herself she'd call him later and dragged herself out of bed and down to her great-aunt's kitchen.

"Good morning, Grandma. Good morning, Aunt Jean."

Her great-aunt turned around from the oven and smiled. A typical white-haired older woman with glasses, she stood about five and a half feet, but she just seemed younger in her ways.

"Good morning, sweetie. How did you sleep? Linda, get her some coffee." She looked toward her sister and handed her a coffee mug. Turning back toward Callia, she said, "I made muffins."

"I know. I smelled them all the way upstairs." Callia took the cup of coffee with a smile and sat down at the round kitchen table.

The two older women sat down with her a few minutes

later. They all sat in silence, but Callia could tell they were anxious to speak to her about the vision.

"Grandma, the two of you are making me nervous. What was in this vision? Was it about me?" She searched their faces, hoping if it was about her it wasn't too bad. She knew if it had been good news her great-aunt would have just told them on the phone.

Aunt Jean spoke up first. "It was about you, but I'm a little worried."

Callia's stomach dropped. Did it have to do with Varek?

Impatiently, she asked, "Well, what is it? What's going to happen, Aunt Jean?"

"I saw someone with yellow eyes around you."

A half-breed? Her grandmother had warned her many times about dating humans because of the half-breed issue, but hearing this made Callia sigh with relief now.

With a smile, she said, "Aunt Jean, you don't have to worry. I'm with my destined one now—an Aeveren male. I'm sure she told you." She knew full well her grandmother had told her aunt the whole story, complete with added color commentary.

"She did. It's just that my vision was very clear. Yellow eyes."

"Well, you don't have to worry. Varek isn't human, so any children we'll have won't have yellow eyes."

They'll have beautiful, deep, dark eyes like his, hopefully.

Her grandmother's eyes shimmered, and she said, in an almost squealing voice, "Children? Ooh! Will it be soon?" Her delight brightened the faces of both Callia and her Aunt Jean.

Callia reached out her hand and touched her grandmother's. "I promise, when it happens, you'll be the third person to know."

She blushed at the idea that she was referring to sex with Varek with two elderly women—sex she hadn't had yet but had thought about in detail.

Knowing that her aunt's vision wasn't about her burgeoning relationship with Varek allowed her to relax. She began to nibble on the top of a blueberry muffin now that her stomach had begun to settle down.

But Callia could see that Jean wasn't quite ready to let the situation go. Her expression had returned to one of concern.

"That's all well and good, sweetie, but I want you to be careful."

Callia turned her attention to her aunt again. "Why? Half-breeds aren't dangerous. Why would I need to be careful?"

"I had the sense that there was danger around the yellow eyes." Aunt Jean took Callia's hands in hers and held them. "Your grandmother and I worry about you, Callia. We just want you to be safe and happy."

Smiling because she knew Varek would have something to say if she was ever not completely safe, Callia squeezed her great aunt's hands. "You don't have to worry. If anyone can keep me safe, Varek can."

"Why is that, dear?" her grandmother asked with a hint of suspicion in her voice.

Callia hadn't told her about his background, his time in

Nil. Even though she believed in the infallibility of Aeveren biology, she may be concerned that her granddaughter's destined one was a murderer who had spent three lifetimes in Nil.

"Because Aeveren males are always protective of their destined ones. Isn't that what you've always told me in all those stories all those years?" She hoped neither woman sensed she was intentionally trying to change the subject.

She knew she'd have to tell her grandmother about Varek, but she planned to wait until after she'd met him and seen how happy they are together.

Of course, that happiness had to happen first. So far their time together hadn't been full of bliss, but she believed that once he stopped fighting what their biology had already determined was to be, they could be quite happy. She liked what he looked like—in fact, she found him almost irresistible with those deep, dark eyes and that beautiful mouth—and could accept what his past was. People made mistakes, sometimes very tragic ones. She also liked how she could be with him. Other men, Aeveren and human, didn't seem to like her strength and willfulness, but Varek did, as far as she could tell. She was herself with him.

Thankfully, Callia saw her great aunt had other things on her mind that would keep her grandmother busy. She watched as the two older women turned to the discussion of the comings and goings of other Aeveren they knew.

"I'm going to take a shower now," she announced as she rose from the table to make her escape.

"Okay, sweetie. We'll have to leave in a bit, but we'll have dinner later and talk more."

Callia left them to discuss some man they had both known for years who had left his wife for a much younger woman with badly dyed hair and fake breasts. As she exited the room, the words "old fool" and "gold digger" had made their first and undoubtedly not their last appearance.

As she climbed the stairs to her room, she hoped Varek was still at the house so she could talk to him. He didn't have a cell phone, so she could only reach him at home. She could try the orphanage, but then she'd have to deal with Jessica's twenty questions about him.

With the cell phone to her ear, she listened as her home phone rang and thought about getting him a cell phone of his own. Had he ever had one? The sound of her own voice on the other end of the line roused her from her daydreaming about cell phones and time and she closed her phone before the voicemail prompt had finished.

I'll try him later.

She flopped down on the bed and continued to think about him. When she closed her eyes, she could see him perfectly. She imagined him standing in front of her in her apartment, his body almost looming over her. He could look almost frightening at times, but he didn't scare her. He excited her. His darkness. His powerful features. His commanding voice. All of it was incredibly attractive to her.

She smiled as she remembered with amusement his surprise when she'd told him she wasn't a virgin.

A virgin wouldn't be able to handle him. A man like him needed a mate who could deal with what his past had made him. A man like him had demons in him that he fought every moment of the day. He needed someone strong enough to show him that even when those demons rose up and threatened to swallow him whole that he was still loved and someone who knew because of those demons he needed her more than ever before.

Callia found herself fantasizing about him, his mouth on her skin, nibbling and licking as he made his way to her most sensitive spots. His passion in the room at the orphanage the day before told her he would be more than other men she'd been with who had been kind respectful lovers. They hadn't been bad or entirely unsatisfying, but they had never been what she wanted, what she needed.

She needed a lover who knew how to excite every inch of her, who knew that gentle and sweet wasn't always what a woman wanted. She needed one who knew how to please a woman and was powerful enough to take her places she may not know she wanted to go. She needed a male who could possess her.

She believed Varek was that male. She wasn't blind to the demons he might have. He had obviously been in love with the female who had been his first destined one. Jessica had told her that one of the few things she found out about him when she checked him out with the Council was that he murdered his first destined one and her lover as they had sex in his bed. Males who aren't in love don't murder someone out of passion. Those feelings don't ever fully go away, but Callia knew she could show him what loving someone who loved him in return felt like.

But the more devastating demons were those from three lifetimes in Nil. She'd only heard stories about the place, but it was said to be worse than any human prison. She knew his body showed the effects of his time there. When she'd run her hands over his back the first time they'd kissed, she'd felt the scars all over his skin. Whether he'd been attacked or had gotten them fighting other inmates, he had experienced considerable pain from the cuts that had left those scars.

His way with her and others showed how long he'd been away from kindness and care. He was gruff when he didn't need to be, but he was getting better as he got used to life outside of Nil. Callia believed that inside him, past the sexiness, the roughness, and even past the demons, there was a good man. That man showed himself whenever he was around the children of the orphanage. With them, he was kind and caring. She noticed how he softened his voice when he spoke to them and kneeled to be at their height so he didn't intimidate them. She knew that children could sense if someone should be feared, and they had accepted him without a second thought. Even Tia, who spoke to very few adults, especially men, had taken to him immediately.

As Callia thought about all the things that came with Varek, she felt sure that biology hadn't made a mistake. He was just what she wanted and needed, and she was sure she was just that for him. Now if only he could see that as clearly as she did.

By four o'clock Callia heard her grandmother and great aunt come up the driveway. She had spent the day relaxing and thinking about Varek, but now she was afraid she'd have to talk to them about him. She knew they meant well, but she wasn't as innocent or naive as they thought she was. She hadn't been for a long time, she thought, as she remembered someone from several lifetimes ago.

"Natalia, you know I love you. You know that." Marco held her arm, refusing to let her go. Natalia felt pain radiate from where his fingers had begun to bruise her skin.

"Release me. If my father sees marks on my arms, he'll hunt you down and kill you slowly."

Marco eased his grip but wouldn't let her go. "Tell me you love me! You must! You wouldn't sneak out to see me if you didn't!"

Natalia looked into his eyes, so full of young love...lust. Years before, Marco had looked at her as a boy looked at a girl not yet grown into herself. They had lived in Urbino all their lives and Natalia had grown into an Italian beauty, a fact that hadn't escaped Marco's notice.

For months she had been sneaking away from the eyes of her parents to spend time with him. Two years older than she, he would soon be forced to leave home to find work and he knew his absence likely meant another man would take her from him. Too young to marry at almost sixteen, Natalia secretly adored him but kept his feelings at arm's length, even if she didn't keep the rest of him that far away.

"Marco, you know I like you," she said as she leaned in to touch her lips to his ear.

"Like! You don't kiss me like all you feel is like for me. Why do you tease me like this?"

Marco released her arm and pulled her body to his. His hands explored her back and drifted down to her buttocks, squeezing them. His mouth kissed hers passionately, his tongue plunging in to find hers.

Natalia felt the hardness of him push against her belly. His thrusting took her breath away, and she felt her legs go weak.

"Marco, someone will see us!" She tore her mouth away from his to look around the hillside. The sun in her eyes, she couldn't see anyone nearby, but was cautious nevertheless.

In a voice that told her what Marco wanted and he didn't care who was watching, he whispered, "There's no one, Natalia. Kiss me."

Marco maneuvered her behind a large tree and gently pushed her against its trunk. As he kissed her, he unlaced the front of her blouse to get to her breasts. His head dropped, and she felt his mouth on her nipple, sucking tenderly but eagerly. Natalia thrust her hands into his light brown hair and twisted the soft waves around her fingers, exciting him more.

He caressed her skin beneath her breasts. He sucked until her nipple was hard, and achieved the same result with the other one through gentle pinching.

Natalia became wet from his attention. She closed her eyes, too delirious from excitement to care if anyone was near.

In her ear, Marco whispered, "Please." She knew what his

plea referred to, and she slowly knelt on the ground and looked up at him. He looked down at her with half-lidded eyes, waiting for her to do something, anything to end his waiting.

She unfastened his pants and released his erect cock from under the fabric. It jutted out away from his body toward her. She touched the length of it gently and curled her fingers around it, stroking lightly. She watched as his eyes rolled back into his head in pleasure.

She licked her lips and wrapped them around the head. Marco moaned her name and shoved his hands into her hair in a movement not meant to force her head down but to plead for her to take more of him.

Slowly, she took his thick erection into her mouth as far as she could, stroking the rest of the shaft not in her mouth. Eyes closed, she teased his skin with her tongue, focusing on the sensitive area under the tip. She opened her eyes to see him staring down at her in lust.

He quickly lifted her from her knees and brought her mouth to his. Hoarsely, he told her, "Lay down, Natalia. Now."

As she lay on her back, lifting up her skirt, Marco appeared over her, his skin still glistening from the moisture of her mouth. He brought the tip of his cock to her entrance, pressing slowly into her. They had been together before, but he had been her only lover. He knew this and moved slowly as he entered her.

Overcome by desire, after a short time he was unable to continue his slow pace and plunged quickly into her. Faster and harder, he entered her, each time touching a spot deep inside her that sent waves of pleasure throughout her body.

Natalia felt her climax reach its height and dug her nails into the smooth, tan skin of Marco's back. She pulled him to her, wrapping her legs around his waist to bring him closer. He covered her mouth with his and kissed her deeply as his orgasm began on top of hers, flooding her insides with warmth.

As he lay on top of her, still inside her, Marco whispered, "I know you love me, Natalia."

She kissed and held him silently, keeping her feelings to herself so when he left he would never know how much she'd miss him.

Callia smiled at her memories of her time in Italy with Marco. He'd been her first in her fifth lifetime, and she'd loved him. But she'd known they weren't made for each other. Marco left a few months after that day, just as she knew he'd be forced to, and she never saw him again. She'd spent the rest of her life in Urbino, alone with her family in the rolling hills of central Italy, tending to the house, going to the market every Saturday, and celebrating at the Festa del Luca each August. It had been a happy lifetime, in part because of her time with Marco. While there were others after him, Marco had been the one who'd made her happiest.

As Callia walked to the kitchen to greet the elderly women, she wished she could remind them that this was her seventh lifetime and she knew a little bit about life, but they saw her as such a young Aeveren, both in this lifetime and in the reincarnation cycle.

"Callia, my sister has been telling me about how you were called to your mate. It's very romantic," Aunt Jean said with a wink.

"Jean, don't tease her. It's her first time."

Callia saw the look on her grandmother's face that showed she was trying to stop her sister from going any further.

"Sweetie, I've decided to go back tonight instead of tomorrow. I hope you don't mind."

Thrilled by her grandmother's news but not wanting to hurt her great-aunt's feelings, Callia nodded and sat down at the kitchen table.

"What time are we leaving?"

"About an hour. You better get your things ready."

Callia could tell her grandmother was trying to get her out of the kitchen before her Aunt Jean began again about Varek. She knew she had very few things to pack. Silently she thanked her and smiled as she got up to leave the room to get ready to leave.

An hour later, they kissed Aunt Jean good-bye and started back for New Hope. Callia drove the three and a half hour trip, and they arrived home a little before nine o'clock. Callia parked her car at her grandmother's, where she always kept it since she didn't have any place for it at her house, and thanked her grandmother for everything. Before she left, her grandmother called after her to call as soon as she got home so she wouldn't worry.

Callia quickly walked the few short blocks to her house, hoping Varek was home. She wasn't sure what she would say to him, but she knew her brief time away had cemented her feelings for him. She wondered, however, what his feelings were. He'd made it clear that he didn't want her seeing anyone else, but she didn't know if he felt any more than that.

Her heart began to race as she walked up the steps to her front door. When she opened the door, she saw the rooms were dark. Let down, she dropped her bag near the door with a thud and went to her room to change into clothes for bed.

She looked at herself in the mirror and said to herself, *I guess it's early to bed for me. And this is different from not having a destined one how?*

She heard a noise in the living room and when she went to see what it was, there was Varek in the white shirt she'd given him and smelling like women's perfume.

Callia stood in her nightshirt staring at him, stunned. Women's perfume?

Varek turned toward her, thrilled to see her. "You're home? I thought you'd be home tomorrow."

"I'm sure you did. By the smell of you, I'm sure you're disappointed."

CHAPTER EIGHT

V AREK KNEW SHE SMELLED THE perfume from the woman at Jake's. He hadn't done anything with her, but he knew her perfume clung to him. If he were to be honest, he was happy it did because it made Callia jealous. He would never touch another female, but as he looked at her glaring at him from across the room, he saw just the thought made her crazy.

Before he could reply, she turned and walked down the hall to her room grumbling about how this wasn't her idea of a good night. He walked after her and caught her by the sleeve just outside her door.

"I missed you." He knew he smelled like another woman, but he hoped she saw the look in his eyes that told her he wanted her.

"Don't touch me. You smell like whoever you were with tonight. I see this destined one thing means a lot to you."

Callia looked at him in disgust. He was wearing the white shirt she was sure would look good on him—and did it ever—but now she thought of him wearing it with someone else.

Varek stared into her eyes and saw not jealousy but hurt. "I wasn't with anyone else, Callia. Jake's is a small bar and a woman was wearing a lot of perfume." He intentionally softened his voice to let her know he was sorry she was hurt.

"Good night, Varek."

As she opened her door, he grabbed the doorknob and held the door. "Can we talk?"

"Not with you smelling like *that*."

"I'll shower. Give me ten minutes."

Callia nodded and went into her room. She wanted to kick herself for how she'd acted. Jealousy wasn't something she wore well, and she knew any control she'd had over the entire situation with Varek had probably evaporated because of her outburst.

What did he want to talk to her about?

Ten minutes later he knocked on her door. She quickly debated with herself as to where to speak to him, where she could consider her turf, and found it amazing that after only such a short time, the apartment had ceased to be only hers. Still undecided about where to talk, she opened her bedroom door and saw him standing in front of her in a grey T-shirt and jeans. He'd bought new clothes.

He looked sexier than she'd ever seen him before. His black hair was still wet and glistening, and his skin was damp. His shirt fit his body like his black one had and strained against his muscular chest. For a moment, she was lost in how incredible he looked.

Varek stepped forward to enter her room, but she stopped

him. "We can talk in the living room."

He led the way down the hall, wishing she would have let him into her bedroom. He wouldn't force himself on her, but he wanted them to start acting like Aeveren destined for one another should.

He sat on the couch, expecting her to do the same, but looked over at the opposite end from where he sat and found it empty and Callia standing three feet farther away. Varek's impatience grew. His desire for her had been pressing on him for over a day already, and his body was in need of release. Her insistence on challenging him was certainly exciting, but his need for her had pushed him past the verbal sparring stage. He didn't know how much longer he'd be able to keep this up.

Attempting to keep his voice casual, he looked up at her and calmly said, "Sit." When she remained still and silent, staring at him, he added, in a voice that contained just the hint of a growl, "Please."

Callia was no longer angry by the time she entered the living room, but she was aroused by how he looked. As she gazed down at him, she felt a rush of excitement when she spied the erection in his pants. *Had he come around to agreeing with nature?*

Determined to play his game, she relented and sat on the couch at the other end, facing him. She hoped the look on her face said, "You want to talk. Okay. Talk." She was pretty sure she knew how this would end, or how she wanted it to end, but he wanted to talk first, so talk they would.

Varek saw she wanted to play. Her expression made it

obvious. But he did want to speak to her before anything else. He felt she deserved to know some things before she got into anything more with him.

"How was your trip?"

"Fine. I went to see my great aunt in New Jersey."

Good. She was speaking.

"It must have been a long drive. Come here and I'll rub your back."

A very slight smile formed on Callia's lips. He held out his hand toward her for her to come to him.

Callia stood up and moved to sit next to him, but Varek opened his legs and guided her between them. As she sat down, she felt his erection push against her lower back and then his hands encircled her neck tenderly. His palms rested against her neck for a few seconds before he began running his fingers over the skin on her shoulders and collarbone.

His hands were large and strong, each one able to cover one of her shoulders. But he wasn't massaging away any tension as much as he was creating some in her by grazing his touch back and forth between her neck, her shoulders, and down to her collarbone just underneath the top of her nightshirt. Callia closed her eyes and parted her lips as she began to breathe heavier, her body pushing softly against his.

The skin beneath his fingers warmed as he let them dance over her. She felt so good he considered forgetting the talking and skipping to what he'd planned next. But she needed to know.

He moved her hair and placed a kiss on the back of her

neck, lingering there as his hands returned to stroke her collarbone. She sighed gently and moved back toward him. If he didn't say what he needed to say, he'd have to say it after they slept together, and that wouldn't be fair to her.

"Callia, I need to tell you something." As he spoke, he moved his fingers slowly up and down her throat. When she moaned in agreement, his fingers felt the vibration from the sound she made.

"You know why I'm here…and where I came from."

Callia felt like the movement of his hands had hypnotized her and his words sounded like they were coming from far away. She whispered yes, but only vaguely knew what she'd agreed to.

Varek sensed she wasn't paying attention, but he loved the reaction she gave him to the touch of his hands on her body. She needed to know the truth, though, so he stopped and simply spoke.

"I…" He knew he should continue and tell her that if he didn't find the murderer that they'd force him back to Nil, away from her and any child they might conceive that night. He knew she should know before taking that final step with him, but he couldn't bear losing her. So he told her a truth, just not the one he should have told her.

"I saw a lot in Nil. Went through a lot. Did a lot of things," he said quietly.

Callia was completely alert as he spoke now. She wanted to turn around to see his face, but his arms held her in position as he hugged her close to him.

She heard the pain in his voice and yearned to say something to take it away. "I know. I can only imagine how bad it was."

Pulling away from him, she wriggled out of his hold and stood up over him as he watched her. Maybe she didn't want to be with someone who brought that past with him.

Callia sat down quickly on Varek's lap, facing him. The fear of rejection in his eyes melted away when she leaned in to kiss him.

"No matter what you saw or what you did, you're the one I'm meant for." As she spoke, she looked into his eyes and stroked his cheek with the back of her hand.

Varek knew he was about to do the wrong thing. He hadn't told her what could happen if he failed to find the murderer. He knew he was being selfish. He didn't care. He'd find some way to not fail. He needed to feel Callia next to him, be inside her, and have her inside him.

All the lifetimes alone, the desire to be with her, her body pressed against his caused something to rise like a fever inside of him. His mouth touched hers, eager and waiting for him, and he thrust his tongue into her mouth.

His hands slid down to her bare legs, straddling his sides. His touch on her thighs made her sit up higher on him, and the wetness of her panties brushed against his stomach. She sat back down, and he ran his finger up the center of the wetness, feeling her through the cotton fabric.

Callia kissed him deeper and harder, feeling her orgasm begin its travel from deep inside her. She prayed Varek would slide his finger inside her before she came, desperate for any part of him inside her. She opened her legs wider to help him reach the spot she knew would feel like heaven with his touch.

Varek read her clues, pushed her panties aside, and ran his finger through her wetness to where he could push into her. She sat down on his finger and began to tighten around it. He moved slowly so he could stroke her tender, soft wall inside, and she exploded around him as she pushed against his hand and sobbed his name through her climax.

When she ceased quivering, he lifted her off him and took her hand in his to lead her to his room. As he closed the door behind him, his conscience briefly won the struggle over his body and he asked her if she had a condom. When she sweetly but almost breathlessly answered that it wasn't needed since they were meant for each other as she worked his button and zipper to free his cock, the last chance he had to protect her from what might happen slipped away, and he let it go without a fight.

Callia sensed his hesitation and wanted to reassure him that no matter who or what he was, she accepted him. She ran her hands over his back and sides, feeling scars she hadn't noticed the first time she had touched him, and kissed him deeply, hoping to encourage him to not hold back.

As if a switch were flipped, his reluctance disappeared and the deep need in him took over. He tore her cotton panties from her body and in one swift motion stripped the nightshirt from her. Just as quickly, he got rid of what was left of his clothing and pushed Callia against the wall.

Varek felt like a mad animal had been set loose in him. He looked at her standing naked in front of him, wanting him, and any semblance of civilization seemed out of his grasp. He picked her up by her waist and positioned her over his cock. He slid into her, wishing he had been more gentle. She felt unbelievable. She was wet around him, and when she wrapped her legs around his waist, he buried the final inches of his cock, her moans telling him it felt just as incredible for her.

Callia held him tightly around his neck and kissed him like his mouth held the very thing she needed to live. He held her to him, but he tried to shield her from the shock of the wall hitting her back every time he thrust into her.

She felt his orgasm begin, and his hands brought her to the base of his shaft. Warmth flooded her insides, and as he finished, she let her head rest on his shoulder, her fingers stroking his damp hair lightly.

Varek stood still inside Callia, holding her close as her soft breath caressed his neck. He hadn't felt this good in so long, he almost didn't know how to react. He slowly lifted her off him and set her on her feet on the wood floor.

She looked up at him, her face flushed and her hair in sexy waves framing her face. As he bent down to kiss her, she took his face in her hands and touched her mouth to his in a soft kiss.

In a husky voice, he whispered, "I'm sorry it took me so long to realize how wonderful you are."

Callia smiled and kissed him again. "I'll forgive you if you promise it will always be that great with us."

Varek's eyes grew even darker than they usually were, and a devilish smile lit up his face. "That? That was just a parched man having his first drink in ages. Now you'll see what it's like when I take my time with you. Get on the bed."

Giggling, Callia joked, "There's that tone again," as she sprawled across the queen-sized bed.

Standing over her, his eyes traveling over her naked body as his own body showed evidence of being ready again, he reached down to stroke her inner thigh and said in a low voice, "You want me to be sweet and kind?"

"No, I want you to be just what you naturally are." She loved the idea of this powerful man sexually in control of her, possessing her.

Varek slid his hand up her thigh to touch the slickness between her legs and grinned. "Good. I wouldn't want you any other way. I love making you weak and when you say my name as I make you come."

Callia closed her eyes and moaned as Varek slipped between her legs and ran his tongue up her moist sex. He held her to the bed as he licked, sucked, and stroked her to orgasm, this second one even more powerful than the first.

Varek slid up her body until his face met hers, and he kissed her. He rolled over onto his back and lay there stretched out next to her. Callia thought to herself that he was the most masculine man she'd ever seen. She ran her fingers over the taut muscles in his stomach and wrapped them around his erect cock. She stroked up and down, lingering on the head, and heard his moans of approval.

"What are these marks?" she asked as she touched his sides near his hips.

"Brands."

"You were branded?"

"When I was punished in Nil."

"What for?"

Varek remained quiet for a minute and when he spoke again, his voice was low. "Callia, I did what I had to do to survive. That meant defending myself and making sure anyone who wanted to kill me…couldn't."

Callia ran her finger tenderly over the marks. Three were different than the rest of them. Each of these brands looked like an x with a hash mark on each leg of the x.

"What do these three mean?"

Varek looked down at where her fingers lingered, but he didn't have to. He knew the marks she referred to. The only marks he wore on the outside of his body that told the world he was a murderer.

"That's the symbol for killing someone in Nil."

Callia didn't know what to say. Varek's past didn't frighten her, but it was totally foreign in her world.

He pulled her up to him and looked into her eyes. "I'm not the animal I had to be in there anymore. I would never hurt you, Callia. I promise."

Varek held her to him as she drifted off to sleep, kissing the top of her head and stroking the soft skin of her shoulder. He thought about how much he wanted to make her happy and wondered if three lifetimes away from kindness and good had made him into the one of the monsters he had fought and killed in Nil.

Callia awoke as he thought about his time in hell and propped her head up on her hand. Varek looked at her as she lay staring at him.

"You remind me of a boy I knew in another lifetime." As she spoke, she slowly traced the outline of his lips.

"A boy? Did you like this boy?"

"Very much." She continued touching his lips lightly with her forefinger and, after a minute or so, spoke again. "But I never told him how much I cared for him, and when he went away, I never saw him again."

Varek stared, silently commiserating with her as he admitted to himself he had lost the chance to let others know how he'd felt about them and feeling the ache of regret pinch at him.

"He wasn't meant for me, so I justified never letting my real feelings show because of that, even though he told me he loved me all the time." As she spoke, her expression became distant.

"Callia?"

When she heard his voice, she came back from the memory of long ago and to the reality that she had waited almost seven lifetimes to finally have.

"Varek, I don't want you to be like that boy. I don't want you to ever be unsure about how I feel because one day something might happen and I'd never want you to think back and wonder 'Did she love me?'"

Varek's heart jumped. "You love me?"

Callia smiled. "In some ways, I loved you from the moment I laid eyes on you. In other ways, from the first time your lips kissed mine. And in other ways, from the first time we made love tonight. And I'm sure, in the future, I'll realize more moments that make me love you all over."

Kissing him sweetly, she laid her head on his chest over his heart and wrapped an arm around him. His body felt strong under her. He played with her hair and stroked her back, and Callia closed her eyes and enjoyed the closeness that she'd waited so long for.

Varek wanted to tell her the truth. She'd understand. She'd stand by him. She loved him. He knew all these things but couldn't bring himself to say the words for fear he'd lose her. His mind tortured him, plaguing him with guilt, but then it rationalized his sin of omission with ideas about how telling her would ruin this beautiful moment or hurt her unnecessarily. In an effort to silence both sides' tug of war in his head, he squeezed her tight and quietly said, "Don't ever think I'm anything less than crazy in love with you."

Callia pressed her lips to his powerfully built chest and whispered his name. Her grandmother had been right. All he needed was a little convincing. She wondered if her grandmother had a little of the "gift" her sister had.

CHAPTER NINE

CALLIA AWOKE AND KNEW VAREK wasn't next to her before she opened her eyes. She had to get to work, but she wanted to see him. However, before she could get out of bed, the door to his bedroom opened and he walked in with breakfast in bed for her.

"Oh, my God! You're so sweet! You didn't have to do this for me."

Varek bent down, kissed her lips lightly, and placed the tray over her legs. "I know I didn't, but this is how good people are to one another." Grinning at her, he ordered, "Eat."

Sitting next to her, he watched her eat and thought about how beautiful she looked lying in his bed with his T-shirt on. "Do you have work today?"

Nodding, Callia finished eating a forkful of scrambled eggs and took a drink of tea from her morning teacup.

"I have a few leads the children gave me the other day. I'm looking for a half-breed." Varek took a triangle of buttered toast and saw a surprised look on Callia's face.

"Half-breed? Yellow eyes!" Everything her great-aunt had

said about her vision flooded back into her mind. "My Aunt Jean said she saw yellow eyes."

"Callia, what are you talking about?"

"My great-aunt has the ability of precognition. When I went to see her, it was because she had a vision of me around someone with yellow eyes. She's worried I might be in danger. The murderer is a half-breed?"

Varek became serious, his tone full of concern. "Callia, I want you to listen to your aunt. Aeveren visions have meaning. I don't want you hurt."

"Varek, I don't have any children. I'm not a parent...yet." She playfully put extra emphasis on the last word and smiled at him.

"Don't joke about this. I want you to be careful, and from now on, you don't walk home from the orphanage in the dark without me."

Callia leaned forward to kiss him, but he stopped her. "I'm serious. Promise me you'll be careful."

"I promise. But I really don't think it's necessary."

"Did your aunt tell you anything else about her vision?"

"No."

"I want you to call her today and ask her if she remembers anything more. Let me know what she said when I get to the vet's to walk you to the orphanage."

"To and from?" Callia loved the idea of being protected by him, but teasing him was so much fun.

"Don't make me go all Cro-Magnon on you. I will." Varek smiled as he took the tray and empty dishes from Callia's lap.

"Time for work."

As she watched him leave the room, she stretched, her stomach full and her heart happy.

Varek heard Callia start the shower and thought about joining her for a moment but decided against it, knowing she had to get to work and if he joined her, she'd be late or not get there at all. Her body felt so good against his, soft and yearning for his touch. Her mouth, her tongue, on his skin made it feel more alive than it had in lifetimes.

He felt his body begin to harden and reconsidered his decision not to get into the shower and continue what they'd been doing earlier, but the sound of her turning the water off made the choice for him. Instead he returned to his bedroom and put his T-shirt back on, her beautiful scent drifting up into his nose.

A noise in the distance made him freeze as he got to the hallway. Police sirens and the screaming sound of an ambulance made his heart sink. Unable to move, he stood in shock and felt everything go dark.

DERRICK JAMES HEARD THE SIRENS as he sat in his living room eating a breakfast of over-easy eggs, rye toast, and orange juice. The sound of them finding the evidence of his sixth murder just streets away from where he sat was like music to his ears. He stopped dunking his toast in the runny, yellow yolk and listened to the chaotic world outside as the end of the bread soaked up the liquid.

This one had been particularly easy. Just after ten he had arrived at the house on Church Street and waited until his victims settled in for the night. He had watched them for days and knew their schedule. The father left for work at eight-thirty every morning. The mother took the little girl to play dates with other Aeveren children each day at ten. Father, mother, and baby girl reunited each day at five-thirty for dinner at six. The child was put to bed at eight, and at ten-thirty the parents retired to their bedroom, the father first and the mother following after she lingered in the kitchen to turn on the light on the back of the stove and then walked first to the side door in the kitchen and then down the hallway to the front door to check that the doors were locked.

By morning they were both gone and the little girl was an orphan. He hadn't bothered to wake them up as he had with the first five sets of victims. He found as he watched them sleep together that he didn't feel the usual surge of hate come over him.

He had spoken to the mother just days before as she shopped for food at the market. He had intentionally backed into her cart with his, and she had been apologetic and concerned she had broken his eggs. She had looked into his yellow eyes without flinching, and the kindness he found in her eyes had pleased him. She had to die, but he remembered her kindness and made it quick.

The father got no such reprieve.

Derrick James finished his breakfast and washed the dishes, along with the frying pan. When he was done, he changed out of his stiff, bloodstained clothes. As he stood naked in front of the mirror in his bathroom, a tiny spot of blood near his right shoulder caught his attention. The rage that had been absent when he killed the parents overtook him, and his mind raced with words like sickened, mutants, and contaminated. Long after he had scrubbed the skin near his shoulder raw, he stood in the shower with scalding hot water burning his back and neck.

Back in front of his map of New Hope, his skin hurting from the pain of his shower, Derrick James placed the yellow pushpin into a spot on Church Street. He opened a new plastic case of pushpins and dumped them into the old box, mixing silver and gold pins with the other colored ones.

Hours later, after pacing through his home thinking about his own family, he stopped in front of the map and played with the plastic pushpins as they sat in the container. He looked at the map for a long time and finally looked down at the pushpin in between his thumb and forefinger.

"Tomorrow I look for silver."

JOHN CASEY HAD SEEN MANY murder scenes in his time on the force in Albany, but these six in New Hope were different. He took a breath and walked toward the bedroom. Leaning against the door frame, he saw the coroner, a man in his fifties named Gene Dizer, standing next to the blood-soaked bed and surrounded by evidence there had been a murder committed there.

"I don't know where your victims are, Case, but I can tell by the amount of blood here at least one person was killed here. Maybe two, just like the others."

"How the fuck do two victims just vanish?"

Casey's voice was a clear indication to everyone in the room that he was near his breaking point. "Six murders and we haven't found any of the victims from the previous five murder scenes. Where the hell are they?"

The coroner shrugged and appeared as bewildered as everyone else in the room. "I can tell you that whoever is taking them, they're being clean about it. There's no proof these people ever left this bed once they got in it last night."

Casey turned to one of his officers. "Did we get to talk to the child?"

"Sir, we tried, but just like with the other killings, they don't know anything."

Casey walked out of the bedroom and down the hall into the kitchen as he spoke. "Where is the child now?"

"With her relatives. We called them when we found a list of numbers on the refrigerator."

"Find me their address. Maybe they know something."

The officer hesitated, and Casey looked at him impatiently. "Sir, how are you going to tell them the bodies are gone?"

"The same way I did with the last five families. I'm not. And hopefully they'll be like the other ones and won't ask."

Casey left the house and walked to his car to wait for the address. As he sat down behind the wheel, the question of why none of the victims' families had ever asked about their loved ones' bodies gnawed at him as it had since the case began. He was certainly thankful to not have to answer the question of where the bodies were, but each time he'd met with the families, he'd waited for the dreaded question to come up, hopeful that at that moment he'd have an answer that didn't make him sound like a rookie cop. But professional embarrassment aside, he was angry that in the months since this case began he'd not been able to even find the slightest clue about where the victims had been taken. Or why.

THE AEVEREN COUNCIL CHAMBERS RUMBLED with the sound of discussion. In room 80, the members assigned to the New York area sat listening to the details of the most recent murders in New Hope. Once again, both parents had been murdered and a child was left orphaned. This time, an aunt had been able to take the child, so at least she didn't end up in the orphanage.

"Don't we have someone working on this in New Hope?" one of the members inquired.

The head of the Council of New York rifled through papers on the table in front of him until he found one with the official seal of Nil on it. "Yes. Varek Leale." His voice boomed with anger as he said the name. "He was released from Nil for this a few weeks ago."

He turned to an assistant and bellowed, "I want to see him. Get him here now!"

The assistant shuddered as the chamber shook and in fear handed the head of the Council a document he had just received.

"Your honor, he's been recalled to Nil."

"Fine. Let them deal with him."

CALLIA DRESSED FOR WORK AND expected to see Varek waiting for her, but he was nowhere in the apartment. As she stood in her living room confused, her phone rang.

"Callia! There's been another murder!" Jessica cried into the phone.

"Who?" Callia, like Jessica, knew the Aeveren in town and hoped it wasn't someone close to them.

"I'm so sorry, Callia. It was Dr. Parker. Both he and his wife. Their little girl has gone to Serena's sister's."

Callia was overcome with tears and began to sob. Jacob Parker had been her boss for three years. Everyone loved him, as far as she knew. As the town's only veterinarian, he treated everyone's pets. An Aeveren in just his second lifetime, he teased Callia that she was an old one since she was five lifetimes ahead of him.

Callia thought of his wife Serena, just as young an Aeveren as her husband and their two-year-old daughter. She had just seen her and the little girl the day she had gone to Aunt Jean's. She remembered thinking they were the picture of happiness, an example of what she hoped she and Varek could be someday.

"Callia? You there? Honey, I'm so sorry."

Jessica's voice brought her back to the present. "I have to go. I'm sorry, Jess."

As she hung up the phone, she sat down into a chair and cried, wishing Varek was there to hold her as she mourned the loss of two more of their kind.

VAREK STOOD IN FRONT OF the Aeveren Council in Nil again as he had a few weeks before. He wore the grey T-shirt Callia had worn and jeans. He also wore shackles and leg irons once again, as any other prisoner in Nil would.

He'd been brought there as soon as news of the sixth murder had reached the Council. He knew this would happen if another murder occurred before he could find the killer. He'd failed to do what he needed to do and now they'd take back the gifts they'd given him. He'd be sent back to Nil, this time for eternity. But he didn't care. He'd lost Callia.

He bent his head down to rub his check over the T-shirt. He breathed in deeply and faintly smelled her scent as he struggled to control the sadness that threatened to tear him apart. Tears came to his eyes, and he kept his head lowered.

The Council head called the members to order, and Varek waited to hear his fate.

"Mr. Leale. We had hoped the next time we saw you would be to release you permanently from this place."

Varek stood silently, his head hung.

"Look at us, Mr. Leale."

He lifted his head but made no effort to hide his sadness. For the first time since his first hearing in Nil after killing Neera and her lover, Varek showed remorse.

"We sent you to New Hope to find the murderer. You haven't. Can you report anything—anything new about the identity of the murderer?"

Varek cleared his throat and swallowed hard. "He's a half-breed."

The Council members turned to each other and discussed this in voices too low for him to make out what they were saying. Varek kept his head up but closed his eyes as the sadness of losing Callia stabbed at him.

"Is there anything else you can tell us?"

Varek had no other information, but believing he was a doomed man, he opened his eyes and asked what most Aeveren had asked since the murders began.

"Why can't you find out who he is? At least one of you must be far enough in the reincarnation cycle to have the power to see the future or read minds."

The head of the Council smiled. "If only it were that easy. It's true we possess many powers, including precognition and telepathy, but we are like any other Aeveren. Our powers are no stronger than anyone else's. So we can see the future, but not in a general sense. And we can see nothing about half-breeds. You have helped with that information."

Another Council member spoke. "Mr. Leale, you look different than the last time you appeared before us. You no longer look like a prisoner in Nil. What has changed?"

Varek knew she wasn't asking about his change of clothes or how his hair had grown in. What had changed was inside him.

"The gift you gave me has changed me."

Varek looked down at his hands shackled at the wrists. This was his future, his existence from now on. The love he had felt with Callia would be just a memory he'd eventually have to give up to survive. Again, he'd be alone.

The head of the Council listened as the council member to his right whispered something in his ear. Agreeing, he turned to Varek.

"Mr. Leale, it is imperative this murderer is found. It is this Council's recommendation that you seek help to stop this madman."

Varek looked up at the Council, his eyes moist. He couldn't have understood correctly. Deep inside him, a tiny lick of hope flickered and touched his heart.

"Do you mean…?" His sentence broke off. He was too afraid to say it. He took a deep breath and exhaled slowly. "Are you sending me back?"

The head of the Council smiled again. "Yes, Mr. Leale. You will return to New Hope to find this killer. We are not ready to bring you back to Nil. Yet."

His heart racing and beating wildly, Varek stood up straight. The sadness he thought would be with him forever melted away. "What kind of help are you referring to? Human?" For once, he desperately wished they wouldn't speak in riddles.

"Time is both your ally and your enemy." With that, the Council members stood up to leave the chamber.

Varek said their words over in his head but had no idea what they meant. Who was he to get help from?

"Please! Give me a clue about what you mean—time is my ally and enemy?"

The head of the Council looked down on him. "Right now, time is your enemy. You must find a way to make time your ally and work for you to solve this case. Know that if we had the ability you need, we would be able to make time our ally."

None of this made anything clearer for him, but he didn't care. He was going back to Callia!

"Godspeed, Mr. Leale. Again, take care of the gifts we've given you. May when we meet again be our last time."

Varek smiled and began to say thank you but found himself in the hallway of Callia's apartment, once again free with no shackles or leg irons.

CHAPTER TEN

V AREK SPOKE THE WORDS "THANK you" as he reappeared in Callia's apartment. His wrists and legs free once again, he looked up to see Callia crying on the couch, her head in her hands. He ran to her and put his hand gently on her shoulder.

Callia turned around, her eyes red rimmed and her cheeks tear stained.

"Where were you?" she asked.

Varek didn't think that moment was the right time to explain where he'd been.

"What's wrong?" He sat down next to her and took her into his arms.

"Dr. Parker and his wife were killed last night. I worked for him. Knew them," she sobbed into his chest.

"I'm sorry, honey. I promise you I'll find who's doing this."

"Varek, they were my friends. Not just Aeveren. I want to help you find the killer."

He held her close as he spoke. "I can't risk losing you. No."

Callia pushed away from him and wiped the tears from her face. "I'm not a child! You can use my help. It's not like you have anyone else."

Varek sat back on the couch frustrated. "You don't happen to know how to make time your ally, do you?"

She looked at him, confused. "What do you mean?"

He ran his hand through his hair and closed his eyes. He would have to tell her at least some of what had happened with the Council. Selectively choosing the information he wanted to tell her, he began to explain.

"This morning I was recalled to the Aeveren Council in Nil." Varek saw the look of concern come across her face. "They took me back because of the murders this morning. I thought that was it—that I'd never see you again—but they sent me back to find the killer and told me to seek out help."

"What kind of help?"

Varek shrugged and shook his head. "I don't know. They told me I need to make time my ally."

Callia thought about this but came up with nothing. "I'm sorry, but I don't understand. But we'll find out." She ran her hands up and down his forearm, hoping to comfort him.

"I think it might be some ability Aeveren have that has something to do with time, but I've never heard of it."

Smiling, she jumped up from the couch and ran to the phone. As she dialed, she said to him, "If it exists, then my grandmother will know. And if she doesn't, my great-aunt is sure to!"

"Grandma! I need your help! Is there an Aeveren ability

that has anything to do with time?"

Callia held the phone to her ear, making noises of agreement and looking at Varek. If she could help him, she'd be able to honor the memory of her friends.

"Okay, Grandma. Call me as soon as you know something, either on this phone or my cell. I love you. Bye."

Turning to Varek, she said, "She doesn't know, but she's asking my Aunt Jean. She's a much older Aeveren, so if any ability exists, she'd know."

Twenty minutes later they had their answer.

"My grandmother says yes, there is an ability to manipulate time, but very few Aeveren possess it. My great-aunt told her it's an ancient ability. The problem is that the Aeveren who possess it are usually rogue because it's so powerful."

"Callia, what do you mean by rogue? I spent three lifetimes in Nil and never met anyone with any ability associated with time."

"Aeveren with this ability are too powerful for Nil. The ability allows them to affect the flow of time by slowing it, accelerating it, reversing it, or stopping it. They are beyond the reach of our laws because they can manipulate time."

Varek folded his arms and let his head drop on the back of the couch. As he looked up at the ceiling he thought to himself, *Great. Now I have to deal with fucking wizards.*

"Just how the hell am I supposed to find one of these time manipulators?" Varek said in frustration.

"This is where I can help," Callia said proudly. "My great-aunt knows how to find one, but she won't tell me until she meets you."

"Why?"

"She told my grandmother she would need to know why I wanted to know about this type of Aeveren before she told me any more." Callia traced her finger down Varek's neck, over his Adam's apple, to the hollow at the base of his neck. "But I think she's curious about you and wants to see you."

After exhaling a deep sigh, he turned his face toward hers. "Callia, what did you tell your family about me?"

"Nothing except that you're my destined one. I don't think your past is anyone's business, but I will tell them if you want me to."

Varek knew she was telling him she wasn't ashamed of him, and he loved that. But he never wanted her to defend his past. It was indefensible. He hated the idea of her being associated with it at all.

He leaned over and kissed her. "Any chance your great-aunt has a thing for bad-boy types?"

Callia smiled and winked at him. "You only look like a bad boy. Inside, you're a marshmallow."

Rolling his eyes, he said with resignation, "Then I guess we need to go to your aunt's."

VAREK STOOD JUST INSIDE THE front door of Callia's Great-Aunt Jean's house. As he looked around the modest living room with its pale green carpet and cream-colored walls, he thought to himself that it didn't seem like the type of home someone who knew Aeveren with advanced abilities would live in. He had pictured somewhere more...modern. But her name *was* Great-Aunt Jean, so the flowered patterned couch and lace tablecloth on the side table did seem more appropriate than minimalist designs with stainless steel. He let his gaze follow the line of pictures on the wall in front of him and chuckled to himself for imagining Callia's aunt's house as Lex Luther's hideout instead of an ordinary old lady's house.

"Callia, sweetie! Twice in one week! Come here and give me a kiss." Her Aunt Jean wrapped her arms around Callia and looked over her shoulder at Varek, examining his face like an inquisitor. She stood back from her and smiled.

"And this must be Varek," she said as her gaze moved from her grandniece to the male standing behind her.

Varek saw her inspect him like he was something she'd never seen and wasn't sure she liked having in her house. Her face remained sweet like it had when she looked at Callia, but her eyes told a different story.

Callia took his hand in hers and moved next to his side. "Yes, this is Varek."

He knew she hadn't told anyone about him, but he wondered how difficult it would be for an ancient Aeveren like her Aunt Jean to find out whatever she wanted about whomever she wanted. Extending his hand, he said in a confident but calm voice, "Hello. It's nice to meet you."

Aunt Jean smiled, turned to Callia, and whispered in her ear, "He's a cutie."

Varek heard her and while he didn't agree with the characterization of himself as a cutie, he sensed he'd passed some test. Callia squeezed his hand and turned around to him with a big smile on her face.

"Follow me, you two. We'll sit in the kitchen and you can tell me what my grandniece and her boyfriend want with a tempuster."

Her kitchen was just as normal as her living room, Varek observed. No stainless steel. The three of them sat around a white painted wood table with a bowl of apples and oranges placed in the center. Canisters for flour, sugar, and tea sat on the white tile countertop, along with wire racks holding fresh baked cookies.

Varek took the cookie Callia's aunt offered him and examined the woman. Her white hair made her look much older than her sixty-five years. Small wrinkles marked her face near her faded blue eyes and around her mouth. She was thin but appeared very strong, despite the blue and white flowered apron she wore. As he savored a homemade sugar cookie, he wondered what *her* background was, what kind of things she'd done in the past.

"Aunt Jean, what can you tell us about these Aeveren who can manipulate time?"

"Tempusters. Some of them can slow or accelerate time, others can reverse it. There aren't too many of them who possess this ability. And only a handful can do all these things. Those Aeveren are more powerful than any of the rest of us with our simple abilities."

Callia turned to Varek. "Do you think we'll need someone who possesses all those abilities?"

Before he could answer, Callia's aunt asked him why he was involving her grandniece in any of his issues. Varek had hoped she wouldn't ask that question because he didn't have a good answer. He knew Callia shouldn't be anywhere near any dangerous situations involving killers or tempusters. But he loved having her close, even though it was selfish. He struggled to think of how to explain all of this to the woman who stared intently at him from across the table.

"Aunt Jean, Varek isn't involving me in anything. I want to help catch the person who's killing our people." Callia's voice was clear and strong, and she set her mouth defiantly as she looked at her aunt.

Varek felt her brush her leg up against his, and when her aunt turned to grab another tray of cookies from the counter, Callia's gaze moved to his to tell him she was on his side.

Her aunt sighed and took a bite of a cookie. She turned to Varek and made a clucking sound. "You'll need someone who possesses all the abilities to manipulate time. But you'll need to be careful. These are dangerous Aeveren. Their power makes them believe they're immune to our laws. I can give you the name of one, but I'm not sure."

"Aunt Jean, we can't let any more Aeveren die! We need to find the killer!"

"Callia, I'm worried I'm going to provide you with a cure that's worse than the disease. Beings who can alter time aren't to be trifled with."

Varek's eyes met hers. "I know about dealing with dangerous beings. I spent three lifetimes in Nil."

Callia's great-aunt raised one eyebrow and clucked again. "You're used to murderers and rapists. Tempusters aren't violent. They're manipulative. They possess power gods have."

Varek and Callia sat silently, unwilling to be deterred from what they knew they must do. He gently took her hand in his and squeezed it. He had no illusions about how difficult it would be to utilize the skills of a tempuster and not be manipulated themselves, but he believed the two of them could do anything if they were together.

Callia softened her voice. "Aunt Jean, I know you want to protect me, but I'm a big girl now, and Varek won't let anything harm me." She took her great-aunt's hand in hers and held it.

"Varek, I want you to listen to me very carefully. The Aeveren I'm sending you to is ancient. He is no more or less dangerous than any other tempuster, but he is one of the most powerful. I knew him many lifetimes ago as the brother of my first destined one. He's one of the rarest kinds of Aeveren. He was born with his abilities. My only hope is that he's learned to temper them."

Varek listened closely as she continued.

"Callia, if you get into any trouble, I want you to remember something. Often, we don't realize what we can do until we must do it."

Callia looked at Varek, who was beginning to tire of cryptic Aeveren suggestions, and then back to her aunt, whose eyes were fixed on Varek.

"His name is Amon Kalins. You can find him an hour and a half outside of New York City at this address. Tell him Callia is related to Elan. That might help you. He always liked me."

Callia felt like she was seeing a side to her great-aunt she'd never imagined. She looked at her, stunned.

"Sweetheart, you didn't think I was always an old woman like I am now, did you?" She smiled knowingly and winked at her. "When you get back, I'll tell you about my first destined one. He was a cutie too."

Varek stood and thanked her while Callia gave her a hug good-bye. "Thank you so much, Aunt Jean."

"Remember what I said—*both* of you."

Outside, Varek turned Callia to face him and looked intently at her. "Callia, your aunt is right. Beings that mess around with time are serious. I need you to promise me that you'll listen to me if we get into a situation that might turn dangerous."

Callia smiled. "Not the Cro-Magnon thing again."

"I'm serious. I need to know you'll follow my lead if things get dangerous." His face told her now was not the time for jokes. "I'm not even sure I'm up to dealing with an Aeveren who can manipulate time, Callia. I don't want to have to worry that you're not going to work with me when I need you to."

She put her arms around him and hugged him tightly to her. "Varek, I promise I'll work with you."

As they walked to her car, he turned to her, looking as if he had just thought of something important. "Do you have any powers yet?"

"No. I'm only in my seventh lifetime. And I wasn't born with any that I know of. Why?"

"Nothing. I just wondered what your aunt meant back there when she said that you don't know what you can do until you have to do it."

Shrugging, she said, "I have no idea. It seemed mysterious, didn't it?"

"Yeah." But just like the Council's riddles and strange suggestions, he had a feeling it was something to remember.

He sat down in the driver's seat and turned on the ignition. Callia turned to face him.

"Do you have any powers?"

"Unfortunately, no. I'm not in a life after my twentieth and unlike our time guy, I wasn't born with any." As an afterthought, he added, "Nil would have been much easier with powers."

Callia heard the change in his voice. As she studied his face, she could only imagine the horrifying things he'd been forced to endure in Nil. Those demons she truly believed she could handle hadn't shown themselves yet, but she knew they were part of him, and she accepted them. She didn't press him to talk about his time there, knowing that when he did, she'd be there beside him to help slay whatever demons his past could throw at them.

They drove silently, with Callia thinking about how Varek had changed her life in such a short time. Her thoughts eventually led to the death of her friends, and she sighed as she remembered the reality that they were gone, murdered by the very person she and Varek would bring to justice.

Varek turned as she sighed and saw the sadness cross her face. He reached out his hand for hers, and she laced her fingers in his. As he felt her skin on his, he thought about how he had never believed he'd be with anyone like this again. In love. And loved in return. He wasn't going to let anyone ruin his happiness. If he had to find a murderer and get help from super powerful Aeveren to do it, then damnit, that's what he'd do. He looked forward to a settled life with Callia. His time in Nil had taught him that he was strong, but his time with her had already showed him how vulnerable he could be. Silently, he told himself this time was different. He was different. Callia was a different person than Neera, and he could be the kind of man he needed to be this time.

CHAPTER ELEVEN

⚊⚊⚊✺⚊⚊⚊

T HE DRIVE TO THE TOWN of Cochecton near the border of
New York and Pennsylvania took almost three hours.
Callia's aunt had told them the address, but she hadn't said
they'd be driving to the middle of nowhere. The sun had set by
the time they found the place they were searching for, but they
ignored courtesy and went to the tempuster's home instead of
waiting until the next day.

The home sat alone on a dark, tree-lined road. Callia
noticed as they drove closer to it that the tempuster's house
was isolated, with nothing but fields surrounding it. No
streetlights lit the road to the house, and only the moon
illuminated the way.

Varek turned to Callia as he shut off the engine but could
only make out the outline of her face in the dark. He leaned
toward her and kissed her ear.

"Are you ready?"

Callia stared at the tempuster's house. One light lit up
window on the far right side of the enormous home. The rest
of the house was dark. A chill ran up her spine, and she took a

deep breath.

"Yes. Let's go."

Varek led Callia to the porch, holding her hand tightly in case anything came toward them in the darkness. The cold March air bit at his skin, and he wished he'd bought a heavier coat than the leather one he wore. As they walked, they stepped carefully on the nearly iced-over pavement that led to the front porch. Winter still held reign over the area.

The giant Victorian-style porch allowed Varek to walk to the lone lit window, but he saw no one as he peered into what looked like a library.

"Do you see him?" Callia whispered.

He walked back to join her in front of the door, shook his head and rang the doorbell. Callia grabbed his hand as they waited for someone to answer, squeezing it hard when the door opened, frightened by what lay behind it.

A man stood looking at them in surprise through the glass. He was dressed in black and white clothes, but his face was nothing less than sinister, with a jagged scar that slashed from the outside of one emerald green eye to the corner of his upper lip. He slowly opened the door and spoke to them.

"Can I help you?"

Varek noticed immediately that the man had a foreign accent but couldn't place it.

"We're here to see Amon Kalins."

"Your names?"

"Varek and Callia."

Before the man could close the door, Callia chimed in

with, "Please tell him I'm related to Elan."

The door closed and they stood in the cold, waiting for the tempuster to come to the door. Instead, five minutes later, the man returned and opened the door to let them into the house.

The inside was warm, and Varek removed his coat and turned to help Callia out of hers. The man they assumed to be the butler took them, draped both coats over his arm, and gestured to them to follow him.

Varek examined the dimly lit hallway as they followed the man. Mahogany wood and paneling lined the hallway, creating a warm feeling. Sconces on the walls flickered and threw enough light for him to see the artwork hung near the lights. The pictures looked like Americana, and Varek wondered what kind of ancient being would design his home like that.

Callia peeked into each room they passed only to find them fully furnished but uninhabited. She touched Varek's arm to get his attention.

"Varek. It doesn't seem like anyone else is here. All of these rooms are dark," she whispered.

They came to the end of the hallway and stood in front of a closed door at the back of the house. The light under the door indicated this was where the owner of the home was. The man opened the door and stood aside to let them pass but didn't announce their arrival to anyone. Varek and Callia found themselves in the room with the door closed behind them.

Callia began to speak, but Varek stopped her with a shake of his head. He quickly scanned the room but saw no one else.

But he sensed they weren't alone.

Leaning in to him, she whispered, "Where is he?"

Before he could answer, they heard the doorknob turn, and they turned to find themselves face to face with the Aeveren tempuster. Amon Kalins stood facing them in the doorway. Taller than Varek by mere inches but leaner, he seemed bigger than life. His long, pale blond hair, his most noticeable feature, hung to the middle of his chest. Running a very close second were his eyes, which were a color close to ocean blue, except near the pupil where they became the darkest blue he'd ever seen. The entire effect was almost magical. Dressed in all black and wearing a long black coat, Amon Kalins looked like a sorcerer.

Fucking wizards, Varek thought to himself.

The three of them stood silently, Varek and Callia taking in the sight of one of the most powerful members of their people and Amon sizing up the visitors to his home.

"Callia, Gethen tells me you are related to Elan. How is she?" His voice was husky and low. As he spoke, he slid out of his coat.

"She's fine." Callia felt like she should say something else but was uncomfortable. His deep blue eyes stared into hers like he was searching for something in her through them.

"And this is…" Amon's voiced trailed off as he turned his head to look at Varek. A sinister smile drew the corners of his well-formed mouth up slightly, and he said in a mocking voice far different than the one he'd used with Callia, "…your brother?"

Varek hoped one of Amon's powers was telepathy and intentionally spelled out in his mind exactly what he thought the tempuster should do to himself. Callia saw his body tense and diplomatically answered the question while she attempted to avoid eye contact with Amon.

"No, Varek is my destined one," she said in a voice full of pride as she smiled at Varek.

Amon walked between them and, in a deep, hollow voice, said, "Ah, young love." He sat in a dark leather chair and extended his arms out to indicate they could seat themselves in the two chairs facing him. Behind him hung full-size portraits of fierce-looking warriors.

Varek kept his eyes on Amon, jealously watching him stare at Callia like she was something he wanted to taste. He sat in the chair closer to the tempuster and silently hoped this meeting and their entire acquaintance with Amon Kalins would be brief.

Callia struggled to avoid Amon's gaze and looked instead over his head at the warriors' portraits. She felt his eyes on her and knew without even looking at Varek that he was watching the other man.

Amon thought to himself how easy it would be to dispose of the beautiful female's destined one and considered doing so but decided not to until he'd heard the reason for their visit. Then he'd seriously consider how to rid her of Varek, whom he knew already didn't like him.

"You didn't come to see me to admire my ancestors' portraits, carina, so what can I do for you?" He knew without even moving his eyes from Callia that Varek disliked the pet name he'd chosen for her. Carina. *Little one.* He did enjoy when visitors came.

Callia recognized Varek should explain their situation but believed Amon's preference for her required her to answer. As she prepared to speak, she offered Varek her hand and held his tightly, hoping to remind him of how much she loved him.

"We need your help. We have to find who is murdering Aeveren in New Hope. We need you to use your…abilities to help us capture him."

As Callia spoke, she felt like Amon's eyes were enveloping her. They were almost hypnotizing, and she began to fear that they were connected to some unknown power he possessed.

He answered in a voice like a deep purr, "We?"

This time Varek spoke, his voice the one he'd used in Nil. "Yes. We."

Amon pulled his gaze from Callia and turned toward Varek. Callia watched as his deep blue eyes became almost blue-black.

"And I would do this, why?" The purr in his voice changed to a growl.

Varek thought to himself that Callia's aunt had been wrong. Amon was just as vicious as any prisoner in Nil. He also quickly assessed the male sitting in front of him and, not knowing what other powers he possessed in addition to manipulating time, decided for the time being to be more diplomatic.

"Because it would help us save Aeveren." His tone was

matter-of-fact but less aggressive than before.

Callia knew this standoff between the two men was getting them nowhere. She thought maybe a trip down memory lane might persuade Amon to help.

"My great-aunt said she knew you when she was your brother's destined one."

Amon's eyes shifted back toward her and transformed back into their beautiful ocean-blue color. For a moment, his face continued to show the anger he'd felt for Varek, but as Amon's eyes met hers and he moved to face her, his expression softened and he smiled as if he realized what she was doing but would indulge her for now.

"I did. She made my brother very happy."

Callia had hoped he would be a little more forthcoming, but she saw she was going to have to work to get him to talk. His demeanor had changed for the better, so she felt she was at least succeeding at that.

"When was that and where?"

Please let his answer be more than a date and location.

Amon smiled and showed a set of beautiful, white teeth. His eyes seemed to dance as he looked at her. Callia hoped he was preparing to tell them a story or at least a memory that would take longer than a few seconds to relay.

"I knew Elan in one of my early lifetimes in Greece. She was a beautiful young girl, and my brother fell in love the moment he saw her. They were well-suited for one another. Dmitri was fortunate to have such a mate." Amon spoke slowly, as if he was remembering a series of events in his mind and was narrating them.

Callia looked forward to hearing about Dmitri from her aunt after she and Varek found the murderer and retired to a life of boring bliss. But now she found herself curious about Amon in that time.

"Did you have a destined one then?"

Callia saw instantly from the cold look that came over his face that she had ruined the light mood she had worked for. She watched as his body became rigid, and for the first time since they'd met him, Amon seemed uncomfortable. It left as quickly as it had come, but he returned to dealing with her far more guarded.

"While reminiscing is pleasant, carina, I must ask you to leave." His face showed no emotion, and Callia knew she'd lost the advantage. When he stood up to leave, Callia grabbed his hand and looked directly into his eyes.

"Please don't leave!" she pleaded. "I'm sorry if I offended you by my question. Please help us. We need you."

He stared intently into her eyes, and for a moment, there was nothing but her eyes and her touch on his skin. Amon regained his senses and found Varek standing at his side, barely containing his aggression. Amon restrained the desire to attack him, admitting to himself that Varek was most likely physically superior to him. He sat down again, and when Callia moved her hand away from his, he noticed it with regret.

His composure regained, Amon looked up at Varek. "Please be seated. Your destined one is quite persuasive. I will help you."

Varek reluctantly took his seat again, his patience with the tempuster almost at its end.

"Fine." *Now, I'll do the talking.* "We need you to go back to when the murders began and find out who the murderer is. Once you do that and tell us his identity, we won't bother you anymore." *And you can take your wizard self right out of our lives.*

Amon seemed to listen carefully, but said nothing when Varek finished speaking. Callia wondered if he was considering how they would pay for his services.

"We don't have much, but we will find a way to pay whatever you want." Using the money she'd been left after the death of her parents was a last resort, but if there was ever a desperate time, this was it.

Amon looked at her and smiled. "I can travel to any time in the past that I choose. Any event I want to experience is there for me. As an Aeveren in my forty-seventh lifetime, I know how to get anything I want, including money. I own homes around the world, can afford anything I desire. There is no amount of money you can offer me."

Callia stared at him, worried he'd changed his mind.

"Don't worry, carina. I do this as a favor to your aunt. No payment of money is needed."

Tremendous tension ebbed away from her, and she relaxed back against the soft leather chair. She turned to Varek but noticed he still looked tense.

"If you'll wait here, I'll return with the information you

want," Amon said as he stood and walked toward the door.

Callia realized they'd barely given him any details about the case. "But don't you need to have us tell you more?"

Amon turned to look at them over his shoulder. "I may travel back in time hundreds and thousands of years, but when I'm here, I read the newspaper." He paused and raised his eyebrows. "Unless there's something you know that the papers don't."

"He's a half-breed," Varek said flatly.

The tempuster grunted in disgust. "Yellow eyes," he said coldly. And then right before their eyes, he disappeared.

Callia and Varek looked at one another, each one searching as if to ask the other where he went.

"Do you think we can trust him?" she asked as she stepped next to him and wrapped her arms around his waist.

"No." He wanted to add that he hated the way Amon looked at her, but he didn't want to sound like a jealous teenage boy. He held her close to him and ran his hands through her hair as she rested her head against his chest.

Callia gave him a little squeeze and looked up at him. "Thank you for letting me handle that. It showed you trust me, and you don't know how important that was to me.

Varek smiled at her and kissed her forehead. "Thank God you did because I wanted to kick his wizard ass, and that wouldn't have gotten us anywhere."

"Cro-Magnon."

As they stood there, they realized they were no longer alone. Somehow, in the blink of an eye, Amon had returned and was standing behind them.

"I found your murderer. Damned, half-breed."

"Who is he?" Varek asked, ready to leave and hoping the butler was already walking down the hall with their coats.

"I don't know his name yet, but I'll return with you when you go home tomorrow, and I'll find out then."

The last of Varek's patience evaporated. "Why the hell couldn't…" His voice broke off when Callia stepped between him and Amon.

Hoping to diffuse the situation, she calmly said, "Okay. Thank you, Amon. Do you know where we can find a hotel near here?" *In the middle of nowhere.*

"You will stay here. Gethen can take you up to one of the bedrooms right now."

As much as Varek didn't want to stay in his home, he knew finding somewhere to sleep was going to be next to impossible where they were, and sleeping in the car wasn't something he wanted to do. Grudgingly, he agreed and followed Callia and the butler, who seemed to appear out of nowhere, up the staircase to a fully made-up room on the second floor.

Exhausted after a full day, Varek fell back onto the bed along with Callia, and in very little time, they were both fast asleep in one another's arms.

AMON REMAINED IN HIS STUDY thinking of the night's events. It had been nothing for him to find out Derrick James's identity, and he could have stopped him from ever killing anyone, if he had been so inclined. But he preferred to spend more time with Callia, so he'd drag out his assistance for as long as possible.

He leaned back in his chair, stretching his long legs in front of him. When he was completely relaxed, he let his mind open and waited patiently until it found hers upstairs above him. He had instructed Gethen to put his guests in the room directly above the room he sat in, unsure that he'd be able to reach her if she were farther away. He'd never had as much control over this power as he had over his others, so using it successfully wasn't a sure thing.

This time he wouldn't attempt to introduce anything into her mind. Now he just wanted to linger among her thoughts to know her better. But the temptation was too much and before he could consciously stop himself, he had inserted the idea of him into her mind. He waited excitedly to see what her subconscious would do but saw nothing in her mind about him.

Disappointed he couldn't manipulate this ability better, he relaxed his mind more to enjoy his own thoughts of her. Before he could let his mind wander to where his body was urging it to go, he felt a tiny pull in her mind. Returning to her thoughts, he was thrilled to find that the simple idea of him planted in her mind had blossomed into something much more. He felt her eyes on him, her gaze gliding over his features, lingering on his hair. She avoided looking at him in her dreams as she had earlier, but he sensed pleasure in her thoughts about him.

As he found that kernel of attraction in her mind, he fought not to fully insert himself into her thoughts. To overpower her might bring her temporarily to him now but to wait and slowly introduce himself to her would increase the pleasure of that moment when she finally offered herself to him completely. Satisfied, he closed his mind to hers and reveled in his thoughts of her, happy to let them overwhelm both his mind and body.

CHAPTER TWELVE

B Y NINE O'CLOCK THE NEXT morning, the three of them were driving toward New Hope. They sat in silence, each one absorbed in his or her thoughts. Varek thought in disgust of the male in the backseat, sure that he'd lied the night before about not knowing the murderer's name. As he drove over the country roads back toward New Hope, he decided Amon had either not even gone back in time or had, in fact, learned the killer's identity and was withholding the information to use to his advantage at some point in the future. Whichever it was, Varek knew he wasn't to be trusted alone with Callia. He grimaced to himself and looked over at her in the passenger seat beside him as she quietly gazed out the car window, lost in thought. Reminding himself that she wasn't Neera, he turned his attention back to the road.

Callia watched the trees with their still bare branches fly by as she thought about last night's dreams. She struggled to remember bits and pieces, but remembered quite clearly Amon in them. He had appeared suddenly as she dreamed about the orphanage and the children, or at least that's what she thought her dream was about. It was all very hazy, except for the parts with him. Those were jarringly clear. He stood before her in a dimly lit room and though he hadn't spoken to her, she knew what he was thinking.

She blushed and quickly turned her head away from Varek's view. She wondered why Amon had appeared in her dream and why she felt like she did. She hadn't felt any attraction to him as they spoke in his study the night before. No doubt females found him attractive. That was for sure. His eyes were beautiful, almost enchanting, and his hair gave him the air of something mystical. Beyond that, his chiseled face with its aquiline nose and perfect mouth made him seem almost regal, and his body, under clothes that revealed enough taut muscles to convince any female that his was a body best felt on top of hers, promised pleasure. Callia could certainly see his appeal, but she wondered why her dream had been so sexual when she hadn't consciously even registered mild attraction the night before.

She loved Varek completely, and she was sure the guilt over her dreams was written all over her face. He'd obviously sensed something about Amon. His jealousy was unmistakable, but he had nothing to fear from her. She finally had a destined one, and she adored him. She wasn't going to give that up for anything, not without a fight.

Callia turned to gently touch Varek's arm and smiled sweetly at him when he responded. She sensed Amon's eyes on her, and when she turned toward him in the back seat, his gaze moved from her hand on Varek to her eyes, startling her.

Suddenly it occurred to her that he might possess the power of telepathy. Was he reading her mind right now? Did he know what she'd just been thinking about him? Quickly, she turned around and returned to watching the countryside out the window.

Amon's gaze slid from the back of Callia's head back down to her hand. When she'd touched his the night before, he'd experienced a sensation that was almost electric. It traveled up his arm to his chest and slowly infused his skin all the way down to his legs, causing him to fiercely want her right there in his study. If they'd been alone, he would have taken her in his arms, pressed her to his body, and taken possession of her mouth with his, invading its warm moisture with his tongue, as he pushed his erection into another area of wetness. She'd beg to have him inside her, and he'd have to control himself to ensure he didn't allow himself to give in to her pleas too soon as she had a powerful effect on him. One touch had told him she could possess him like only one other had. As he sat watching her from the back seat, he knew he began to crave her touch already.

Cursing his weakness, Amon pushed the thought of her soft body yielding to his desires out of his mind. Of all his powers, the purely mental ones were his weakest. Although he had been born in his first lifetime with powers, an incredible rarity among their race, the mental abilities had come much later in his reincarnation cycle, and they were also unique to him. He couldn't read minds or see the future, but he could connect his mind to another's and sometimes was able to insert an idea into the other person's mind.

But this power had never developed as his ability to teleport or his ability to manipulate time, which nature had allowed him to hone to perfection. His power to make and control a mental connection to another depended greatly on his control of his desires and emotions, which was also lacking in such a powerful being, Controlling them required constant effort, and sometimes they overwhelmed him. At those times, his mental powers were nearly useless. He warned himself that if he didn't control his desire for her beginning at that moment, any future attempts to connect to her as he had the night before would probably be futile.

Twenty miles outside of New Hope, Callia's curiosity about Amon's abilities finally won out. Turning her head to face him but avoiding his gaze, she asked, "Amon, is the power to affect time your only ability?"

Varek was surprised by her question but not displeased. As far as he was concerned, any knowledge they possessed about their new partner would help them.

He lifted his gaze to the rear view mirror and looked back at Amon. "Yeah. Do you have any others?"

Amon stared back at Varek's eyes in the mirror and considered how much he should divulge to the male he didn't like and the female he already liked too much. Obviously, he wouldn't tell them about the mental power. He could live with that sin of omission, but a little show of his force might impress each of them in the way he desired.

Slowly, and in a deep voice, he began. "I can slow and

accelerate time and reverse it. I'm particularly adept at stopping time. Of course, I can teleport, but I can also do that within time in addition to through it."

Callia had turned around in her seat and was listening intently, curious about the details of his abilities. "What do you mean 'within time'?"

Amon straightened his body in the seat and grinned. "Watch."

Varek looked back in the mirror to see Amon disappear. "Where did he go?" Callia exclaimed.

On the road about two hundred yards in front of the car, Amon reappeared moments later. Varek slammed on the brakes to avoid hitting him, and Callia pushed her hands against the dashboard to avoid being thrown against it. The tires skidded and squealed as Varek slowed down from seventy-five miles an hour to a dead stop in the last hundred yards. Just as the car reached Amon, Callia screamed, and he disappeared. Seconds later, he reappeared in the back seat of the car, his slightly windblown hair he smoothed with his hands the only evidence that he'd ever left.

Varek jammed the car into park and spun around to face him. "What the fuck is wrong with you?" he barked, his voice a mixture of fear and rage.

"You could have been killed!" Callia screamed.

Both stared with wild eyes at the being in the backseat.

"I wouldn't have been killed. I'm an ancient Aeveren who's possessed these powers for forty-seven lifetimes."

His tone revealed a cockiness that irritated Varek to his

core. Unable to control himself any longer, Varek grabbed Amon by the collar, pulling him up off the seat toward the front of the car. Staring into the tempuster's surprised eyes, he bellowed, "I've had enough of you and your wizard bullshit!"

Gently placing her hand on his shoulder, Callia said nothing but she calmed him enough for him to admit he didn't want to fight Amon, so Varek released him with a push back toward the seat. He turned back around and started the car as he mumbled, "Asshole."

Callia tried to relax but still felt the adrenaline pumping through her, mixed with anger at Amon. "You might not have been killed, but we might have. Did you consider that?" she asked, her eyes flashing wildly at him.

Amon's emotions began to spin out of control inside him. He could handle Varek's fear and anger. In fact, it made him feel powerful, but Callia's anger affected him differently. Her unhappiness with him made him feel regret and a strange sense of pain.

In a quiet voice, he said, "I'm sorry, Callia. I didn't mean to endanger either of you."

As he spoke, his eyes turned a translucent shade of ocean blue, a reflection of the emotions inside he struggled to control.

Callia groaned and turned around in her seat still irritated. *If he thinks changing his eyes to an even more beautiful shade of blue and saying he's sorry in that sad voice is going to fix things, he's got another thing coming.*

They arrived at Callia's apartment around one o'clock

after dropping her car off at her grandmother's. An awkward silence remained between them, and Callia happily excused herself to take a shower. Varek would have preferred to retreat to his room or any other place where Amon wasn't, but he interpreted Callia's instructions to entertain their guest as requiring him to remain in the same room with him. Unhappily, he played host, offering Amon a seat in the living room and something to drink.

Varek studied the tempuster in the environment he thought of as his own and disliked his findings. Amon seemed strangely comfortable, whereas he wasn't, and in the bright light of day in the middle of the living room, he seemed even more impressive than at his own home the night before. Scowling, Varek glared at him as his confidence continued to irritate him.

Amon watched Varek as he still seethed over his trick in the car, and he fed off that anger. He nonchalantly looked around the room and guessed Callia and her destined one hadn't been living together for long. The apartment's decorative touches all pointed to it being hers, not theirs. He waited patiently for Varek to speak, enjoying the standoff.

"So what *did* you find out about the killer last night?" Varek knew his voice sounded exasperated but didn't care.

Amon answered, "I only found out what he looks like."

"Well? What does he look like?" Varek's frustration with his wizard nonsense had reached a boiling point.

Amon took his time answering, further infuriating Varek. "He's average height—maybe five-nine or five-ten. Blond hair—short. Perfectly average, run-of-the-mill, blend-into-the-woodwork person, except for the fact that he's a murderer."

Debating as to whether or not to tell him about Derrick James's contact lens color, he finally decided that the disclosure of this wouldn't disrupt any of his plans. "He covers his yellow eyes with dark blue contact lenses. I assume you'd have to be very close to him and focused on his eyes to be able to pick out the yellow."

Varek thought about this information and then turned to Amon. "If you can travel back in time, why didn't you stop him?"

The disapproval in his tone bothered the tempuster, but not as much as if Callia had asked the question.

"I can't do that."

"Why?"

"It's not my destiny."

This, of course, was pure bullshit. He could have stopped him before he killed anyone, but that would've meant not seeing Callia anymore. He could certainly go back in time and meet her before Varek, but he preferred not to manipulate time or to at least keep it to a minimum with the ones that truly interested him. He'd work a little mind mojo on her but hoped he could have her in the present time.

Varek snorted in disgust at the idea that stopping the killer was his destiny and looked with relief down the hall as Callia came toward the living room. He gruffly excused himself and met her as she entered the room to give her a kiss and whisper "I love you" to her. She smelled clean, and a wave of resentment came over him. He would much rather make love to Callia than leave her to entertain Amon while he washed up.

He ran his hands down her back and squeezed her bottom, wishing time guy would get the hint and teleport somewhere else, preferably far away. When he didn't, Varek left to shower, relieved at least that his time with Amon was over for now.

Callia watched Varek leave and also wished they could have some time alone. She looked forward to the end of his work for the Council and the happy life with her destined one her grandmother had described to her. But at that moment, with one of the most powerful Aeveren sitting in her living room preparing to help them catch the killer, that life seemed far in the future.

She sat down across from Amon and noticed he still wore his coat. "Would you like me to take your coat?"

Amon stood and practically slithered out of it. Just as he had the night before, he wore all-black clothes. Callia took his coat by the collar, and he watched in disappointment as she removed it from his grasp without touching him. When she returned to her seat, he looked at her as he fought the craving to touch her hand.

"I'm curious. Why do you live in that house when you said you own houses around the world?"

"Is there somewhere else I'd be better suited for?" Amon asked as he thought of the home he'd like to take her to.

"No. I guess that since I've lived here this entire lifetime, I might be feeling a bit of wanderlust."

"Where would you like to go?" He imagined asking her

that after she surrendered to him. He would take her to his Italian villa, his mountain home in Germany, the home in Greece. Wherever her heart desired.

"Oh, I don't necessarily want to go anywhere. I just wondered why you spend time in a big Victorian home in the country surrounded by no one."

"I like the quiet."

Amon looked into her eyes, knowing he made her uncomfortable. He hoped she would betray some interest through her nervousness.

Callia sat quietly and lowered her eyes. Her hands fidgeted in her lap, and she wished she'd followed her friends' advice and purchased a television for the living room so she wouldn't have to sit uncomfortably with him looking at her.

"Where else have you lived?" He wanted to learn more about this female who interested him so.

"A few different countries." But then almost as an excuse for what sounded like a very boring existence so far, she added, "I'm only in my seventh lifetime." Varek's words about not trusting Amon rang in her head, but the silence was awkward, so she continued. "I think I liked Italy of all the places other than here."

"Where in Italy?" As Amon asked, his mind pictured her at his villa.

"Urbino. It's a small town in central Italy."

"I know of it. I've been fortunate to spend two lifetimes in that beautiful country, one in Rome, many lifetimes ago, and one in Sicily. I own a home near Castelmuzio."

"Il Castello! I remember the castle there! It's been so long since I thought of that. What a beautiful region for a home!"

Her excitement touched him. He had never thought much of that home any more than any other of his homes. They were things he collected more than lived in or enjoyed. They were things to spend money on, nothing more. But the idea of her there with him made his Italian villa more special than anywhere else in the world at that moment.

In perfect Italian, he said, "I would love for you to come to visit me there."

Heat rushed to her face as she blushed at his offer. His voice, speaking Italian, sounded so sensual and lush. She was embarrassed at how much it affected her.

Her voice shaking, she replied, "That's very nice of you. Perhaps Varek and I could come to visit sometime."

Amon listened for the sound of running water and knew Varek was still in the shower. "Please speak to me in Italian. It's been so long since I've heard it other than from my own mouth." He leaned toward her, imploring her to acquiesce with his eyes.

Do as I ask, carina.

"I haven't spoken Italian in lifetimes. I'm sure I've forgotten it. And I'm sure my accent would be a disgrace compared to yours."

She was rambling, but his gaze focused on her so intently that she felt wrong not to do as he requested. Her voice shaking even more now, she nervously said in Italian, "I'm sure your home is lovely. Thank you for the invitation."

She instantly felt guilty and jumped up from her chair when she heard Varek open the bathroom door. "Excuse me."

As he watched Callia hurry out of the room, Amon sat silently, pleased that he had been successful at tempting her. He repeated her words and delighted at the sound. Alone, he closed his eyes and fantasized about her skin under his fingertips yearning for his touch, coming alive as his lips traveled over her body. He would take her to Italy and she'd be his, and no one—not her destined one, not the Council— would be able to stop him.

I'll wait patiently for your surrender, carina. You will be mine.

Callia reached Varek just as he entered his room and pushed him inside, closing the door behind them. Standing with his hair wet and with only a towel around his waist, Varek wondered why Callia was in his room instead of entertaining Amon.

"Callia, is something wrong?"

"No. I just wanted to tell you I love you."

Just being near him made her stomach flutter, proof to her that whatever had crossed her mind in the living room was nothing. She wrapped her arms around him, feeling his damp, bare skin under her hands as she ran them over the scars on his back and the brands near his hips. She heard his heart beat faster as she touched him and felt him harden under the towel.

"Callia, if we don't stop now, I'm going to want you right here. I'm just about to the point of no return already," he said breathlessly.

"I'm sorry," she said, backing away from him.

Stroking her face, he said, "It's okay. You know there's nothing I'd like more than to spend the afternoon making love to you, but we need to find the killer and then send Amon on his way. But tonight I want to pick up right here." He stopped speaking to nuzzle her neck and pull her to him.

Controlling his desire, he backed up a step. "Okay, let's get going. I'll be right out, so tell him to get ready." Varek bent down and planted a soft kiss on her lips before turning away to get dressed.

Callia felt the tightness in her lower abdomen that always came when she wanted Varek. She happily reminded herself that she experienced nothing like that with Amon, even when he spoke Italian, and made her way back to the living room to announce to him that it was time to go.

CHAPTER THIRTEEN

D ERRICK JAMES PACED BACK AND forth through his house, unable to shake the sick feeling he'd had for hours. His head throbbed, his skin felt like he was being scratched with razor-sharp pins, and he was sure he was being watched. Over and over he told himself he was just being paranoid.

The cops don't know anything. They don't even have bodies since the freaks disappear when they die. Nobody knows anything.

No matter how he tried to convince himself, he knew something was wrong. He sensed it. Something was very wrong.

He continued to pace, checking out the windows as he passed them for anything suspicious. But everything seemed suspicious now. A red car seemed too similar to another red car that had passed fifteen minutes earlier. That old man had never walked his dog past the house before. Other people walking down the street appeared too interested in his house.

He stopped in front of his map of the killings. Now it

didn't please him as it always had. To him, the map was evidence of his failure. There was no silver pushpin.

Flashes of a memory of the last killing had begun to haunt him. Someone had seen him. He was never fully able to reconstruct the memory, but he remembered seeing a man. A man had been with him in the house on Church Street when he killed those parents. He had seen his reflection in the mirror for just seconds, but when he turned to face him, he had disappeared.

Maybe he was never there.

He was there.

He hadn't been able to remember anything more about the man except his long, blond hair. He wondered if he was an angel.

He'd been sent to stop him. They had sent him to stop the killings. But five wasn't enough. They didn't understand why he killed. They wouldn't understand until more died.

Derrick paced again, unable to get the man out of his mind. He was coming for him. He would end this life for him and there would be no others. The curse of being only part Aeveren was knowing some got to live again, but he would cease to exist after this lifetime.

He obsessively watched out the window now. The man was coming. He felt it. There would be no silver pushpin.

AMON LED VAREK AND CALLIA to Derrick James's house right outside of New Hope. The three of them stood outside their car, parked across the street. To Callia, it looked like every other home in suburbia with hedges, shutters, and a sidewalk to the front door. She had a difficult time believing that inside lived a murderer who hated their kind.

Varek and Amon had fewer illusions about the situation they were about to confront. For Varek, the house looked much like any of the houses he'd been to on a murder case as a cop. Murderers lurked in all types of places, including pleasant residential houses. For a moment his mind went back to the outside of the house he'd shared with Neera and his little girl.

That was the house of a murderer too, he thought.

For Amon, what he saw when he looked at the house was the next step toward having Callia all to himself. The person inside the house meant nothing to him. He'd watched Derrick James as he murdered his most recent victims, but other than that brief encounter he had no more interest in him other than what would happen when the half-breed was eliminated. Varek would be called back to Nil because his job for the Council would be finished, and Amon knew there was no way murderers earned release from their sentences in Nil for a little bounty-hunter work, no matter what the Council had promised. Some yellow-eyed half-breed was not going to be Varek's get-out-of-jail pass. Forty-seven lifetimes of experience assured Amon of that.

Turning to Varek and Callia, Amon informed them of his plan. "I'll teleport in and restrain your murderer and then you come in."

"Before we decide on that, Callia, I think you need to stay

here. I don't want you in there, honey." Varek hoped for once Amon would be a help instead of a hindrance and agree with him.

"Why?" Just the tone of her voice told Varek this would be an uphill fight.

"Because it's dangerous, and I don't want you to get hurt."

"Varek, I'm not playing this Cro-Magnon thing with you now. Why can you two go in but not me?"

"Because this is my responsibility and I have experience as a cop. And Amon at least has some abilities that may help."

Amon agreed with Varek, as distasteful as that was. "He's right. You might get hurt. Stay here."

"No! I'm coming, so whatever plan there is better include me."

Varek knew he was getting nowhere with Callia, so he turned to Amon. "I need you to find out if there are any weapons in there before we come in."

"Fine. Anything else?"

"No, that's it. Go in, check the place out, and come back and get us."

Amon disappeared a second later, and Varek nervously looked up and down the street hoping no one noticed a six-and-a-half-foot-tall man with long blond hair just vanished into thin air. Thankfully, the street outside Derrick James's house was deserted at that moment.

Inside the house, Amon appeared in the hallway and began to slowly walk toward the living room and the sound of a television. Three steps down the hallway he saw Derrick

James. Immediately, he saw his bright yellow eyes that made him almost resemble a bug.

"Are you an angel?" the man asked, his voice full of fear as Amon continued toward him.

Amused, Amon smiled. He stopped next to him, towering over him by at least eight inches, and chuckled ominously in a very unangelic way.

"No. Not an angel."

"Then what are you and why are you here?"

Amon considered playing with the man's fear for a brief amusement but decided against it.

"I'm here to stop you."

Derrick James looked up in terror at the stranger who stood in his living room. Amon's blue eyes changed right in front of him to almost black, frightening him even more.

"Are you a demon?" he asked, his voice screeching in fear.

"No, not a demon either." Amon's voice, low and hypnotic now, seemed to calm the man.

"Then what's wrong with your eyes?"

Again, Amon laughed. "You're one to ask."

The man realized in horror that he didn't have his contact lenses in. Another person had seen his yellow eyes!

"Let's put it this way. I'm the exact opposite of you. What you possess only partially, I possess in abundance."

"What are you going to do to me?"

"I told you. I'm going to stop you. If it were up to me, I'd have killed you already. But this is someone else's responsibility. I'm only involved for the…fringe benefits, let's call them."

Confused, Derrick James moved toward his desk where he kept his gun, hoping to kill the angel or demon or whatever the hell it was that stood in his living room. Before he could reach it, Amon took three great steps and reached the desk before he did.

"No you don't. You might hurt someone else with this gun, and the only person getting hurt here is you."

As the words left his mouth, Amon disappeared and reappeared outside to signal to Varek and Callia to come in. He then reappeared in the living room with the man again.

Derrick James began frantically rambling about the inherent evilness of Aeveren and his destiny to show everyone that evil so they'd pay for the way he'd been treated.

Amon stood listening with little interest and less sympathy. This crazy man with the yellow eyes had begun to irritate him. He may not agree with anything the Council did, but he had little patience for some fucking half-breed's rantings about how all Aeveren were evil freaks.

"Enough! You'll be lucky if I don't kill you myself!" he roared in a voice that made the man stop dead.

Amon knew he couldn't kill Derrick James. Oh, he was fully capable and after just that short time with him wanted to, but if anyone was going to kill him, it would be Varek, just to make sure he would be going back to his rightful place in Nil.

Amon moved to the front door and opened it to let Varek and Callia in. For a moment, Derrick James looked stunned that now there were three strangers in his living room.

Handing Varek the gun, Amon casually remarked, "He's crazy."

"Who are you? Why have you come here?" Derrick James screamed, his voice rippling with fear.

Varek moved slowly toward him, gun drawn. "You can't keep killing people. I'm here to stop you."

"They're not people! They're freaks!"

"No, they're Aeveren. Now you're going to come with me."

"No!"

He lunged for Callia, who stood looking at his map of the crimes. Before Varek or Amon could rescue her, he held her in front of him with a knife from his jacket pointed at her neck. The tip of the knife pressed against her skin as he pulled her tightly to him.

"Please don't do this! Maybe we can get you help!" Callia knew her words were lies, but the point of the weapon in the hands of a murderer made her desperate.

Varek stood horrified and enraged as the man threatened Callia. Because he was standing so close to her, there was no way Varek could get a clean shot. Maybe he could talk the man out of it, but he'd kill him if he had to, if it was a choice between his life and Callia's.

She looked terrified as he ranted about how taking another Aeveren life would be no loss. Varek pointed the gun at Derrick James's head knowing he had no shot but sure he had to bluff.

In a calm voice, he said, "Let her go. If you don't, I'm

going to kill you. All I need is one shot."

Amon watched the entire scene in rapt attention. He couldn't let Callia get hurt, but if he teleported behind the man, he ran the risk of him plunging the knife into her neck. Angry at himself for not seeing the knife before calling them in, he scanned the scene in front of him while his mind scrambled to find a solution before her emotions made him unable to focus on anything else.

He leaned over to Varek and whispered to him. Varek nodded and kept his aim on James.

Amon looked at Callia, whose eyes were fixed on Varek. In Italian, he calmly said, "When I call you carina, I need you to duck. Do you understand?"

Callia nodded.

In Italian, he added, "Don't worry. I won't let you get hurt."

"What is he saying?" James yelled at Varek. "Tell me!"

"I don't know. Ask him."

He turned his attention to Amon and for a moment loosened his grip on Callia, giving Varek a clear shot.

Amon thundered, "Carina!" and Callia ducked. Varek's shot hit James in the head, sending him backward to the floor.

Callia ran to Varek and buried her head in his chest. As he tried to soothe her, Amon walked over to the body and stood staring down at him.

He turned to Varek and grinned. "Nice shot." Then he mumbled to the body on the floor, "I guess now you're going to meet some angels...or demons. Whichever."

Varek ran his hand over Callia's back to comfort her. She held him tightly, afraid if she let go the Council would take him away for Derrick James's death.

Amon stood looking at the body lying perfectly still on the floor. He had killed a few Aeveren in his forty-seven lifetimes, but it had been many years since he'd had a part in a human's death. He studied the body, amazed once again at the finality of it.

He turned his attention to Varek and Callia huddled close together a few feet away. "We need to leave here."

Varek whispered in Callia's ear, and she reluctantly released him.

She looked first to Varek then to Amon. "What will happen to him? Should we call the police?"

"When we get home. Now we need to get out of here." Varek grabbed her hand and began to walk toward the door as Amon followed them outside, closing the door behind him.

AN HOUR LATER, THE NEW Hope police gathered in Derrick James's house. John Casey stood in front of the map of the murders studying it. As he did, he fondled the container of pushpins, standing it on its one side and then the other.

Turning one of his officers, he said, "Did we find anything to connect him to the murders other than this ghoulish map?"

"Sir, we found clothes with dried blood on them in the bathroom. We're still looking."

"Good. Keep looking. If this is the guy, I want to be able to put this case to bed."

The coroner came through the door barely able to contain his excitement. "Case! Have you found the guy? One of your officers said it looks like this homicide victim is possibly your killer."

"I don't know yet, Gene. But this map shows the exact locations of each of the murders so far."

Gene Dizer knelt next to the body to perform his preliminary investigation. "Gunshot wound to the head. That's the cause of death. And it's pretty recent. Other than that, take a look at his eyes. You don't see that color eyes too often, do you?"

Looking up at Casey above him, who had a look of disgust on his face as he glanced at him, the coroner joked, "At least you have a body this time, Case."

The policeman sneered as he returned the jab. "Real fucking funny, Gene. When can I know something other than what any of my rookie officers can tell me just by looking at him?"

Gene Dizer smiled. "Same as always. I'll know more in twenty-four to forty-eight hours."

As his assistant covered Derrick James and wheeled him out of the house with the aid of one of the officers, the coroner turned to John Casey, who remained standing in front of the map.

"Poker tomorrow night still on?"

Casey turned to him and smiled. "You know I can't say no

to taking your money."

"Six o'clock then."

"See you then, Gene. Thanks."

As the coroner left the house, an officer came in to report that no one in the neighborhood had seen anything suspicious any time during the afternoon and no one really knew the victim.

"Okay. Take the map and make sure they dust the place for prints."

Standing alone in Derrick James's house, John Casey wondered if he or anyone else in New Hope really knew what was going on.

CHAPTER FOURTEEN

N ONE OF THEM SPOKE ON the ride to Callia's. When they returned to the apartment, Varek wondered why Amon was still around. He'd done what they'd needed him to do. He could go now.

Callia was exhausted and wanted nothing more than to get into bed and cuddle up to Varek, and she also wondered why Amon hadn't left to return to his life. She put a kettle of water on the stove for tea and sunk into one of the kitchen chairs, unable to get the sight of the killer lying dead on the floor out of her mind.

Varek felt her sadness but not for Derrick James. The ability to feel remorse for one who had killed innocents was absent in him, he guessed because of his time in Nil. No, the sadness he felt was because she had been exposed to such ugliness, to death, to danger because of him. He regretted that he was so in love with her that he couldn't refuse her when she insisted on helping him catch the murderer.

He stood watching her and promised himself he would make it up to her. Now they would have a life together, just as the Council had promised. But as he said this to himself, he saw everything go dark in front of him.

They weren't done with him yet.

Callia saw Varek disappear and cried, "No!" She frantically grabbed for him but felt only air. "No! They can't do this! We did what they wanted!"

Amon stood near the front door. He had always known Varek would be called back to the Council. Murderers didn't receive a reprieve, no matter who they found for the Council. He wouldn't have agreed to help Varek if he thought he'd be freed.

But Amon's emotions began to overwhelm him as he watched Callia cry over the loss of her destined one. He felt her sadness, not because Varek was gone, but because she affected him so strongly. He might be happy Varek was out of the picture, but she was devastated, so Amon felt devastated. Never had he known any being who caused him so much turmoil as she did.

He took a step toward her, wanting to console her but unsure if he could withstand the emotions it would release in him. He gazed down at her with her head in her hands, hesitant to allow himself to be so close to her. The shrill sound of the tea kettle whistling startled him, and when Callia jumped up to remove it from the burner, he backed up against the counter in surprise.

Callia stood over the stove, tears again rolling down her cheeks. Consumed by loss and loneliness, she wrapped her arms around her body, needing to be held. Hearing a voice behind her, she spun around, surprised to see Amon, whom she'd forgotten was still there.

Wiping her tear-stained cheeks, she apologized and offered him something to drink. He shook his head and took a step toward her with open arms.

"Come here, carina."

Callia staggered toward him, finally resting inside his arms, her head on his chest. For Amon, the feelings she brought out almost overcame him. He fought back the urge to hold her to him and take her across time and space to somewhere he knew could make her happy again. Somewhere he could give her whatever her heart desired. Somewhere he'd willingly become a slave to her love.

No. Now isn't the right time.

"Callia, everything will be okay. I'm sure he'll be back just as soon as the Council's finished hearing what happened today."

Amon didn't believe that any more than he wanted it to happen, but he knew she needed to believe it to trust him. Slowly, he moved his hand up and placed it gently on the back of her head. Excitement raced through his fingertips and up his arm. Amon used every bit of strength he possessed to keep himself calm. Her body pressed against his made the task almost impossible, and her sobbing caused her to press closer to him, straining his control.

"Why would they do this? Why? How can they be so cruel?"

Amon silently said in Italian, *Don't cry, carina. Let me take you from your pain.*

"Shhh. It will be okay."

Amon closed his eyes as she began to cry again. Her emotions stabbed at him. Her breasts moved up and down against his body, making him desire her despite the suffering her anguish caused him. The smell of her hair filled his nose— a fragrance that he would forever associate with her. Her soft hair brushed across his lips and tempted him to kiss the top of her head to comfort her, his carina. He yearned to allow his body and emotions to do as they begged.

"Callia, why don't you go rest? I'm sure after you take a nap, he'll be back and all will be well."

Callia nodded sadly. "Are you leaving?"

"No. I'll stay until you find out what's happened."

"Thank you. I'm sure you'd rather be back at one of your homes. You've been very kind."

Amon resisted the temptation to brush a stray tear from her cheek. His eyes explored the depths of her sad, hazel eyes, and he pushed down emotions that surged through him. "There is nowhere else I'd want to be."

Callia forced a weak smile and slowly walked to her room. Once she closed the door, he relaxed on the couch and concentrated on willing his body to do the same as the pain of her emotions ebbed away. Every moment spent near her heightened his emotions, and he struggled to control them, knowing his patience with her would be rewarded soon.

Amon gradually felt the tension drain from his body, and he cursed his emotional nature. As he lay stretched out on her couch, he considered entering her mind, but even a being like him had the ability to feel sympathy. There would be time enough for what he desired later.

Closing his eyes, he let his mind drift to another who'd affected him so. He had loved her completely, had been willing to never use his powers again if she'd said the word. His third destined one, Sevine.

The soft summer breeze drifted over his skin and refreshed him. He was conscious of another nearby and struggled to focus on his work. Something stirred in him, giving him notice that his time alone had come to an end.

Behind him he heard footsteps and turned to see her. Her pale grey eyes, wide with fear, stared up at him and she stood frozen, afraid to move.

"Please save me." Her terrified voice sliced through him.

He heard horses coming through to the clearing and quickly motioned with his head for her to hide in a small hut just feet away from where they stood. She scurried into hiding, and he waited to see who she so desperately didn't want to find her.

Five men on horseback rode up, all with weapons, and stopped in front of him as he stood with his shovel beside the gravel pile he had been spreading. One man spoke with a strange accent.

"You there! Have you seen a girl come through here?" As he spoke, he and the four others scanned the area for any sign of her.

He looked up at them and forced a look of ignorance on his face. When he spoke, he feigned irritation. "I've seen no one but you. Who do you seek?"

The lead man glared down at him and grunted. "An ungrateful whelp." His tone was sharp and full of anger.

"What is your name?" barked the head horseman.

"Lucius Salvius."

Lucius stood silently, developing a dislike for the man who spoke. He wanted to ask what the female had done, but this wasn't the one to tell him, so he said nothing.

"She's not here! Let's move!" With this, the five men rode off away from Lucius's property. He waited until they'd disappeared and went to find her. She sat huddled behind bags of feed for his horses, shaking with fear.

Lucius stood over her, feeling a tightness around his heart. She seemed so frightened and was so innocent compared to the men he had just encountered. Something in him made him want to protect her.

"They are gone. You can come out now. It is safe, I promise." As he reassured her, he extended his hand to help her up. Accepting it, she stood up in front of him, her head down.

"What is your name?"

She lifted her head and straightened her back. "Sevine."

"Sevine, why are those men after you?"

"I refuse to marry the one you spoke to," she said uneasily, looking away.

He could certainly understand why a woman would refuse to marry the man he had spoken to. But he sensed she objected for reasons other than his appearance and brutish manner.

"Have you been given to him in marriage?"

Sevine's eyes filled with tears but her voice told him she was angry as well as sad. "No! He killed my parents when I was a young girl, and he has kept me with him all these years until he was ready to marry me. I escaped the first chance I got." She paused and then looked down before she spoke again. "Please do not let him have me," she whispered.

Lucius felt that tightness even more as he looked at her staring down at the ground while she pleaded for help. His heart told him to take her in his arms and never let her go.

Sevine waited for him to speak and when he stood in silence over her, she looked up at him, her eyes wide. "Please...I can help around your house, help your wife cook, and I can clean. Please let me stay."

He shook his head. "I have no wife." His voice betrayed his loneliness. "I am alone."

Lucius wanted to let her stay. They were both alone, in need of the other.

He nodded and gently touched the hair that framed her face. He would let her stay.

"Oh, thank you so very much!" She wrapped her arms around his bare torso and hugged him tightly, touching his muscular back with her hands.

His eyes closed, and he reveled in the feel of another next to him. He gingerly stroked her hair as she continued to thank him and promise he would not regret letting her stay. She felt so good pressed against him. He had missed the touch of another for so long.

It took just days for him to realize she was his destined one, *but he knew he had been in love with her from that first moment of closeness. Sevine was a much younger Aeveren, so it took longer for her to know he was the one for her. He waited for her to realize fate, and when she did, he told her about his abilities. Instead of the fear he had experienced in previous lifetimes when he told others of his powers, Lucius saw acceptance from Sevine, and his feelings blossomed under her care.*

For Sevine, he was what she had always wished she had in her life: a powerful male to protect her.

Amon breathed deeply, enjoying his memories of Sevine and their time together. She had been the great love of his existence, and he longed for a love like hers to end his loneliness.

His body strained in anticipation, waiting for her to touch anywhere to ease his tension. Her mouth hovered near his erection, and he silently begged her to place her lips on him. She enjoyed teasing him, knowing that when he was finally able to hold back no longer, their lovemaking would be passionate and explosive. His power and urgency excited her, and once she had realized the effect she could have on him, she exercised it often. For Lucius, all he knew was that she was like nothing or no one he had ever experienced in all his lifetimes and all the places he had traveled to. Every touch from her made him feel alive.

Sevine brushed her lips delicately across his hip bone and lightly dragged her tongue over toward his other hip, allowing her cheek and chin to glide across his hard cock. His ragged breathing told her that her teasing affected him just as she liked. Soon he would be close to losing control and would take her, possess her with a passion she craved.

He buried his hands in her hair, tugging her toward his cock, wanting the feel of her lips and tongue on his hot skin. She resisted him but quickly flicked her tongue over the head to taste the musky, salty moisture there. His cock jerked at her touch, and Lucius pushed his hips upward. The tension in his body made him ache for her.

Sevine's hands massaged his sides, and she slid her body up his until her lips met his. Straddling him, she moaned just above his face as she slid over his erection, making it slick.

Lucius arched his body to enter hers, but she rolled her hips to avoid his entry. He pulled her close to him to kiss her passionately and groaned her name, wanting the exquisite relief he would find inside her.

"Sevine..." His body craved hers more than he could handle. He pulled her tightly to him and kissed her deeply. Her whispering his name inched him closer to the edge.

He grabbed her hips and rolled her onto her back under him. Bending his head down, he drew a nipple into his mouth, pulling gently as he sucked with his lips and grazed it with his teeth. Her skin tasted sweet.

She opened her legs wider for him, urging him to move his mouth to between them. Wanting the taste of her again on his lips, he slid down, kissing her stomach, and ran his tongue up her moist sex. His tongue and lips slowly brought her to the edge and backed off, twice, three times. Now he was in control, and *he watched her yearn for the relief only he could give her.*

The sight of her complete surrender to him made him lose control, and he rose up over her and plunged himself into her, the place he had been so many times before but still brought him immeasurable joy.

Over and over, he thrust into her, moaning in pleasure. Each thrust into her depths was followed by the slow withdrawal from her and the sensation that her body, desperate to keep him inside, closed around him.

Sevine grabbed his shoulders and held him to her, wanting to feel every inch of him touch that spot inside her that made her body melt. His breathing raced to a pant next to her ear.

"I need you. I need this. Come for me, carina. Come for me."

Lucius drove his cock into her and felt his orgasm explode into her as he pumped faster, bringing Sevine to the brink of shattering. In her ear, he demanded in a raspy, sex-filled voice, "Come for me, carina."

Sevine's climax overwhelmed her, and she dug her fingernails into his shoulders and down his back. As she shook from aftershocks, he stayed inside her, never wanting to leave. She kissed his cheek and over to his ear, whispering, "I am yours, Lucius. No other man could ever make me feel the way you do, bring my body the kind of pleasure you do."

Lucius, still hard inside her, lay listening to the words of the woman he loved, wanting to spend eternity with her.

Amon felt a heaviness in his chest he always did after

thinking of Sevine. Lifetimes together gave him thousands of memories, all of which should've made him happy but only left him with an aching loneliness.

But now he'd found someone who made him feel like he had with Sevine. Callia stirred something in him, just as she had. He felt alive when she was nearby. He felt love inside him when he touched her. Just being next to her made the loneliness of lifetimes without another in his world evaporate. He would love and be loved again.

That she had a destined one meant nothing to him. Aeveren laws had never meant much to him—he had powers that made them inconsequential. Now it was just a matter of deciding how to achieve his goal.

Amon weighed the pros and cons of his ideas. He could take her and go anywhere in time where they could live happily. But she'd still know about her destined one, and that would ruin their happiness.

He could go back to some point in Varek's lifetime before he was sent to Nil and kill him. He had deduced from their conversations that he was sent back to the lifetime in which he committed his crime, so he could use that. But Amon thought to himself that this seemed too elaborate and might get Varek out of spending any time in Nil.

No, the idea that made the most sense was to go back in time before Callia met her destined one and get her to fall in love with him first. Then when Aeveren biology called, Varek would be in New Hope and Callia would be with him.

In Italy, happily in love.

CHAPTER FIFTEEN

T HE AEVEREN COUNCIL CHAMBERS IN Nil buzzed with energy. Council members spoke to one another, one occasionally loud enough for Varek to hear his part in the conversation. Bits and pieces of various discussions floated down to where he stood on the level below the Council members' tables. While he couldn't understand what they all spoke about, he sensed they were excited about something. He assumed the excitement was about the end of the murders in New Hope and hoped they were happy enough that Derrick James had been stopped to overlook the fact that he had killed him.

Varek looked down as his wrists as he waited for the proceedings to begin. For the first time in three lifetimes, he stood before the Council without shackles. He prayed this wasn't an oversight they'd correct once they began to focus on the fact that he'd murdered again. He hadn't intended on killing James, but the man had given him no choice. He had to defend the woman he loved. He didn't regret protecting her, but he wondered now if he had ruined this lifetime and possibly more because of his actions.

The head of the Council called the meeting to order, and Varek waited to hear if he'd be allowed to return to Callia and the happiness he'd been denied for lifetimes or if he would return to Nil as a prisoner to be punished once again. As he listened for their judgment, his mouth was parched, and his heart hammered against his chest.

"Mr. Leale, we extend congratulations and gratitude for stopping the murder of Aeveren parents in New Hope. Your success has impressed this Council."

Varek knew by the tone of the last words the Councilman spoke that there was more to come. Would it be *"but you murdered another so our agreement has been voided and you must return to Nil?"* The anticipation made his stomach churn.

Another Council member took a stack of papers from the head Councilman and seemed to scan the information for a minute. When he looked up to focus on Varek, he removed his glasses and cleared his throat.

"Mr. Leale, you've become acquainted with a very interesting individual in completing the task we set before you."

Varek looked up at him, unsure of what he meant. Who was he referring to? Callia or Amon?

Almost in answer to his silent questioning, the Council member answered, "Amon Kalins."

Sensing nothing good was to come, Varek nodded but offered nothing more.

"What do you know of Mr. Kalins?"

The chamber fell silent as every other Council member stopped what they were doing and waited for his answer. Varek's mind filled with a laundry list of things he knew about Amon, all reasons he disliked him.

He's a pain in the ass, a manipulative bastard who hits on the person I love.

But Varek sensed they didn't want to know his personal feelings on one of the most powerful Aeveren to ever exist.

"I know he can manipulate time and teleport back in time and within the present time."

The head Councilman spoke again. "Have you witnessed him manipulating time, Mr. Leale?"

"Other than his claim that he went back in time to find out the identity of the murderer, no, I haven't witnessed him using his power."

"Have you witnessed his teleportation power?"

Witnessed it? I almost ran the son of a bitch over when he put himself in front of a moving car going seventy-five miles an hour, the cocky bastard.

"Yes, I've witnessed that." Varek wondered where this line of questioning was going.

"Have you witnessed any other powers?"

"According to him, he doesn't possess any others." A chill ran up Varek's spine. Had Amon lied about what powers he had? "Does he have others?"

The head Councilman inhaled and exhaled slowly. When he spoke, his tone was more serious than before. "That's what we'd hoped to learn from you, Mr. Leale. We suspect he possesses additional powers now."

Varek's stomach knotted. Callia was alone with Amon. God knows what he was doing. "Additional abilities? Like what?"

Methodically, the Councilman listed the various possibilities that may have occurred in Amon. Some didn't concern Varek, such as an increased ability to heal quickly, but others were disconcerting, particularly the abilities associated with the mind.

"So you're telling me he may be able to control other's minds?" He knew his tone was disrespectful, but he found it incredible that they'd brought him back to Nil and left Callia with Amon knowing he may be able to manipulate someone's mind.

"We don't know. But we do know it's possible. Amon Kalins is a very powerful Aeveren—possibly the most powerful of our race. In addition, he's an ancient one who's had many lifetimes to hone his powers and very probably gain new ones."

"What do you mean gain new ones?"

"Mr. Leale, Amon Kalins is a rarity among Aeveren. He was born with powers instead of gaining them later in the reincarnation cycle. He's been able to manipulate time since his first lifetime, but just as most Aeveren come into their powers after their twentieth lifetime, he's gained powers as he's continued through lifetimes. We knew about his ability to teleport in present time, and we've heard rumors of what seem like other abilities he possesses now."

Varek felt real fear for Callia's safety now. "Are any of these powers dangerous?"

"We don't know."

These were exactly the words he didn't want to hear. His destined one was alone with Amon and might be in danger, and he was standing in the Council chambers in Nil discussing the tempuster's possible abilities.

"Then you need to send me back to Callia—you know, one of those gifts you gave me—right now before she gets hurt."

"We can't do that yet."

Rage flowed through Varek, his hands tightening into fists at his sides as his words exploded into the chamber. "What the fuck do you mean you can't do that yet? I did as I was instructed. I found your murderer and stopped him. I get to go free now. That was the deal!"

The head Councilman leaned forward and spoke in a calm, almost condescending tone that only served to enrage Varek more. "We understand your feelings, but we can't do that now. We…"

Before the Council member could finish his statement, Varek interrupted. "The fuck you understand my feelings! I'm just a tool to you, something you can use to your own ends! You don't even care why that damned half-breed was killing our people! But what about Callia? You care nothing about endangering an innocent female just so you can keep pulling my strings and send me on another fucking errand that you can't seem to do with all your power?"

The Council members stared down at him in stunned

silence, and Varek expected the shackles and leg irons to fasten around his wrists and ankles at any moment. He knew he'd gone too far, but he didn't care. All he cared about was Callia.

He waited as the Council members spoke in murmurs above him, his mind racing through the various methods Amon may have harmed her already. He felt sick at the idea that he may have already taken her back in time to someplace he'd never be able to reach and she was lost to him until their next lifetime. His body grew heavy at the thought of her gone from his life so soon after he'd found her, and he wasn't sure he'd be able to take much more of the Council's officious discussion of his life. He closed his eyes and attempted to steady himself for what was to come next.

"Mr. Leale, we don't want to endanger your destined one, but there are bigger issues here."

Looking up at the man, he sighed. "Not to me."

"We will honor our agreement, but we will require you to perform one more task before we can do so."

Varek wasn't stupid. He knew what they wanted him to do. He just couldn't understand why they needed him to do it.

"And if I do this, you'll release me free and clear? No strings attached?"

"Yes."

Varek knew he had no choices, so he took a deep breath, exhaled in a mixture of disgust and resignation, and asked the question he already knew the answer to. "What do I have to do?"

"Capture Amon Kalins."

"How the hell am I going to capture one of the most powerful of our race? I have no powers, and we don't even like each other, so it's not like I can get close to him." Varek's exasperation filled the chamber, and as he looked at the Council members' faces, he saw guilt and realized what they'd done.

"This was your plan all along. You knew I wouldn't be able to stop the murderer without help from someone able to go back in time. You told me as much." Varek stopped, and his mind reluctantly moved to thoughts of Callia. "Did you manipulate Callia and me to be drawn together because she's related to an ancient who would lead us to Kalins? Were we just pawns who didn't know any better?"

I love her. Please don't say we aren't destined for each other.

"Mr. Leale, it's true we knew you'd most likely require some kind of aid to find Derrick James. However, we cannot control Aeveren biology outside of Nil. When you were released, what had been stripped from you when you entered this place was reinstated. We knew you would be given the gift of a destined one when you returned to your lifetime, but what we did or didn't know about who your destined one was isn't important. That you are destined to be with one who comes from a family with an ancient who knew how to find Amon Kalins is just a fortunate coincidence."

Varek relaxed, relieved that they hadn't orchestrated his love for Callia or hers for him.

"Or perhaps it's fate," the Councilman said with a grin.

"So how am I supposed to capture Kalins?"

The Council sat silently.

"Are you telling me you want me to catch him and bring him back to you but you can't tell me anything that could help me?" he asked.

Out of the corner of his eye, he saw one of the Council member's pages approaching him with something in his hand. The page held out what looked like a charm, and Varek took it.

He held it in his hand, feeling its coldness against the center of his palm. As black as night, the object seemed to be carved out of some dark stone.

"What am I supposed to do with this?"

"That is a charm to travel through time. We are giving it to you to help you find Kalins."

"Great...what's the catch?"

"The catch is that with great power, such as what this talisman affords you, comes not only great responsibility but great choices."

Varek sighed and placed the object in his front pocket. *More riddles and platitudes.* He knew asking them to clarify this would be of little help, so he chose to stick with basic usage instructions.

"So how does it work?" *How do I get to be Varek the Wizard?*

"All you need do is use your mind to transmit your intentions to the talisman. But beware, you must be clear about where and when you wish to go or you may find yourself in difficult situations."

Great. More difficult than capturing an Aeveren with near-

superpowers?

"Why don't one of you capture Kalins? At least you possess some power, unlike me."

The Council looked at Varek intently, and he thought he saw sadness creep across their faces.

"You asked that question once before, so perhaps it is time to answer it for you. Just as that talisman you possess imparts to you great power, so do we have great power. But as you now know that with power comes responsibility and choices, we have always known that as we know we may not leave this place once we've made the choice to serve our people on this Council. We must rely on those individuals like yourself who we deem worthy of our faith to carry out our deeds."

Varek understood all too clearly the feelings the Council must experience. Three lifetimes believing he'd never be free had in some ways made him as clinical in his thoughts as they seemed to be.

The Council members stood to leave the chamber, but Varek had one more question to ask.

"Wait! Please!"

The head of the Council sat down again and the other members stopped in their procession.

"What if I run into problems or need to come back to speak to you?"

Smiling, the head Councilman simply said, "You now possess the power to return here at any time."

With that, they filed out of the chamber, and he waited to be sent back to Callia's. Standing alone, he waited but nothing happened. He took the talisman out of his pocket and held it in his hand once again.

Take me back to Callia's.

Instantaneously, he was in his room in Callia's apartment, thankful that he hadn't returned right in front of Amon. Varek stuffed the charm back into his pocket and walked into the hallway. The apartment was silent, and he felt panicked at the thought that Amon may have already taken Callia.

As he entered the living room, relief swept over him when he saw Amon resting on the couch.

Perfect. I can grab him and take him back to the Council before he can even wake up.

Amon sensed another person in the room and opened his eyes to see Varek standing over him taking something out of his pants pocket. He quickly stood up and faced him.

"Back so soon?"

Just as Varek began to reply, Callia's door opened and she appeared in the doorway. When she saw him, she ran to him, her arms open.

"Varek! Thank God you're back!"

He pushed the talisman back down into his pocket and wrapped his arms around her.

"I missed you so much. I thought they'd taken you back." As she spoke, tears flowed from her eyes. She held him like she was afraid to let go, for fear they might take him again. In her ear as she rested her head on his chest, she heard his heart beat wildly.

"Callia, don't cry. I'm back for good." He stroked her hair

as he repeated the words. "I'm not going anywhere ever again without you."

Callia stepped back, and he caught her face in his hands. She looked up at him with wide, moist eyes.

"They let you go for good? You never have to go back to Nil again?"

"I did what they wanted, so the deal was I would be free, and here I am." Varek didn't want to lie outright to her, but with Amon standing right next to him, hanging on every word, he couldn't say what he wanted to. That would have to wait.

Callia smiled and hugged him again. She let her body mold to his, in love with the sensations she was experiencing with his return. Behind her, Amon cleared his throat.

"I think it's time for me to go." Amon reached for his coat slung over the back of the chair and slipped into it.

"Amon, I can't thank you enough for everything thing you did. You were truly wonderful to me when I needed someone." She walked over to him and wrapped her arms around him. "Thank you so much for everything you did for us."

The feel of her body next to his set alarms off throughout him, and he quickly remembered to make sure his face didn't betray anything he was thinking or feeling as he stared into Varek's black eyes.

Callia returned to Varek's side, and Amon stood awkwardly, hating the feeling that he was an intruder. He smiled and turned to leave.

"Where will you go?" Varek asked, instantly hoping Amon

wouldn't suspect anything.

Amon turned to face him, thinking the question was odd coming from someone who had wanted him out of his life almost immediately after meeting him. Raising an eyebrow, he answered, "I'll probably just go back to the lonely Victorian home where you found me." He turned to Callia, and in Italian said, "I look forward to seeing you at my home near Castelmuzio, carina."

Callia smiled, and Amon left them holding hands in her living room. Varek brought her hand up to his lips and kissed it softly.

"What did he just say?"

"Just that he wants us to visit him at his home in Tuscany, near the village of Castelmuzio—Il Castello."

Varek pulled her to him and bent his head down to her ear. "Right now, I don't want to go anywhere else other than one of the bedrooms down that hallway, and I don't want to think of anything but making love to you, least of all visiting him anywhere."

He tipped her head up toward his and leaned in to cover her mouth with his. Their kiss was deeper than ever before because they'd each believed they'd lost the one they loved more dearly than any other in the world.

Callia looked up at him and traced her finger over his lips. "So you're going to tell me what's going on later, right? I don't need to know now—I don't want to know anything other than how you feel inside me right now—but later, you need to tell me."

Varek looked confused, and she smiled as she tugged his T-shirt out of his pants. "I know you, Varek, and I could tell you were holding something back before."

She unfastened his pants and lightly dragged her hand over his abdomen. He groaned and put any thoughts of capturing Amon Kalins out of his mind as he led Callia to his bedroom.

CHAPTER SIXTEEN

A MON SAT PENSIVELY IN HIS study thinking of Callia and Varek. That she would soon be with him and they'd travel to Italy delighted him. He replayed the same fantasy over and over again of her in his garden surrounded by beauty and running to him to wrap him in her arms as she had Varek. The jealousy he had felt stab him as he watched them embrace had been replaced by a sweet anticipation of what would soon be his.

He stood up from his desk and stretched his arms over his head to relieve tension. Just the idea of her was enough to excite him, but with no chance of having her at the moment, he had to be content with either himself or traveling to one of the females he frequented. He thought about it and decided although it would be more hassle than being alone, it would be immeasurably more pleasurable with another.

Reclining on a couch, he deliberated over who and when, deciding on a female he had encountered on one of his visits back to eighteenth century France.

A French farm girl will do the trick.

With that choice made, his mind turned to the question of Varek. Amon wondered how he had been allowed to leave Nil and return to Callia. Was the Council truly that grateful for his ending the murders in New Hope? He mulled this over and decided that the Council did not let murderers out of Nil for what he'd done for them. No, he was still working for them, but doing what?

His ego made the conclusion that the Council had sent Varek back to capture him an easy one. But his ego also saw this as insulting. Varek had no powers, nothing to equal his abilities.

Do these ridiculous Council members believe they can stop me with simple brute force?

The idea made him chuckle, and a sinister laugh rose from his belly to his throat. Varek wouldn't even be a good adversary in the fight for Callia's affections. He would be even less in a fight to capture him for the Council.

Amon ran his hand over his stomach and let his head fall back on the leather arm of the couch. His time with Callia had affected him so much he found it difficult to want another. His hand slid down the front of his pants, and he closed his eyes. He was already rock hard. Remembering the special talent the French farm girl could perform with her tongue roused him from his reluctance to move from the couch, and he stood up. Straightening his shirt, he thought about where he wanted to go and looked down to see the obvious bulge in his pants.

It won't take too much of her tongue this time.

Smiling, he focused on eighteenth century France and a

farm in the Limousin region and disappeared from his study.

VAREK LED CALLIA INTO HIS room and closed the door behind them. Standing there in front of him, she looked so unbelievably sexy, but he didn't want this time to be fast and hard like the last time. He kissed her gently on the lips and began to slowly undress her as Callia reached for his clothes and worked to remove them.

"Callia, I want to make love to you slow and sweet."

As he spoke, his hands slowly traced her curves, lingering on her breasts. The sharp intake of breath when he gently squeezed her nipple told him she was as excited as he was, but he wanted to prolong the pleasure of their lovemaking this time. He wanted her to truly know what it meant to be made love to.

Callia lay on the bed and welcomed Varek to her with open arms. He rested much of his weight on his forearms, so he didn't hurt her. Kissing down her neck to the hollow at its base, he groaned against her skin as he softly pressed his lips against it. Her hands ran through his hair, tugging as he nipped lightly at her collarbone.

Varek slid up her body to kiss her lips again, and moaned into her mouth when she slid her tongue over his. When she sucked his tongue into her mouth, his cock hardened even more.

He loved the taste of her, the feel of her mouth on his, the sensation of her tongue gliding over his, mingling with his.

Her sensuality excited him more than he ever thought possible. She teased him, made his skin feel like he was on fire. Her body moved under his, building his passion.

"Callia, I need you. I don't want a life without you." His voice was passionate, full of emotion.

He looked into those beautiful hazel eyes of hers like he was searching for himself in her. Did she love him as deeply as he loved her?

He doubted she could love him because of her, the one before Callia. His fear of love shone in his eyes.

She loved him as she had loved no other in seven lifetimes. She loved him as easily as she breathed.

"Varek, there is no life for me without you. Your happiness is my happiness, your sadness my sadness. I am your destined one. I love you."

As he closed his eyes, he cradled her face in his hands and kissed her sweetly. She was his. His Callia. The one who helped him see that he could love again.

He moved his body down hers, kissing her breasts and stomach slowly. Each spot he kissed he touched with his fingertips as if he couldn't bear to leave any part of her but craved the parts he hadn't touched yet. As he moved down her body, his silky, black hair feathered across her skin, exciting her even more. He kissed one spot while caressing another.

His mouth reached her sex and just the brush of his lips made her tremble. He skimmed over where she so desperately wanted his mouth and kissed her soft inner thighs. His desire increased, and he began slowly sucking her skin and flicking his tongue up her leg. But what he truly desired waited for him, needy and wet.

Varek moved slowly between her legs, teasing her with his fingers all around where he desperately wanted to place his mouth. Callia lifted her hips, hoping to persuade him to do just what he wanted. He moaned sensually and placed a hand on each of her hips, pinning her lower body to the bed. He licked his lips, and the warmth of anticipation ran through her, making her wet.

He hovered over her sex, his hot breath exciting her even more. And then with just the soft tip of his tongue, he touched her slick skin. What felt like electric shocks raced into her body, touching her deep inside. Each drag of his tongue became more insistent until he was fully tasting her with his whole mouth.

Varek expertly ran his tongue over her most sensitive spot and more shocks shivered into her. Pleased by her reaction, he repeated the action but finished by sucking on her swollen nub, bringing her closer to orgasm. Once more, this time with the addition of two fingers slid inside her, sent her over the edge and she desperately grabbed handfuls of hair as she pulled him closer. He rode her orgasm, his mouth savoring everything she offered.

When he lifted his head, Callia's eyes were closed and she bit her lower lip. Still enjoying the aftershocks, she smiled when he climbed up toward her face.

Without a word, she urged him onto his back so she could give him the kind of pleasure he'd given her. She kissed down his torso while her hands stroked his sides and then his lower abdomen and hips. His thick erection strained as her lips teased his skin, and she took it in her hand, almost wrapping her fingers around it. A moan escaped from his mouth as she licked the head softly.

As she took his cock into her mouth, Varek opened his eyes to watch. The sight of him disappearing into her, combined with the feel of her tongue gliding over the head and shaft, almost made him come. Callia stroked under his cock and gently squeezed each time her mouth traveled up to the head to suck greedily.

Varek felt his orgasm begin deep inside him and hoarsely said, "I can't hold back anymore." He exploded into her mouth and groaned as she sucked him to the end.

Callia rose up to his face, placed a kiss on his nose and nibbled his ear. Still hard, Varek rolled her onto her back and placed himself at her entrance. Slowly he thrust into her, stretching her to accommodate him.

"Take me. Take all of me, Callia."

Callia arched her body toward him and grabbed his shoulders, pulling his chest to hers. Each time he pushed into her, he touched a spot that felt like heaven. She let out a cry as her body exploded in ecstasy, calling out his name in a satisfied moan as waves of pleasure swept through her.

Varek felt her come, her insides squeezing his cock toward his own orgasm. So close, he drove in and out, in and out, waiting for his own climax. When it came, he buried himself into her as deeply as he could, flooding her insides with him.

He opened his eyes to see her eyes, half-lidded and signaling her satisfaction, gazing up at him. Her hands moved up and down his back in long, lazy strokes, relaxing him even more. He kissed her and pushed the sweat-dampened strands of hair from her forehead and cheeks.

Slowly, he left her body and rolled over onto the bed, exhausted. Callia rested her head on his chest and curled up close to him. As he absentmindedly stroked her hair, he closed his eyes and let himself enjoy the bliss of the moment he found in her body pressed to his.

Callia traced his jaw line with her finger and he sighed, telling her he hadn't dozed off.

"Varek, we need to talk about what happened when you went to the Council."

A mild growl told her he was going to be obstinate.

"You need to tell me. We're in this together."

Still wanting her, Varek thought about the other things he'd prefer to be in together. His cock twitched against his belly and just the thought of Kalins made him jealous and possessive. He rolled Callia onto her back and bent his head down to kiss her. She could sense immediately that something in him had changed.

"Ready to go again?" she playfully asked. She felt his hard cock graze her inner thigh, answering her question.

Varek's eyes shone like black satin, and his face looked like sex—wild sex. He spoke into her ear, his voice a ragged purr. "Roll over. Get on your knees."

Pursing her lips, she teased, "Mmmmmm…Cro-Magnon."

She got up on her knees and planted her hands in front of her on the bed. He came up behind her and grabbed her hips with both hands, positioning her in front of him. One hand slid down between her legs, a finger sliding into her slick heat.

Bending down next to her ear, he groaned, "You're so ready for me."

Callia wiggled her behind against him and heard him say, "Greedy" as he pulled her back to him, teasing her with his cock at her moist entrance.

"Tell me what you want."

Pushing against him as he brushed against her clitoris, Callia turned her head and in a breathless voice pleaded, "Please...now..."

From behind, Varek plunged into her. With his hands on her hips, he pulled her down onto him and pushed her to the tip, prolonging the intensity for both of them.

But his body wanted more than teasing, and he began to pump wildly into her as he pulled her back to him. He rode her like a male possessing a female.

Callia felt more turned on than she ever thought possible. He controlled the pace, the force, her. His power felt so good pounding into her. Behind her, Varek breathed heavily, moaning softly as he pulled her to him.

Her orgasm took her over. In a deep, hoarse voice, he talked her to her climax. "Come for me, Callia. Come for me."

Utterly satisfied, she dropped to her forearms, and the change in angle brought his orgasm fast. He pulled her to his body as he pulsated inside her.

Sated and knowing he had brought Callia as much pleasure as she had him, he reluctantly eased out of her and lay down next to her.

Smiling, she said to him, "I love it when you're like that."

"Some twenty-first century female you are," he said jokingly and kissed her lips.

Callia smiled, thinking she was perfectly fine with how their relationship had turned out. He respected her and treated her as his equal partner, and she knew he adored her. But she loved the part of him that took control—his power was one of the most attractive parts of him.

Later, after they had spent time enjoying just holding one another silently, Varek knew he had to discuss with Callia what he had to do. One more job to do for the Council and he'd be free to settle down into a life with her, maybe start a family, and live out this lifetime loved by a wonderful mate and looking forward to many more lifetimes with the gift he'd been so fortunate to receive.

Still naked, Callia sat up and leaned back on her hands, and Varek propped himself up on his elbow, a measure of how comfortable they had become with one another.

Looking up at her, he spoke, his voice serious. "Callia, I have to do something else for the Council before they'll let me go."

She couldn't help the frown that showed her unhappiness with what they were doing to him.

"What? What do you have to do?"

Varek sighed. "I have to capture Amon and take him back to Nil."

"I knew it had something to do with him. You were obviously holding back when he was here."

Varek thought for a second and decided not to say anything that showed his jealousy. He had just given Callia multiple orgasms and knew she loved him as much as he loved her. He didn't want to ruin things by being snide about Amon Kalins.

"But Varek, how are we supposed to capture a tempuster?"

"We?" he said, lifting both his eyebrows.

"Don't start with this again. I'm not going to sit here in New Hope while you do this."

He didn't want to fight her, but he didn't want her anywhere near Amon. He resigned himself to her will, but told himself he'd find a way to involve her without letting her be in harm's way.

Varek walked over to his pants and pulled out the talisman, holding it up to show her. "This is how we capture him."

Curious, Callia kneeled on the bed and looked at what he held in his hand. "What's that?"

"It's a talisman that allows me to travel through time."

"Can we both go at the same time?"

"I don't know, but I need to figure out how to find him first."

"He said he was going back to the place where we found him." Callia thought about her conversations with Amon. "I know he has a home in Tuscany too."

"That helps I guess, but he could be anywhere."

"Did they give you anything to counter his ability to

teleport?"

Varek shook his head. In fact, the Council had given him more help with this than they had to catch the murderer, but he knew he'd need more than just getting through time.

Callia sat down on the bed. She thought for a moment and shrugged. "You know, Varek, I think I could be very helpful with Amon."

"No."

"Varek, I know he likes me more than you. I think I could make him lower his defenses so you could capture him."

Varek sat down on the bed. There was no way in hell he wanted to use Callia as bait to trap Amon.

"No."

Callia sat up on her knees and kissed his cheek. "You know it would work."

Varek turned to her, his face deathly serious. "I know that I don't want you that close to him. What if he took you somewhere in time and I couldn't find you?"

She took his face in her hands and looked into his worried eyes. "You forget. I'd still know you're the one for me, no matter where he took me. I don't think he'd do anything to harm me. And you'd be able to find me. I know it."

"Callia, listen to me. You underestimate Amon Kalins. He has no restraint, far too much power..." Varek hesitated and then continued, "...and he wants you."

She kissed his worried brow and smiled. "I don't care what he wants. I love you."

Varek forced a smile. "Well, I love you, and that's why I'll think of another way."

CHAPTER SEVENTEEN

A MON REAPPEARED IN HIS HOME on the New York-Pennsylvania border. It was dark by the time he returned from his pleasure trip to rural France, and he made his way to his bedroom after questioning Gethen about any visitors who had come while he was gone. No visitors yet.

He removed his clothes and changed into silk pajama bottoms. As he lay in bed, he mulled over his time with Callia. Even as he'd been standing in that orchard with another female's mouth on him, he'd thought of Callia, each touch of the woman's tongue adding another level to the fantasy he'd constructed of her surrendering herself to him.

There had been so many since Sevine had left him. Most were meaningless comfort he couldn't feel anything for even if he wanted to, which he didn't. Some had been more than just things to amuse him. Some had come close to touching his soul, but no one since Sevine had.

Not until Callia.

Lifetimes had passed without him feeling a connection to another, but he'd never forgotten the sensation of wanting to be with someone—really wanting another, not just wanting to fuck someone. He'd never forgotten how his heart raced around someone he truly cared about, how he doubted himself in the face of a woman he adored. He, who could flow through time effortlessly, make it stop, bend it to his will, doubted himself only for a few others in his forty-seven lifetimes, and now he felt the insecurity of needing someone again. It made the last time he had someone all come back to him.

The coldness of the room made him shudder. The servant fumbled in his attempt to start the fire, and he nervously looked around, anticipating a beating from his master. The sharp strike of a third match led to a tendril of smoke that rose from the firewood piled in the fireplace. The servant quickly shuffled out of the room, his head down in frightened deference.

Riordan angrily paced back and forth across the wood floor, each step resulting in a sharp creaking noise behind him. His hands balled into tight fists at his side, the muscles in his body aching from the tension that strained them. His anger coursed through his body, making it difficult to think of anything else.

The longer he waited, the angrier he grew. He felt trapped in the dark, paneled room but couldn't leave. Not without speaking to her. On one of his passes across the room, his anger exploded at one of the ornately carved chairs, and he kicked it with enough force to make it skid across the floor and strike the wall next to the fireplace. The sound of it crashing against the wall startled him out of the furious trance he had slipped into. Taking a deep breath, he picked up the chair and placed it once again in its traditional home before he turned to look expectantly at the door, hoping she would come through it at that very moment.

Riordan cursed out loud at his need to see her. He couldn't let her leave him. She was his destined one. There was no way she could leave him. Aeveren biology was more powerful than her feelings on this matter. At the thought of her out of his existence, his stomach knotted. Just then, she walked in and greeted him with a look of disgust.

"Sevine, I've been waiting here for almost an hour!" As he spoke, he walked toward her, his arms folded over his chest.

"Riordan! I haven't been Sevine for almost twenty lifetimes!" she snapped. "Stop calling me that. My name is Frederika."

He stepped within an arm's length of her, and in a voice far quieter than before, he began again. "Frederika, we need to talk."

Maneuvering around him, she walked to the fireplace and turned to face him. "We have nothing more to talk about, Riordan. I haven't changed my mind."

Each word she spoke felt like knives stabbing him. He took a few steps toward her and stopped himself from taking her in his arms, knowing she would just push him away.

"I will not let you go," he said in a resolute voice that barely hid his sadness.

"You have no choice."

He knew her unwillingness to discuss this with him meant she had already done something to leave him, but he wouldn't give up. He couldn't. He took two more steps toward her and reached his hand out to touch her shoulders lightly with his fingertips. The softness of her dress against his fingers stilled him.

"Please..."

Frederika looked into his eyes. His fingers stayed on her body as she moved. She looked up into his eyes and sighed in resignation.

His light brown hair fell free from its tie at the back of his head and onto his face, creating a harried look in him. Even though he'd been sixteen different men—sixteen different loves of hers—and looked nothing like when she'd first met him on his farm in the Italian countryside at the height of the Roman Empire, he still had something of the face of Lucius Salvius, the destined one she'd first fallen in love with so many lifetimes before.

He didn't wait for her to agree to what he had to say. He began to plead his case.

"Frederika, you are my destined one. We're meant for each other. Until you move on, you're mine." His voice was deep and masculine, but he made sure to soften it enough to let her know that beneath biological forces, he truly cared for her.

He gazed into her violet eyes and waited for her to speak, but she said nothing. Her silence encouraged him, and he continued.

"I love you. No matter what has happened, we have lifetimes of memories together."

He abruptly stopped when she began shaking her head in disagreement and backing away from him.

"*No! You cannot do this!*" *He stepped toward her and took her face in his hands.* "*Nothing has happened that cannot be made right.*" *His voice sounded painfully desperate now, but he didn't care.*

Frederika lifted her hands and placed them over his. "*I can no longer be your destined one. I cannot remain with you knowing what you've done with your powers.*" *She released his hands from hers and stood in front of him, her face dispassionate.*

Riordan let his hands drop. He scanned her face for some remnant of love, some leftover emotion for him, but found none. He had finally pushed her away with his actions. She had finally gone through with the threat she had voiced so many times before.

"*I never did anything to harm you. I never meant anything but to show you my love.*"

Frederika shook her head again. "*You don't care for others any longer, Riordan. Perhaps it was inevitable that your powers would lead you to disregard others' feelings. The ability to manipulate time is a great temptation, one that you have not been able to deny. I overlooked much, and for that I am ashamed, but when you began to manipulate me with your powers, I could overlook your behavior no longer.*"

Riordan stood in front of her, struck by the cold, analytical tone of her voice. It was true. He had used his powers indiscriminately in the past to punish his enemies and to arrange things so his life with her could be easier. And it was true that she had never condoned his using his powers toward such selfish ends and had become more and more unhappy about his actions as the years passed.

His jealous manipulation of time to separate her from another he feared would take her from him had been too much for her to bear. She'd known deep in her heart that he'd been responsible for her human friend's disappearance but hadn't wanted to believe it for a long time. When she'd finally asked him if he'd had any part in his absence, Riordan had blithely admitted it to her as the tears streamed down her face. When her sadness became too much for him to bear, he'd attempted to reverse the wrong he'd done but found that his manipulation of time had resulted in her friend's death.

But Riordan hadn't anticipated that Frederika's love couldn't be won back. Day after day, he assumed her heart would open up once again for him when her grief had left her, but instead her heart grew hard toward him, incapable of forgiveness.

With his last chance to regain the love of his destined one at hand, he pleaded with her. "Please, Frederika. I know I have done things...things that have caused you pain. Please give me the opportunity to show you how much I love you, how much I need you."

Frederika pushed past him and headed for the door. He grabbed her shoulders and spun her around toward him, unwilling to accept that he'd done something that couldn't be changed.

"I will not let you go."

Knowing all too well he wouldn't, she'd found an Aeveren

experienced in the magick of the ancient ways of their race to help her escape his grasp. With the magick she'd gotten from him, she was prepared for anything her husband could attempt with his powers.

"Riordan, your future has been cast by your actions. I will not remain with you. If you persist in your refusal to let me go, I will be forced to use the ancient magick of our people to bind you from using your powers on me."

He staggered back as if he'd been struck across the face, in shock that she'd gone to such lengths to be released from him. He'd truly lost her if she was willing to delve into Aeveren magick, a dark area of their world most of their race refused to even acknowledge.

Riordan instinctively reached out for her in his despair, his mind not registering the idea that she was the one soul no longer available to comfort him. Her reaction hurt like salt in a wound. She recoiled from his touch like he was a monster.

Afraid that he'd try to force her back in time with him, she began chanting the spell she had obtained.

"By the will of Kronos, by the hand of tempus…"

Before she could speak the final lines, Riordan put up his hands in front of him and stepped back in fear that she might bind his powers completely. For a long moment the two who had been with one another for seventeen lifetimes—across the span of history from a simple farm life in the powerful Roman Empire, to the harsh world of the Norsemen on the shores of the North Sea, to survival from the Black Death, through the demise of their lives at the hands of Spanish conquistadores as their

Aztec Empire fell, to their current lifetime as English nobility—the two who had been destined for no others looked at one another as the world began anew for both of them. Riordan felt the emptiness of being alone again in the world stab at him, a feeling he hadn't experienced since the day Sevine had entered his life.

He hung his head and in a voice soft as a whisper said the words he'd never imagined could leave his lips. "I release you from being my destined one."

Then he was alone again in the room. In the world. Years passed and then centuries. He became different souls but was always alone for he had a destined one but couldn't be with her.

Amon stared at the far wall of his bedroom. He couldn't think of Sevine anymore. Centuries of loneliness threatened to crush him, but Callia brought a sense of relief to him, and his mind began to race with a plan to finally bring him what he'd missed for so long. With just a thought, he alerted Gethen he needed him and leapt out of bed. When the servant appeared, he was already in action.

"Ready yourself for Italy, Gethen." As he spoke, Amon moved around his bedroom excitedly.

"What shall I pack, master?"

Amon stopped, thought for a moment with his eyes closed, and then leveled his gaze at his servant. "Pack nothing."

"Nothing, master?"

"Nothing. We are going back in time."

Gethen lowered his head in a respectful nod and turned to

leave to attend to his duties.

"One more thing."

The servant turned to receive further orders.

"I want no one else at the villa when I arrive. I won't be alone."

"Yes, master."

With the servant gone, Amon relished the excitement he felt at the anticipation of finally having Callia for his own. For the first time, he rejoiced at the thought of the future this lifetime held.

CALLIA WOKE UP IN VAREK'S arms and craned her neck to look out the window. March had come in like a lion and the past week had been cold, but as she watched the world outside from the comfort of their bed, she thought she saw the first signs of spring. The sun shone and from inside it looked like a beautiful day. She imagined many days like this in their future—waking in each other's arms, the sun streaming into their bedroom.

She snuggled up close to his body, and he sleepily wrapped both his arms around her. Awake now, Varek kissed the top of her head and groaned out something about not wanting to ever leave the bed or her.

A half hour later Callia roused herself from her romantic daydreams and left the warmth and safety of his embrace with a soft kiss on his lips. Varek rolled over and continue to sleep as she left to shower.

When she returned, dressed and ready for their day together, she woke him again.

"Varek, time to wake up."

Sighing, he slowly opened his eyes to the daylight. Callia's face was just what he'd always love to see first thing in the morning, he thought.

"Where are you dressed to go to?"

Callia playfully tugged at the covers and she found Varek naked and showing his muscular body to her. She leaned down to kiss him, and he pulled her on top of him, unbuttoning her jeans and pulling her sweater up over her ribs.

"Varek, we need to get going," she said with a chuckle.

He grunted and clasped his hands behind his head on the pillow. "Fine, but when all this business with the Council is over, I want to spend a week relaxing and never getting out of bed."

"Two weeks." Callia smiled and put her clothes back in order. She sat down on the bed and leaned over his body. "Varek, when things settle down, do you know what you want to do?"

"I hadn't really thought of it." He wondered what he could do when he finally got his life back.

Callia kissed him and stood up to go. "I want to visit the orphanage before we get going today. I'll be back in a little bit."

Varek sat up and swung his legs out of bed. He rubbed his face and stood up to take Callia in his arms.

"Tell Tia I said hello. I've missed her."

"I have too. That little girl is easy to fall in love with."

Callia kissed him goodbye, and Varek walked to the shower thinking about the orphanage, which always led to thinking about his little girl. Varek told himself that after he caught Amon and finished his work for the Council he'd find his daughter and try to make up for all the years he'd missed. He may not ever get her forgiveness, but he had to try.

I promise I'll be the man I should have been, Christina.

A summons from the Council forced him to cut short his shower. A few rushed minutes later, he was dressed, his shirt sticking to him in spots because he hadn't dried completely, and he left for the Council's chambers in Nil.

Callia spent thirty minutes at the orphanage telling Jessica the details of her life for the past few days and playing games with the children, who had missed her terribly. She hated to leave them but she knew she needed to be by Varek's side in the days to come.

As she stood at the front door of the orphanage, Tia hung on to her hand, not wanting to let go. She looked up, her green eyes full of sadness, into Callia's, breaking her heart.

"Please don't go, Callia," she pleaded in her tiny voice.

Callia crouched down next to her and smiled. "Guess who wanted me to tell you he misses you?"

Tia didn't waver. "Please don't leave."

"Sweetie, I promise Varek and I will be back in a few days, and then maybe we can go to the park for an afternoon. Would you like that?"

"You won't be back with Varek." Tia's words sounded certain.

Callia kissed her forehead and squeezed her hand as she stood to leave. "I promise, Tia."

Tia watched from the front window as Callia walked down the sidewalk from the orphanage and vanished from view.

VAREK ARRIVED AT THE ORPHANAGE about an hour later after returning from his meeting with the Council that included more information about the job he had to do. He walked into Jessica's office casually and asked where Callia was. The response he got took the wind out of him.

"Varek, what are you talking about? Callia hasn't been here for months. Why would you ask about her?"

He didn't need to ask Jessica to explain what she meant. He knew Amon had done something to time and had taken Callia. Varek staggered out of the administrator's office into the hall and saw Tia standing there.

"I told her she wouldn't be back."

Varek stood looking at the little girl but heard little of what she said, his mind racing to figure out what had happened. Realizing she was speaking to him, he strained to focus.

"What, Tia?"

Tia repeated what she'd said and stepped closer to him. She took his forefinger and wrapped her hand around it.

"Please bring her back."

"Tia, did you see Callia today?" Varek worked hard to keep his voice calm as he looked down at her.

"Yes."

"Did you see her leave?"

"Yes. I watched her walk away down the street. She promised me she would come back with you, but I know she can't."

Varek gently pressed her for the reason why.

"Because she's gone."

"Do you know where she is?"

"No, but I know she's not here anymore."

Varek knew this too, deep in his heart. There was a loneliness he and the little girl felt now that Callia was gone.

Picking Tia up, he hugged her tightly. Her little arms wrapped around his neck and she put her head on his shoulder.

"I promise I'll find her and bring her back to us, honey."

As Tia watched Varek walk down the orphanage's front steps to the sidewalk below, he vanished too.

Moments later, he was standing in the Council chambers in Nil, demanding they tell him what happened.

"You know as well as we do what has happened," the head Councilman said flatly.

Varek felt like the huge chamber was closing in on him. He was in no mood for Council riddles.

"Then tell me how to fix it!" he bellowed, his voice reverberating off every surface in the room.

"He has changed the course of events so she has never met you. She knows only him now. But even Kalins is not more powerful than Aeveren biology."

"So we're still destined for each other?"

Varek felt a huge sense of relief come over him. She was still his. Still his Callia.

"Yes, but Kalins will still wield tremendous power over her."

Varek didn't want to know why but asked anyway, unable to stop himself. The Councilman's words almost knocked the wind out of him.

"She is with him."

An anger he hadn't felt since he was a prisoner in Nil came over him. She was with Amon. He felt a murderous rage creep throughout his body.

"Keep in mind what your assignment is, Mr. Leale. Kalins must be brought to Nil."

Varek nodded once and took the talisman in his hand.

He's going to beg for Nil when I get a hold of him.

CHAPTER EIGHTEEN

A MON STOPPED IN FRONT OF the window of the New Hope Grocery and admired what he saw. His pale blond hair was cut much shorter than he'd worn it for lifetimes, but he liked his new look. So did the women who stood behind him. He turned to look at them and smiled a perfect grin at the three pretty twenty-somethings in skimpy summer clothing.

He looked around as he leisurely walked down First Street. New Hope, New York was a typical small town. The patriotic flags left over from the town's Fourth of July celebration still billowed in the breeze near the tops of telephone poles. Away from the shops and businesses section of First Street, homeowners mowed their lush, green lawns and tended their gardens, which were coming to full harvest this third week of August.

Since he'd begun dating her two weeks earlier, Amon knew Callia would be walking home from her job at Dr. Gordon's veterinary clinic to grab a bite to eat before she went to the orphanage to visit the children. They had been out several times already, and Amon believed she was falling for him. She loved how attentive he was, evidenced by the excitement on her face as she saw him now walking toward her to escort her home.

Unable to stop herself from smiling, Callia worried about looking overeager but admitted to herself that she was thrilled to see Amon on her walk home. She knew he wasn't her destined one, which disappointed her and once again made her question why she had never been given a true love destined only for her, but she was very attracted to him and enjoyed their time together. He seemed to know her so well from the moment they met, and he certainly was a delicious substitute until the universe decided to send her the real thing.

As he watched her walk toward him, Amon's stomach did a turn. She wasn't the most beautiful female he'd ever desired—in fact, he'd found the incredibly beautiful women in this world were never as great as expected—but he felt an attraction to her that was undeniable. That they hadn't slept together was entirely her doing. He would've had her the night they'd met, not by coincidence, as she walked back home from the orphanage at dusk one early August night.

"Amon! What are you doing here?" she asked, her voice betraying that she'd hoped he would meet her on her walk home as he'd done the day before.

"I wanted to see you." His voice made her feel like a silk robe was being draped over her skin.

Callia's heart skipped a beat. He was so good-looking, his deep blue eyes staring at her as if he wanted her as much as she wanted him at that moment. She had a hard time thinking clearly when he looked at her like that.

"I'm on my way home before I go to visit the children." As she spoke, he slipped his arm around her and gently pulled her to him. She looked up at his face, but her focus was entirely on his body touching hers.

She felt the taut muscles that hid behind clothes press against her, hardness that seemed at odds with the deep softness of his voice as he whispered to her.

"Callia, I have to go away to my home in Italy."

With his body so close, she found it almost impossible to understand what he was saying. The effect he had on her was nearly mesmerizing.

"I want you to come with me. It would be a nice vacation." As he spoke, he closed his eyes and he focused his mind to enter hers. He sensed she might be reluctant to go with him, so he wanted to place a gentle suggestion in her mind. Nothing much, but just something to help her give in to her desires. And his.

Callia finally heard what he was saying, and her first idea was to regretfully say no—she barely knew him! But on second thought, she told herself that chances like this didn't come along every day and she should take this one.

"Okay, it sounds like fun. I'll have to tell Dr. Gordon I need some time off. How long will we be gone?"

"As long as you like."

The idea of such a gorgeous man taking her to Italy and letting her decide for how long overwhelmed her for a moment, and she found herself gazing dreamily up into his blue eyes. Reality surged back quickly, however, when she realized she didn't have a valid passport. Crestfallen, she dropped her gaze and frowned.

Amon lifted her chin with his forefinger and smiled. "Carina, you've spent too much time among humans. We're Aeveren, and you have the good fortune to be traveling with one who can teleport."

He let his finger linger on her chin, and then he bent down to kiss her, barely able to control himself. Her brief sadness at the thought of not being able to go had made his emotions surge, first in a delicate stab of pain and then in desire.

Callia kissed him passionately, making control even more difficult. Reluctantly, Amon pulled away, aware that they were still in New Hope.

Soon enough, she'll be mine.

"Let's get you ready. I'll get you everything you'll need when we get to my villa." The sooner he got her away from her familiar surroundings, the better.

"Okay, but I need to let my grandmother know and call my boss, and I'd like to tell the children that I'll be gone for a couple weeks."

Wanting to leave at that moment but realizing he had to be patient for just a short while longer, he told her he'd come back for her at her apartment at eight o'clock.

For almost the next three hours, Callia explained to those closest to her that she was going on a spontaneous trip and promised she'd be careful. Dr. Gordon was happy to hear she was finally taking a well-deserved vacation away from New

Hope and told her to enjoy herself. Jessica at the orphanage was thrilled and nearly cooed when Callia let it slip that she was taking the trip with a man. But the child Callia was closest to at the orphanage, Tia, was sullen.

Callia's grandmother was just as unhappy at the news of the trip. After raising her when her parents died and knowing she was not one for spur-of-the-moment decisions, her grandmother was leery of such a spontaneous vacation. But Callia assuaged her fears and explained away all her objections by telling her she just wanted to take a chance for once. In the end, only Tia disagreed with her going, and Callia chalked that up to the fear of loss many orphans experienced and promised herself she'd remember to send her a postcard and bring her back a souvenir from Italy when she returned.

Amon spent the time congratulating himself on getting Callia for his own. It had been so easy to outsmart Varek that he almost felt bad for him. In minutes, she'd be gone from the only place he knew to find her. And if he did, it wouldn't be for months, more than enough time for her to fall in love with him and willingly choose to stay in Italy as his wife. He'd deal with the destined one issue if and when it came up.

At eight o'clock, he arrived at Callia's apartment and found her excited about the trip. Her enthusiasm touched him. After hours of enjoying the idea that his plan was finally coming to fruition, he'd forgotten that the reason he wanted her—needed her—to be his was because she made him feel things he hadn't felt since the loss of his destined one lifetimes ago. She made him feel happy.

"I'm so happy to be going to Italy. I lived there a few lifetimes ago, and I loved it!" Callia knew she sounded like an excited schoolgirl, but Amon's smile told her he was charmed by her exuberance.

"Do you still speak Italian well?" he asked, knowing the answer.

"No, I'm afraid I only really understand some of it when people speak it. My Italian isn't up to snuff."

In Italian, he told her, "Don't worry, carina. We'll practice and you'll sound like a native in no time." He saw the effect his speaking Italian had on her, just as it had that day they'd sat together in the very room they were in now.

Callia listened as Amon spoke in Italian and felt the sensual sound of his words touch her deep inside. She thought once again that it was a shame he wasn't her destined one. He possessed almost everything she'd ever wanted in a man. What he didn't have she didn't precisely know, but she believed she'd know it if she ever saw it in a man.

"Time to go."

Amon held his hand out toward Callia, and she placed hers in his.

"I've never done this before, Amon." At that moment, she realized she'd never known any Aeveren who possessed the advanced power of teleportation. She also realized with fear that she knew very little about this man, who was obviously a very powerful Aeveren.

Amon took her in his arms and held her tightly to him. A shiver of apprehension over who she was with and what she was about to do ran up her spine. But his deep, silky voice telling her not to be frightened calmed her, and she closed her eyes. Her head on his chest, she waited.

Concentrating his mind on his villa in Italy, Amon pressed his cheek to Callia's hair and saw her apartment and New Hope fade away.

VAREK STOOD OUTSIDE THE COUNCIL'S chambers and considered where Amon could have taken Callia. Drawing a blank, he waited, frustrated that the talisman hadn't taken him to Callia's Aunt Jean's after he'd focused his mind on her home. He realized that the magick of the charm enabled him to travel through time but not teleport through the present, like Amon could.

They couldn't have given me that power too? he thought to himself.

Concentrating on Aunt Jean's house but hours before, moments later he found himself on her front doorstep. As he knocked on the solid wood door, it dawned on him that Amon's playing with time might mean Callia's aunt may not know him or what he needed to talk to her about.

Aunt Jean answered the door, glared at him, and blurted out, "Where's Callia?"

"You know me?" Varek asked, shocked and relieved.

"Answer me, Varek. Where is she?"

Not wanting to have this conversation on Aunt Jean's doorstep, he motioned toward the living room. "Can I come in?"

Inside the house, Varek followed the older woman to the kitchen where they sat at the table they had shared with Callia just days before. Memories of her threatened to overcome him, and he pretended to clear his throat to hide his choking up from emotions.

"Where is she, Varek?" The woman's gaze was penetrating and accusatory.

"Amon took her, and I need your help to figure out to where and when." The sound of the words made him feel weak and useless.

Slamming her hand on the table, she exclaimed, "Damn him!" She stood up and angrily began pacing.

"Did she tell him she's related to me?"

He nodded. "He wanted her"—he began, hesitating before finishing—"to be with him from the moment we met him."

"I've lived many lifetimes, sweetie. I know what he wanted." She mumbled about how she never should have sent her to him. "Sorry. But don't worry. All is not lost. Not by a long shot."

Hoping to change the topic, he asked, "Why aren't you affected by his time manipulation?"

"I don't know, but I suspect Amon's antics aren't as powerful with ancients. I'd bet my sister is affected, though. If Callia went willingly, she'll know where she went."

She dialed the phone, and Varek wrestled with the idea that Callia would ever willingly go anywhere with Amon. She wouldn't, he told himself. *Not if she knew I was in the world for her.*

Back in her chair at the table, the woman appeared to Varek to look happier. "Just as I thought. My sister says she went to Italy at the end of August on a vacation with a man. She called about a month later to tell her she was staying there and was fine.

Varek felt like he'd been kicked in the gut. She had gone willingly, and she'd chosen to stay there with him.

Aunt Jean saw the effect of this information on him and quickly moved to comfort him. "I know it sounds bad, but this happened before you came into her life. She doesn't know her destined one is here for her. You need to go to her. Trust me. Aeveren biology is stronger than any power that damn Amon wields."

Varek took a deep breath, closed his eyes, then opened them. "Where is she?"

"In the Italian countryside between the villages Castelmuzio and Montisi in Tuscany. He owns a house there called Casa Salvius."

Varek thanked her and stood to leave, but she caught his arm. "Be careful. Amon isn't going to give her up without a fight."

"Neither am I."

He had never meant anything more in his life.

Outside, Varek took the black stone talisman out of his pocket and focused on the location she'd told him and prayed he wasn't late. He concentrated on getting to her in late August, right after she'd arrived there, but the talisman wouldn't allow it. He tried one month later, but again it didn't work. Finally, in desperation, he tried the month after that, November. Moments later, he disappeared from the front porch of Callia's great-aunt's house.

SECONDS AFTER LEAVING HER APARTMENT, Callia and Amon reappeared at his villa in Tuscany. What she saw when she opened her eyes stunned her. Amon's villa was something from a picture. Callia brought her hands up to cover her mouth as she gaped at the beauty all around her.

It was everything she remembered from her life in Italy and more. All around her across the vista were rolling green hills punctuated by farms and vineyards. The myriad of pale and vibrant greens and deep yellows danced in front of her eyes. Behind her were rows of deep green Cypress trees, tall and stately as they watched over the gardens and the lane that led to the villa.

She turned toward Amon's home and stood in wonder. An enormous Italian villa, it looked like something out of one of the homes and gardens magazines her grandmother always had on her living room coffee table. Pale yellow with traces of orange, the villa was topped with a roof in a deeper orange. Each window at the front of the home had dark green shutters to shelter the inside from the hot Italian sun. The effect was at once impressive and beautiful and caused Callia's memories from her previous lifetime in Italy to come flooding back to her.

Amon saw her wide eyes and thought she'd been harmed during the trip there. Some Aeveren didn't handle teleporting well, and it had been the first time for her. He put his hands on her shoulders and leaned in from behind her.

"Callia, what's wrong?"

She turned around to face him, and he saw her tear-filled eyes. Before he could ask her again what was wrong, she wrapped her arms around his neck and rested her head on his chest.

"Oh, Amon! It's so beautiful! It's just as I remembered it! Thank you so much for bringing me here!"

Surprised by her reaction, he was suddenly happier than he remembered being in many years. Her soft voice touched his heart, and he lifted her head to kiss her. No one had made him feel like this since Sevine lifetimes ago.

"Welcome to Casa Salvius. Let's go inside." Amon took her hand and escorted her to the villa's front door where a man waited.

"Callia, this is my servant, Gethen. He will see to anything you need while you're here."

The servant bowed and opened his arms to welcome them to the home. "It's an honor, miss. If I may be of any service, all you need do is ask."

"Thank you, Gethen." Callia walked past him and found splendor to rival what she had experienced outside. Amon's villa was a mixture of modern conveniences and traditional, rustic beauty.

"I had it completely remodeled a few years ago. Do you

like it?"

Amon already knew the answer to his question by the way Callia walked through the first floor living and dining rooms, her head slowly swiveling back and forth as she took in the architecture and design of the rooms.

He came up behind her and put his arms around her, his chin resting on her shoulder. She leaned back into his body, sending waves of excitement coursing through him.

"I'm so glad you like it."

"How could I not? It's stunning. The arches, the exquisite frescoes, the beautiful tile floor—this is the most beautiful home I've ever seen." As she spoke, she attempted to take in all the wonderful sights before her.

"Consider it yours while you're here. What is mine is yours."

Amon gently kissed her neck as she continued to admire her new surroundings. The taste of her skin as he lightly danced his tongue down from her ear to her shoulder made him want to sweep her up in his arms and carry her to one of the villa's five bedrooms. Need pushed on him from deep inside, and he knew all he had to do was enter her mind and plant the merest of suggestions to have her and finally quell his desire for her. But watching her reaction to the home and its grounds had stirred another, equally powerful need in him.

He needed her to want him like he wanted her. He needed her to need him like he needed her. He'd fallen in love with her.

"Come. Let me show you where you'll sleep."

A jolt of nervousness hit Callia. She and Amon had never done more than kiss, and she wondered if they would share a bedroom. She couldn't deny her physical attraction to him. She just felt nervous about it. She wasn't a virgin and had some experience in her seven lifetimes, but he seemed far more experienced.

"Amon, how many lifetimes have you lived? I know you told me the other day, but I forget."

He stopped on the third stair of the massive open staircase that gently curved toward the villa's second floor and turned toward her, a devilish grin on his face. "Forty-seven. That's why I sometimes call you carina—little one—even though we're close in age in this lifetime."

"Oh." Callia was sure now he had far more experience than she, and suddenly she felt very unsure of herself.

When they reached the top of the stairs, she looked down the long hallway to her left before following him to a room near the end of the other side of the hallway. As she walked, butterflies fluttered in her stomach.

He opened the door to the bedroom to show her a room with a cherry four-poster bed, a private bath, and a balcony. As with every other room she had seen, this one was superbly decorated and lacked nothing.

"This is yours." He led her into the room and released her hand.

All Callia could think to say was thank you. What else could she say to a gorgeous, sexy man who took her to Italy, to his stunningly decorated home, and didn't pressure her to sleep in the same room with him?

But thank you sounded juvenile, so she said nothing, instead waiting for him to continue.

Amon sensed her nervousness and became excited by it. Pushing that down, he turned to her.

"Would you like to look from the balcony?"

Callia nodded and followed him through the doors outside. The view took her breath away. A picture much like she'd seen from the front of the house met her. Rolling green hills, dotted with villas in the distance, and tall, green Cypress trees nearby with olive trees filled out the scene in front of her.

"Oh, Amon! It's breathtaking!"

Amon realized he had never looked at the surrounding area like this before. He let himself relax and for a moment thought he saw what she saw. Her voice roused him back to reality.

"Amon, why don't you live here all the time? It's beautiful."

The same question could be asked about the other half-dozen homes he owned around the world. The answer would be the same for all of them.

Because without someone to share this with, it's just a house, an empty, meaningless structure.

He decided not to answer, feeling the effect of her emotions already on his mood. Needing to find somewhere to be alone, he turned back into the room and sought some distance from her.

"I'll be in the next room if you need anything. Rest,

explore the house and the grounds, whatever you like. I'll have Gethen prepare dinner in a little while."

Before she could respond, he left and closed the door behind him. Callia stood in the middle of the room, confused at his hasty departure.

Alone in his room, Amon tried to calm his emotions. Callia made him happier than he'd been in lifetimes, but for reasons he was unable to understand, any sadness or anger she felt immediately caused havoc within him. It was getting worse the longer he knew her. The loneliness she'd sensed in him on the balcony became amplified when she'd felt badly for him and had thrown his emotions into turmoil. As he sat on his bed, he rested his head in his hands and tried to calm whatever she'd created in him. He pushed out of his mind that this was a sign he shouldn't be with her, ignoring the obvious in favor of the complete happiness she was capable of making him feel.

A knock at his door startled him out of his thoughts, but he had let Gethen know he needed him, so he told the person on the other side of the door to enter. Thinking he was in the presence of his servant, he remained slumped over, his head in his hands.

Callia slowly entered Amon's room and walked quietly over to the side of the bed he sat on and stood silently in front of him, unsure if she had made a mistake in coming in.

Never looking up, Amon brusquely said, "Gethen, don't just fucking stand there staring at me. Callia needs clothes, and we'll need dinner at five."

Callia stood frozen but very quietly said, "It's Callia."

Amon's head shot up, his eyes a much darker blue than Callia had ever seen them. They startled her at first, but then she found herself almost drawn to them.

Surprised by her arrival and hoping she wasn't unhappy— he couldn't handle any more of the torture his emotions were causing him—he stood up and looked down at her.

"I'm sorry. I didn't know it was you. I thought you were Gethen."

"Amon, I'm sorry if I said something wrong before."

Not only was she unhappy, but she was feeling guilty. Amon was sure he would collapse under the weight of the emotions inside him. All he could think of was getting her out of his room, away from him, so he put his hands on her shoulders to guide her to the door. When he touched her, something snapped in him, and he was overcome by the need to be close to her.

He pulled her to him and covered her mouth with his, one hand grabbing a fistful of hair and tugging her head backward so she looked up at him. His tongue demanded entry into her mouth.

Callia reacted with surprise but quickly reciprocated his desire, pulling him to her by the waist of his pants. Her hands slid up his back, over his shirt, and her nails dragged across the fabric between his shoulder blades.

Amon knew he could have her. He felt the dampness under his fingers as he ran them under her sundress and over her cotton panties. She wanted him. He could fuck her, and it would be the best sex he'd had in lifetimes. He would have what he'd wanted from the moment he'd met her.

But he wanted more. He wanted her to love him.

Callia's ran her hand up and down the front of his pants, eager to wrap her fingers around him. She wanted what he offered: the sex, the house, everything. Whatever he was, she wanted it. She wanted him. Her hands fumbled with the button on his pants. Her fingers slid inside and grazed bare skin, nearly sending him over the edge.

Amon gently pushed her back away from him and breathlessly said, "No."

Callia's face showed her confusion and hurt. He pushed her toward the door, hoping to get her away from him before she spoke, because the pain of her emotions was nearly killing him already without hearing a word from her lips.

Right before he reached the door, he made the excuse that they shouldn't do this now. The moment she turned toward him and asked why, he knew he'd made a mistake. The pain from seeing the hurt on her face and hearing the rejection in her voice made him double over and fall to the floor.

Callia dropped to his side on the floor. "Amon! What's wrong?"

"I'll be fine. Go get Gethen," he said, his voice sounding like the words were being pulled from him.

Callia ran to get the servant, who was already on the top of the stairs. "Something's wrong with Amon!"

Gethen walked to where his master sat on the floor of his room as Amon silently commanded him to keep Callia away. He stopped her as they walked into the room.

"Miss, I will take care of him. I'm sure he doesn't want you to worry. Dinner will be served at five."

Gethen closed the door, and Callia stood staring at the closed door feeling hurt, confused, and rejected. She walked back to her room, hoping Amon would be all right and wondering if she'd made a mistake in coming here.

CHAPTER NINETEEN

A MON FELT THE PAIN SLUICE out of him with each step she took down the hall toward her room.

"Gethen, get me up."

Amon's servant crouched down next to him and pulled his master to his feet.

"Help me over to the bed."

The servant guided Amon to the bed and carefully sat him on the edge. Silently, he stood in front of his master awaiting further instructions and watched as Amon recovered from his attack.

Amon looked up at Gethen and spoke to him in a tone more suited to a friend than a servant. "What the fuck is wrong with me, Gethen? When have you ever seen anyone have this effect on me?"

"Never in all the lifetimes I've been with you."

Gethen had spent centuries as his servant, and the Sidhe had seen countless females near his master, never one affecting him as Callia did. Not even Sevine.

"Then what the hell is going on? I want her more than any

other in lifetimes. What kind of enchantment is causing me to feel pain because of her emotions?"

Gethen was silent but stood thinking of his master's enemies—those who would revel in Amon's misfortunes, no matter what kind. There were many.

"May I suggest contacting Markku? If anyone would know how to diagnose this problem, he would."

Amon groaned and lay down on the bed. His eyes closed, and his face signaled his disgust at the thought of once again dealing with one of the members of the Soren, a rebel sect among Aeveren that sought to exert more control over humans. Their methods were often of the dark magick variety and generally seen as distinctly un-Aeveren.

"Every time I'm forced to be around him I feel sick afterward. I only spoke to him on the phone the other day and he irritated me."

Gethen walked to the bathroom and returned with a glass of water he handed to Amon as he sat up.

"I agree, but if Callia has something about her that has anything of the magicks, Markku will recognize it."

Amon nodded even as his distaste for the man continued unabated. "Contact him and tell him I'll meet him in the village at nine. But that means you'll have to make sure Callia doesn't leave here tonight."

Gethen understood Amon's order but felt the need to ask for clarification. "How forceful am I to be?"

Amon stood and faced his servant. "She isn't to be touched or harmed." He spoke the edict in the tone of a master, but softened it slightly as he continued. "Show her the kitchen. Maybe she likes to cook."

Gethen's usually stony face betrayed a hint of irritation at this suggestion, and Amon, now fully recovered, chuckled. "Not that there's anything wrong with the dishes you make, my friend."

Gethen seemed to realize no insult had been intended, and his face once again resumed its stony composure.

"Go. Find Markku and get him here tonight so I can find out what the hell is wrong and how I can fix it."

CALLIA RESTED UNTIL GETHEN CALLED her for dinner, and she went back down to the expertly decorated dining room. Amon was waiting for her, wearing black pants and a sapphire blue dress shirt, both of which had the effect of making his light hair even more a focal point of his appearance than usual. She had worried after seeing him fall to the floor in pain earlier, but he seemed fully recovered and eagerly welcomed her to dinner.

Choosing a seat opposite him, she said, "I apologize. I didn't realize we were dressing for dinner."

Amon was thankful to realize she wasn't truly sorry and her apology was merely polite manners. He hoped to make it through the meal without suffering any more.

After he helped her slide her chair in, he returned to his seat, assuring her she was dressed appropriately and quite beautifully. Gethen served a chicken dish with fresh tomatoes and garlic, and both Callia and Amon ate silently, one not knowing what to say after the events earlier and one hoping he could keep any potential physical pain to a minimum by saying little.

Ten minutes of silence later, Callia couldn't keep quiet anymore. She needed some reassurance to make her believe she hadn't made a mistake by coming to Italy with him. She decided to start the conversation with a compliment in the hopes that he'd open up.

"Amon, it's so beautiful here," she began with a smile. "Do you think we could take a walk outside after dinner?

Amon saw she was trying to get him to talk, and as much as he wanted to, he knew until he got to speak to Markku, he couldn't be sure any time spent with her wouldn't end once again with him on the ground in pain. But the almost pleading look in her eyes made him give in to her and agree to go.

They walked around the grounds as the sun began to settle below the rolling hills. At first they walked in silence, but throwing caution to the wind, Amon began to tell her the history of the area. Callia listened in rapt attention and when he had finished, they were back in the gardens near the villa.

Callia spotted a bench and grabbed Amon's hand to lead him to it. Seated next to one another, they said nothing but watched the sunset's purples and oranges spread across the sky.

Nervous, she turned to him and took a deep breath before leaning in to kiss him. If he rejected her again, then she'd know she'd have to return to New Hope immediately, before she became even more attached to him.

If he didn't…

Amon sensed her near his mouth, her lips so close he felt her soft breath on his face. Fearing a repeat of earlier but unable to deny his desire to kiss her, he slowly closed his eyes and tilted his head to meet her kiss.

Her supple lips timidly brushed against his, signaling her fear that he would push her away once again. Pleasurable sensations flooded him, causing him to sigh into her mouth in relief. This time her emotions caused no pain, just utter happiness.

Callia read his clues and softly slid her tongue over his lips and into his mouth. When he responded by thrusting his into her mouth with ardor, her body tightened. His kiss promised that his cool demeanor masked a far more passionate man.

In moments, they were locked in a deep embrace, his hand cradling her head as his mouth softly crushed hers in desire. As she ran her hands through his sleek blond hair, pushing strands from his face, he moaned into her mouth.

Callia lightly kissed his ear and whispered, "I love how your hair feels."

Amon remembered the thoughts he had seen the night he'd probed her mind, recalling how she seemed to like his hair then also. As she kissed his neck, giving him excited chills, he dreamily told her that it used to be longer.

Callia sat back away from him with a studied look on her face. For a moment, Amon wondered if anything was wrong. *Does she remember anything?* he asked himself as he worked to keep his expression calm.

"I can see it long, but I like it this way," she said with a smile.

Relief washed over him and he took her hand to walk back to the house. He still had two hours before he had to meet Markku, and he hoped to put it to good use.

Callia wondered if this would be when they finally moved their relationship to the next level. She looked forward to making love with Amon, holding his hand excitedly as he led her up the stairs to the second floor to his room.

Amon wasn't thinking with his head anymore. The feelings she'd created in him in the garden made him want her, and he was willing to risk any amount of pain for the pleasure he'd find buried deep inside her.

He guided her to the bed and laid her down. Standing over her, he momentarily considered what might happen if her emotions affected him now and pushed that out of his mind as he covered her small, firm body with his much longer and muscular frame.

She felt the hard ridge of his erection press into her sex as he kissed her deeply. Running her hands down his broad back, she pulled his shirt from his pants and placed her hands on his bare skin. It was hot, and he moaned into the pillow next to her ear as she lightly caressed his back.

He lifted himself off her and unbuttoned his shirt, shrugging it off to reveal a well-toned chest and abdomen of tight muscle. Straddling her, he kneeled above her, admiring how incredibly sexy she looked lying underneath him on his bed as she slid her fingertips over his ribs and down toward his pants.

Slowly pulling her dress above her hips, he let his fingers graze the front of her panties for evidence she was ready for him. Excited by the moistness he found there, he lingered for a moment, dragging his finger up the center of her sex. Callia let out a sweet moan and reached to undo the clasp of his pants.

Amon waited, wanting nothing more in this world than for her to take his hard cock in her hands, but as she unzipped his pants, he heard Gethen silently alert him to the fact that Markku had chosen to arrive early and come to the villa instead of waiting for him in the village.

He closed his eyes in utter frustration and sharply let his servant know to keep Markku busy. He'd be down in a minute.

Taking her hands in his, he gently squeezed them, hoping she'd understand. "Callia, I need to deal with something downstairs. I promise I'll be back in a little while."

"Oh, okay. I'll just go to my room." She tried not to sound petulant but felt a little needy as she lay there wet and ready for him, cast aside for the second time in just hours.

"No, please stay here. You can take a bath, if you'd like. I promise to get back as soon as I can."

Amon maneuvered off the bed and picked up his shirt. When he was fully dressed, he bent over her still reclined body and kissed her.

"Please promise me you'll stay." As he spoke, he gently opened her mind and inserted the idea of how wonderful a bath would feel.

Callia smiled. "Okay. Maybe I will take a bath while you're gone."

That's my carina.

Amon reached the first floor in seconds and struggled to control his rage before meeting Markku. As much as he disliked him, he had to be nice to him if he wanted answers.

"Markku, thank you for coming. You're early. And you didn't wait for me in the village."

Thanks for ruining what was possibly going to be the best sex I've had in lifetimes.

"Amon. What do I owe the honor of a call from you—well, a call from your man?" Markku obviously had taken offense at the servant summoning him on Amon's behalf.

"Let's go outside. I need to speak to you."

Amon escorted the man outside to a darkened area of the garden. He hoped to make their conversation quick as the smaller man with the perpetually greasy hair and overall grimy look came close to sickening him when he was forced to look at him.

"Okay, Amon. What's up that I needed to get here *tout de suite*?"

"Markku, I've got a situation I need your help with. The woman I'm with has an unusual effect on me."

Before Amon could continue, the other man made a lewd remark and smacked his shoulder in congratulations.

"Markku, pay fucking attention!" Amon barked, no longer able to keep his disgust for the man hidden.

With a sulking look, Markku asked, "Okay. What kind of

effect?"

"Her emotions cause me pain. The negative ones."

"What about the good ones?"

"They're not a problem," he answered, thinking about what he'd left upstairs just minutes ago.

"Sounds like Aeveren magick to me, Amon."

"Details, Markku. Now."

"Well, it sounds like a pretty garden-variety love magick. You only feel happy if the other person is happy, and when you cause them pain, you feel pain. You must have pissed off some lady."

"This doesn't make sense. I was just with someone the other day and had no problems." *No problems at all.*

"Were you in love with that one?"

"No."

"Well, there's the problem. Love magick only works on you if you're in love, big guy."

Amon let Markku's step into familiarity pass unnoticed while he racked his brain for who would've put a love spell on him. Only one woman had ever threatened him with magick.

Frederika. It had to be her.

"So how do I fix this?"

"Depends. I can whip up a counterspell, but that may not work if the one who put the whammy on you used strong magick."

She did if it was her. This is the same woman who threatened to bind all my powers once.

Markku continued. "You can find the spell broad and get

her to remove it."

Amon stood silently looking down at the shadowy face of the man and waited for the next solution to his problem.

"Or?"

"Well, you can just make your current one happy."

Amon scrubbed his hand over his face before telling Markku to see what he could do with the counterspell, even though he feared it wouldn't work.

The greasy man disappeared after agreeing to help, and Amon made his way back to his room to find Callia.

I can just make my current one happy.

Amon found his room empty and cursed out loud. Then from the bathroom he heard the sound of water, and he found Callia naked in the large garden tub full of bubbles.

She smiled at him as he stepped into the room. "I took your advice. I love your tub!"

Sitting on the edge, he ran his fingers through the water to touch her skin. She looked so sweet surrounded by foamy bubbles that he began to harden.

With a devilish grin, she asked, "Want to join me?"

Amon shook his head and held his hand out. "Come."

He pulled her out of the tub, her body soapy and dripping, and grabbed a nearby towel. As he dried her off, he planted kisses across her shoulders and collarbone, tasting the floral sweetness of the bubble bath.

When she was dry, she stood naked in front of him. He ran his hand down her body, over her firm breasts and hard nipples, and across her soft, feminine stomach. He bent his head down to kiss her lips, his tongue finding her tongue, and slid a finger slowly down her wet slit. Callia pulled at his neck, pushing her body against his. As his finger searched for her entrance, she gently bit Amon's lip and moaned.

She released his lip and groaned, "Please" and his mind flashed the vision of her up against the cool tile on the wall as he pounded into her.

Callia felt like she would explode if he didn't give her some relief soon. She unbuttoned his shirt frantically, tugging it off his body, and quickly worked to remove his pants as Amon backed up out of the bathroom and into the bedroom toward the bed. By the time he felt the mattress on the back of his legs, she had his cock in her hands.

Her touch made him lightheaded, his eyes rolling back in his head. Somewhere in his mind he sensed her mouth drifting over his stomach, and he gently yanked her upright. He was sure her mouth on his cock would feel better than anyone's ever had, but that's not what he wanted. He had French farm girls and others for that.

Her eyes, pleading and confused, stared at him as he sat on the bed. He placed his hands on her hips and leaned forward to drag his tongue over her hard nipple. When she moved to straddle him, Amon held her fast to where she was, gently restraining her as he sucked and nibbled.

Callia felt need tighten in her lower abdomen and pushed against his hands eagerly, wanting some part of him to touch her sex, but he was the one in control. Amon's hands slid down her body and squeezed her behind, his fingers coming deliciously close to where she so wanted him to touch her. Needy for relief, she moved one of her hands toward her body, but he caught her by the wrist.

Shaking his head, he seductively raised one eyebrow and licked his lips, his pink tongue making his beautiful mouth even more inviting. He pulled her up on him and his cock teased her as it slid up her moist sex.

Callia whimpered when the tip of his cock grazed her swollen nub, and she kissed him deeply, making keening noises. Her body felt raw and on fire.

"Amon…"

He loved the way his name sounded when she said it. It sounded like a prayer coming from her lips.

She spread her legs and began gently sliding up and down his cock, wanting desperately to satisfy the need he'd created in her. He let her do this until he sensed she was close to tumbling over the edge and pulled her up off him, holding her above his slick cock.

"Amon…please…I need…"

He brushed the strands of hair from her face, and then set her down on the bed on her back. She closed her eyes for a moment, and when she opened them, he was beside her on the bed. He lightly ran his fingertips up her inner thigh, teasing her until her leg muscles quivered.

Amon replaced his fingers with his mouth. His own desire raging inside him, he struggled to control himself as his tongue got its first taste of her sweet moisture. Slowly and deliberately, he sucked her delicate skin and slid his tongue over her sex. Callia's hands in his hair and her whimpers of pleasure urged him on, pleading for more.

His tongue dipped inside her and then traveled to her engorged clit. With his hands, he opened her up and softly suckled it, rolling his tongue over it as he took her into his mouth. She exploded with one last drag of his tongue, coming as he greedily lapped her, wanting to savor her desire. As she shook from ecstasy, his mouth rode each aftershock, bringing her to a second climax. He delighted in the delicious taste of her, licking his lips to get the rest of her into his mouth.

Callia continued to pant as her body came down from two orgasms. She had worried needlessly about his being more experienced. As she lay there with him, softly breathing as he rested his head on her stomach, she couldn't remember a time in any lifetime any man had brought her such exquisite pleasure just with his mouth. She ran wet again anticipating his cock deep inside her.

Amon lifted himself above her and kissed his way back up to her mouth. Cradling her face in his hands, he looked at her with blue eyes that reminded her of deep ocean waters, cool and mysterious. When he began to speak, his voice was deep and hypnotic, edgy with desire.

"Callia, I want nothing else in this world than to make you happy. I would suffer any pain if I knew I made you happy. Stay with me and I promise there will be nothing I won't do, nothing I won't bear for you to be mine."

The words came from deep inside him, from somewhere that he'd hidden away and let ice over for lifetimes. Now that place filled with the feelings she created in him—feelings of tenderness and care. He needed her desperately, couldn't imagine his life without her ever again.

His eyes searched hers for the answer he wanted to hear. In them, she saw passion, but she also found devotion. She felt his body tense, waiting for a word from her.

"Yes."

With just one word, she saw real happiness come over him for the first time since she'd known him. His eyes shone, and his expression looked like he was overcome with joy. Callia loved the transformation just as she had known earlier in the garden that she'd already fallen in love with him. His desire to make her happy met with her desire to do the same for him.

Amon kissed her passionately, his longing stoked because of her acquiescence. She would stay with him and let him make her happy. He wanted to give her every part of him. Everything he was he needed her to want.

"Callia." His voice came out in a groan of need he yearned to fulfill. He guided his cock to her entrance and tentatively pushed against it. "Tell me what you need."

She wrapped her arms around his broad back and pulled him to her. Amon pushed into her in one slow thrust that buried him completely inside her with a throaty grunt. His size pressed against her soft walls that stretched to welcome the sweet invasion, and a sensual sob escaped from her mouth in response.

Amon strained to keep himself from plunging into her, afraid of her reaction. Entering her slowly, he held back, unsure. Callia sensed his hesitation and whispered in his ear, "Make me yours."

"I need you...this...too much...I don't know if I can hold back, carina."

Callia looked into his eyes so full of emotion and said the words he desperately wanted to hear. "Don't hold anything back. Make me yours completely."

Amon placed his hands behind her shoulders and as he kissed her, drove deeply into her over and over. His blond hair fell onto his face and he thrust his hips into her, her hips rising to meet him each time his cock rammed into her.

He pushed everything of him into her—his loneliness of all those years, the hope that he could make her happy, the need for someone to share his life with—hoping to find that sweetness he'd had during all those lifetimes with Sevine.

He touched her deep inside, triggering her explosion. She wanted every part of him, to show him how much she loved him. She held him fast to her, pressing his skin into hers. She was his now.

In a voice full of passion, she whispered, "I love you."

Amon heard the words he'd wished for, had only dreamed he'd hear. The one he'd wanted since she'd first entered his world that dark March night at his lonely house was his. And she loved him!

"Callia, I love you," he said, feeling the loneliness of lifetimes without a destined one ebb out of him.

He wasn't alone anymore. He had one who loved him, cared for him. And he had someone to love.

Callia stroked Amon's face sweetly, blissfully in love with the man who'd given her so much. He closed his eyes, enjoying the feel of her touch on his face so tender and sweet.

In this moment, his thoughts turned to what he'd forced from his mind for days. Varek was her destined one. Not him. But Aeveren biology wasn't going to take Callia away from him. No matter what he had to do, she was going to stay with him.

Forever.

CHAPTER TWENTY

C ALLIA AWOKE TO THE SOUND of Amon's heartbeat against her cheek and his arms around her in an embrace. Above her, she heard his quiet breathing as he slept, his chest rising and falling slightly with every breath.

Not wanting to wake him, she remained motionless as she thought about all that had happened in her life in just a few short weeks. The man of her dreams had swept her off her feet, taken her to his luxurious Italian villa, and had professed his love for her and his desire to make her happy. Callia wondered if she was the luckiest woman on the planet.

That he wasn't her destined one was the only flaw in the seemingly perfect picture. But she knew something of life without a destined one and had learned lifetimes before that love didn't require the help of Aeveren biology to be real. As an Aeveren, she did understand that she would someday have another destined for her. For the first time in seven lifetimes, though, she wasn't wishing for him to come along just yet.

Callia's eyes traveled lower on Amon's body, and she silently admired his long, toned legs. At almost a foot taller than she, he towered over her when they were standing, but now the difference in height seemed to have disappeared, leaving a man whose body was simply long and lean.

She remembered their lovemaking the night before, a passionate shattering of her belief that he was cool and aloof. His intensity in pleasuring her body had shown him to be a powerful and attentive lover, but what had surprised her most was his almost innocent devotion to her happiness, something she hadn't expected in one who had lived so many lifetimes.

Amon began to rouse from sleep, and he stretched his long limbs under her. Callia moved to roll away now that he was awake, but Amon pulled her on top of him.

Sliding his hands down to her buttocks, he squeezed and groaned sensually. "Morning." Even right after walking, he seemed like he couldn't get enough of her.

Callia felt his erection pressed up against her stomach and wriggled slightly as he pushed it near her hips. Amon reacted immediately and nuzzled her neck while he moved his hands to her hips.

"We're not leaving this bed. Ever."

When she giggled, he smiled and returned to nuzzling.

"Amon, what about food? We have to eat."

In between kisses he was feathering along her neck, he mumbled, "Gethen will bring us anything we want."

"What about a shower?"

He moaned near her ear, "I like how you think, carina."

Callia smiled. "I meant something else."

Moving her hair from over his face, he looked at her. "I'm

intrigued. What else would we do in the shower with both of us naked and water running over our bodies?"

"Wash?"

"I promise after what we're going to do we'll use soap to clean up." He smiled slyly and pushed his hips off the bed.

Amon grew more excited at the idea of having her in the shower, her legs wrapped around his waist, the water making her skin glisten as he held her against the marble tile wall and fucked her. With his mind staging this fantasy, his body searched for more immediate enjoyment, and he slid his cock between her legs.

Knowing that if he didn't move at that moment he would take her right there, he breathed deeply and lifted her off him and onto the bed. Rolling off, he turned back toward her lying on the bed with her hair sprawled out on the pillow seductively and held his hand toward her.

She took it and followed him into the bathroom, noticing how incredible his naked body was from behind.

Whatever his faults may be, I haven't seen them yet.

No one had ever done anything like this for her, and as she stood in the shower with the water gently hitting her face and breasts and this sexy man caressing her as he soaped her up, Callia wondered if she was in a dream—and prayed she wouldn't wake up, if she was.

After breakfast, which Amon had served in the bedroom, Callia asked, "The area around here is so beautiful. Do you think we could go sightseeing?"

"Wherever you want to go is where we'll go."

She thought for a minute and excitedly said, "Rome!"

"Your wish is my command, carina."

Amon left her to decide what she'd like to see on their trip while he dealt with household issues with Gethen. Callia repeated his words in her head.

Your wish is my command, carina.

Is there another woman as lucky as I am?

AMON FOUND GETHEN IN THE kitchen "I want you to get Markku back here. Let me know when he's coming, and I'll come back."

Gethen said nothing but dutifully nodded his acknowledgement of his master's orders.

Amon considered speaking to Gethen about Callia but stopped himself. It was at these times when he wished he had someone to share things with. Most of the time, keeping his own counsel was just how he liked it, but something about how she made him feel made him want to tell others.

"I'll…" Amon stopped and began again. "We'll be gone today, and I don't know when we'll be back."

Gethen nodded again and Amon let the word "we'll" reverberate in his head.

We.

It had been so long that he'd said we other than with Gethen that the word sounded odd. *We.* From now on, he would have someone to include, someone to join him.

Amon padded up behind Callia and wrapped his arms

around her. He rested his chin on her shoulder and said into her ear, "Where does my carina want to go?"

"Everywhere!" she said eagerly.

Callia relaxed into his embrace. "As long as I'm with you."

AMON AND CALLIA TOURED ROME as if they were newlyweds. They held hands as they walked the streets, Amon pointing out landmarks and telling her what he knew of the history of the city from his time as a Roman citizen during the reign of Constantine I in the third century.

They threw coins over their shoulders at the Trevi Fountain, visited the Forum and the Coliseum, and spent time at the Roman Pantheon. They ended their day at a cafe relaxing their tired feet and enjoying gelato.

As they sat outside on the sidewalk of the cafe, the city of Rome flowing by them, Callia watched Amon, her heart full of love for him. In him, she thought, she had found exactly what she wanted.

Amon slid his hand across the table and rested it on top of Callia's. Just the touch of her hand had been what made him want her that night he first met her. Something in her had instantly reminded him of his destined one and how lonely he'd been. He continued to be thrilled by her, more each day. There was only one thing he wanted for their life together to be perfect. A child.

He thought about what she would look like pregnant with his child. Glowing and even more beautiful than she already was. Just as Sevine had been when she'd given him his first son.

Just the idea of Sevine usually hurt, but he noticed now with Callia, the loss of Sevine didn't make him ache anymore. He had finally put her behind him. Everything she'd been for so many lifetimes Callia was for him now.

Later that night, after they'd returned to the villa, they lay in each other's arms talking about their day as normal couples in love did. Callia knew in her heart she didn't want to leave him. She'd decided she would call her family and friends in New Hope to tell them she wouldn't be coming back.

As she drifted off to sleep, she rested her head on his shoulder, content in the closeness they shared.

For Amon, these quiet moments in her arms talking, listening to her laugh, were some of the best moments of his existence. Finally, once again he was truly happy. But after the lovemaking, after she had gone to sleep, his mind tortured him.

He didn't worry about Varek finding her. He'd altered time and was assured her true destined one wouldn't even arrive in New Hope until February. He worried Aeveren biology would prevent him from having everything he wanted. Because he wasn't her destined one, it would be more difficult to get her pregnant than if he were the one for her. A cruel reality for many Aeveren.

In the dark as he lay next to her listening to the soft rise and fall of her breathing in her sleep, he cursed the inconveniences of being Aeveren. Destined ones. Rules meant to keep happiness for only some while others suffered alone. Edicts better suited to ancient times than now. A Council that thought it had any real control over anyone but the most powerless Aeveren.

He smiled to himself at the thought of the Council sending a prisoner from Nil—a prisoner with no powers—to capture him. Even if he found Callia, it would be too late. He wouldn't be able to get there because of the binding spell he'd had Markku cast on him. Council fools and a common murderer!

How could anyone defend Aeveren biology? Callia's destined one a murderer who spent three lifetimes in Nil? Amon let his hand rest lightly on the back of her head. Such a sweet and gentle creature with a prisoner. The thought of it made him sick.

Varek could offer her nothing she needed, nothing she deserved. Could he give her homes around the world? Take her to any time and place her heart desired? What could he give her, this murderer who should spend eternity in Nil? And why had he been given such a gift as Callia?

Amon was rescued from his thoughts by Gethen's message telling him Markku had arrived. He kissed Callia softly, dressed in the darkness, and vanished from the room.

Markku stood in Amon's living room appalling Gethen with a long-winded story about some time he had spent in Italy and some female who had shown him the time of his life a few lifetimes ago. Gethen's usually stoic expression slid from his face, replaced with sheer disgust at the visual picture the man next to him painted of his sexual encounter. Amon appeared as Markku got to the point in his story that made Gethen turn in revulsion.

"...and you should have felt that, old man. I don't think I've ever had anything that tight before or since. I fucked that..." Markku's sentence broke off when Amon arrived in the room. "Amon, I was just telling your man about a local girl I had once."

Although he had only heard the end of his tale, Amon knew by the look on his servant's face that it wasn't a story worth repeating. With a wave of his hand, he dismissed Gethen, who gave him a look of sincere gratitude as he hastened out of the room, and turned back to his guest.

"You're even more talkative than usual, Markku."

"Yeah, well you know me. Always got a story to tell."

Before he had the chance to revile Amon with his sexual exploits, he was cut off. "What have you done about this love spell I seem to have on me?"

Markku sat down hard on the leather couch and leaned back, his legs spread. "I cast a counterspell like you said to. Has it helped?"

Amon shook his head and ran his hand through his hair.

"Well, I told you it might not work if the one who used the magicks on you had the good stuff. What about just going to that one and asking her to end the spell? Maybe she's had time to cool down?"

"She's had three hundred years to cool down, as you say. No that's not an option."

Markku shrugged. "Well, if the counterspell doesn't work,

that only leaves you with making your current one happy. Is that working?"

Amon could see in his expression that Markku was hoping he'd share the salacious details of his sex life as he'd done minutes earlier with Gethen. Feeling sick at the thought of the likes of Markku knowing anything at all about Callia, he quickly changed the subject.

"I've got another project for you. I want information on ways to get a woman who isn't your destined one pregnant."

The man looked at Amon in confusion. "What do you mean? It happens every day. Look at all the fucking half-breeds."

"Yes, but I don't want to leave anything to chance. You know that not being her destined one might hinder things a bit."

"Are we talking magick here or something like an herbal concoction?"

"Anything. I want you to find out whatever you can and get back to me as soon as you can."

Markku remained seated on the couch but Amon's silence and the change of his eyes from blue to almost black told him it was time for him to go. He'd seen his eyes change like that before and knew it was a signal that his mood had also changed to one far less affable.

As he walked to the door, he turned back to see Amon watching him. "Was there something else?"

Amon crossed the room in three giant strides and stood in front of Markku, glaring down at him. "From now on, I'll meet you in the village."

After an obsequious nod, an insulted Markku left. Amon reappeared in his bedroom, nauseous and disgusted he was forced to employ someone like Markku to help him with Callia.

As he climbed into bed minutes later, he pressed his naked body against her and reveled in how incredible she felt next to his skin. He fell asleep to the sweetly hypnotic rhythm of her breathing, his mood once again happy.

BY THE BEGINNING OF OCTOBER, Callia had called her grandmother to tell her she'd be staying in Italy with Amon. The older woman made her promise to be careful, but as she was happy to hear her granddaughter so content, she offered little protest to Callia's decision.

For Callia, her time with Amon had introduced her to things she'd never experienced in all her lifetimes. Trips to Rome, Paris, London, and Athens had filled the month of September, each one thrilling her with new experiences Amon seemed to know with ease. At times, she had to remind herself that while he was only six years older than she in this lifetime, he was years ahead of her with forty lifetimes more.

For Amon, life had become one filled with happiness. Pleasing Callia pleased him, and other than his inability to get her pregnant, life was perfect. Markku's report on how to circumvent Aeveren biology had yielded no results, and as October began to wind down, Amon began to feel a sense of unease. Callia sensed no change in him, but Amon knew something was wrong.

Another summons of Markku brought the men together on Halloween night. Amon knew he'd resent being called out on a magickal high holy day, but he didn't care.

Callia was in the village at a party with locals Amon trusted. He would join her after his meeting. While he waited on the road near the edge of the village, Amon tried to content himself with what he knew he had.

It wasn't enough.

He had to make sure she'd be connected to him. Impatiently, he paced in the crisp, autumn air and watched a bonfire in the distance.

"How come you're not out having a good time?" Markku said, chuckling as he walked toward him in the dark. He was dressed in more formal clothes than usual, prepared for the Samhain ceremony he would attend later that night.

Amon was in no mood for banter. He needed answers to his problem, not some light conversation with someone he'd often thought of as something akin to a court jester.

"What else have you found out about non-destined one pregnancies?" he asked in a voice sharp and biting, full of impatience.

"This again? I told you everything thing I know the last time you summoned me."

"And I told you to find out more!"

"There's nothing more to find out. I don't understand what the problem is. Just fuck her like you would anyone else and enjoy it. And if you get her pregnant, good. Personally, I don't see why you'd want a kid…"

Markku's speech abruptly ended when Amon lunged at him, grabbing him by the throat. "Don't ever let me hear you talk about Callia like that again! And I didn't ask for your opinion, you greasy fucking pissant!"

Amon held the urge to snap Markku's neck at bay, barely able to keep the rage that surged through his body under control. He hadn't asked for Markku's opinion. He'd told him to find the answers he needed. He pushed Markku up against a low rock wall on the side of the road and glared down at the man.

"Find out what I want or the next time you'll see what happens when I really become angry with you."

Amon pulled him up by his collar and pushed the man away from him in disgust. "I want to know what you find out tonight." The tone of his voice made it clear it wasn't a request.

He strode away toward the party, sickened by the things he had to do.

Markku stood in the darkness more furious than he'd ever been. Who the fuck did that tempuster think he was fucking with? Why should he help him at all?

He paced in anger as he thought about what he would do to get back at Amon. The obvious choice was to bind his power to control time, but even he didn't want to risk that. Amon had other powers, and more importantly, many supporters in the Soren who could make anyone's life hell if that person got on their bad side. Markku knew, even in his current disposition, that binding Amon's power of time would be a mistake he'd end up paying for royally.

But he had to do something. Amon needed to know he'd fucked with the wrong guy. In truth, he had to admit that was mostly bluster and when he calmed down a bit, Markku ran through the things he'd done for him and chose the easiest and what he considered to be the least important thing he'd ever done for him.

Smiling, Markku remembered the name of the person Amon had ordered him to put under a binding spell. Thinking this might not do much but would at least make him feel like he did something to stand up to Amon, he looked to the sky, closed his eyes, and recited the twelve simple words of the spell to reverse the binding.

"No longer shall this binding be, goddess Keres set Varek Leale free."

Pleased with himself, Markku left the tiny Italian village for his Samhain celebration. It looked to be a good night after all, and he might even get laid.

"GETHEN, DO YOU KNOW WHERE Amon is? He was gone when I woke up."

Amon's servant turned his attention from his silver polishing to Callia and bowed slightly. "Good morning, miss. Would you like some breakfast? Or I can make you lunch as it's near that time."

Callia smiled, a little embarrassed that she had slept in so late. "No, that's all right. I may get myself some tea."

Before she could repeat her question, Gethen quickly put down the flatware he was polishing and walked into the kitchen to get her drink. Callia followed him and, after taking the cup of tea, asked about Amon's whereabouts again.

"Miss, he had business in the village this morning, but I am to provide you with anything you desire."

Callia gently shook her head. "I don't need anything, Gethen. Thank you. I'm just going to relax and maybe read a book until he gets back."

The servant nodded. "As you wish, miss."

AT NOON, AMON BEGAN THE walk back to his villa from the village. He was pleased that he'd been successful in his errand to acquire a case of very rare wine from a local merchant. The quality of the region's wine was one of the reasons he chose to keep a home in this area, in addition to the nostalgia it had always offered him.

As he walked, he scanned the rolling hills in front of him. The memories of a long ago lifetime were interrupted by the chill he felt, and he considered just teleporting to get out of the weather but chided himself for being lazy. He told himself the fresh air would do him good.

Things were better this first day of November, to be sure. He had learned from Markku very late the night before that there was a way to increase his chances of impregnating Callia that could be put in her tea each morning, so he'd instructed

Gethen regarding that. He and Callia had enjoyed a wonderful time out after she'd brought him out of his bad mood from his run-in with Markku and had ended the night in each other's arms, as they did each night. Everything was coming together beautifully.

As he walked, behind him he heard the sounds of footsteps on the dirt path. He turned his head slightly to satisfy his curiosity and saw a familiar face.

CHAPTER TWENTY-ONE

"VAREK."

As he spoke the name, Amon smiled broadly with confidence. He turned his body to face Varek as he silently swore to kill Markku.

He studied the person who stood in front of him, curious as to how he'd traveled back in time. He was just as he'd been when they'd last stood in front of one another, and Amon smiled as he considered the one major difference between that meeting and this one.

He had Callia.

Varek's body shook in anger as he stared at Amon Kalins. He may be branded a murderer forever, but Amon was just as bad. He had manipulated another man's destined one into being with him. His destined one. Varek struggled to control the murderous rage that demanded revenge.

"I've come for Callia." His voice didn't betray his fear that she may be so in love with Amon, fooled by his manipulation, that she'd turn away from her destiny. A fear that made him feel so lost he almost couldn't bear it.

"She's no longer yours," Amon said in a tone that made the statement sound like a verdict being handed down.

"Callia will choose me. I'm her destined one."

Amon snorted in disgust. "Nonsense." Then he regained his composure and spoke the words he knew would devastate Varek. "She's in love with me. And how do I know?"

He stepped forward toward Varek and answered his own question. "I know because she tells me when I take her to places like Rome and Paris and buy her whatever her heart desires. I know because of the way she looks at me, the way she used to look at you."

Varek stood glaring at Amon, hating each word he spoke. Amon knew this and continued, confident his next words wouldn't miss their mark.

"I know because every time I'm buried deep inside her it's me she begs for more and my name she screams as I make her come over and over."

Varek's rage overcame him, and he lunged at Amon only to tackle air after he disappeared. Falling to the ground, Varek quickly spun around to find Amon standing above him, gloating.

He jeered at Varek. "The Council didn't give you anything but the ability to go back in time? You're going to need more than that to beat me."

"You won't get away with this. I won't let you." Even to himself, this sounded pathetic, and Varek cringed inside.

Shaking his head, Amon laughed. "You're too late. I've already gotten away with it. And when we find out she's pregnant, it won't matter what you do. She'll be mine."

Varek stood now, stunned at what Amon had said. "Pregnant?"

"Yeah. It happens all the time between Aeveren who aren't destined ones. Fuck, it even happens with humans. Remember your half-breed?"

The idea of Callia pregnant made Varek's body freeze. Pregnant. His destined one pregnant with another man's child. His past flooded his brain with memories of Neera and the pain of her betrayal.

Amon saw his news had achieved his aim. "Better luck next life," he said smugly before he disappeared from in front of Varek's eyes.

Feeling as if his whole world had been shattered, Varek slowly walked down the path back toward the village. He needed to find somewhere to stay. He wasn't going to give up on her, but he knew his only way to beat Amon was through Callia. If he could see her, get to speak to her, he knew he could get her back.

Amon appeared outside the villa and stood a moment to calm himself. The arrival of Callia's destined one had unnerved him. But he couldn't let her see that because she'd wonder what was upsetting him, or worse, she'd be upset and the pain from her sadness would hit him again.

As he stood with the cold breeze biting at him, he cursed Varek, their race's biology, Markku, and his own destined one for her curse on him. When he could control his anger, he entered the villa and immediately searched for Callia. His eyes darted left and right as he peered into each room on the main floor. As he entered the kitchen, he spotted Gethen at the stove.

"Where's Callia?"

"She said she was going to read. Perhaps she's in the study."

Amon spun on his heels and started to storm out, but he stopped abruptly and turned back toward his servant. "Gethen, I want no one allowed into this house. Do you understand me?"

Gethen nodded. "Yes, master. Is there anything I may assist you with?"

Amon let out a deep sigh. "Varek is here. Somehow he found out she was here. Probably the fucking Council."

"I understand, sir."

"Good. Remember, no one is to be allowed in."

Amon left to find Callia, reminding himself that he needed to calm down before he saw her. At the top of the stairs, he took a few deep breaths and tried to convince himself that everything was under control.

Callia sat on the bed they shared, reading a book she had found in Amon's study. He opened the bedroom door slightly and watched her through the crack, finding comfort in simply seeing her. She was like his drug, his addiction. Just the sight of her in his bed altered his mood. His body relaxed, the anger and fear ebbing away.

He couldn't lose her. She was everything good in him. She had brought back his happiness.

"Carina."

Callia turned at the sound of Amon's voice and smiled. Closing her book, she swung her legs off the bed and stood to embrace him.

As he held her, feeling her body mold to his, she mumbled something, but her voice got lost in his chest. He stroked her hair as he stood lost in her arms and closed his eyes.

"Amon?"

Callia's voice roused him from his thoughts, and he opened his eyes to see her looking up at him.

"Didn't you hear me?"

"No, carina. What did you say?"

"Did your business go well in the village?"

Forcing a smile, he answered yes and explained about the wine.

Callia sat down on the edge of the bed and reclined on her forearms. She looked up at him standing over her and traced his figure down from his head to right near his waist. Her voice sounded husky as she said, "I missed you." She opened her legs and hooked one around his leg, nudging him toward the bed.

Amon let her pull him to the edge of the bed, and he stared at her, needing what she offered for more than physical reasons. He needed to believe what he'd said to Varek.

He looked down into her beautiful face, her half-lidded eyes gazing longingly up at him. Her light brown hair fanned out around her head, framing it as it had all those times he'd playfully pushed her down on the bed and made love to her.

He watched as she licked her lips and bit gently into her lower lip. Even if he didn't love her with his entire heart and soul, he wouldn't have been able to deny her any wish at that moment.

He lowered himself down on top of her and kissed her lips softly. His hands cradled her face, and he ran his right thumb along her jaw.

Callia sensed a difference in him and whispered, "What's wrong?"

Nothing was wrong, and it wasn't that he didn't want her. He did. But a gentleness controlled his attitude toward her now. The threat of Varek didn't make him need her more, but it made him need to know she loved him as deeply as he loved her.

He looked into her eyes, full of concern, and placed a kiss on each eyelid. In Italian, he said softly, "Nothing is wrong, carina."

Amon made love to her sweetly as he'd never done before. His hands caressed her gently, showing her a depth of his emotion she'd never known existed in him. His kisses touched her heart with their softness. His exclusive focus on her happiness surprised her. Their lovemaking had always been passionate, but it had been more intense and physical. Now he seemed purely emotional, needing her happiness to ensure his.

As he whispered words of love to her, Callia heard a question of doubt in his voice. When he quietly dropped his head next to hers, Callia murmured words that made him believe she was truly his.

"Amon, I am yours. There is no one in this world I could

love as I do you."

When it was over, she laid her head on his chest and listened to his heartbeat while she gently ran her hand over his stomach. The gentle touch of her fingers on his skin lulled him into relaxation. He wasn't sure how long they lay there together, closer than they'd ever been before, but he silently swore to himself that he'd kill Varek before losing her to him.

IN A SMALL ROOM AT the village inn, Varek sat drinking his second bottle of wine. It may have been the finest wine in the world. He didn't know and didn't care. He needed it for something other than its taste.

Amon's words repeatedly sounded in his head, torturing him as he sat in the dimly lit room.

She's no longer yours.

I know because of the way she looks at me, the way she used to look at you.

I know because every time I'm buried deep inside her, it's me she begs for more…

Varek slammed down another glass of wine, feeling its warmth as it slipped down his throat. He drank to escape the pain of the reality Amon had forced upon him, but instead of allowing him to run away, the alcohol forced painful memories from his past to his present, causing old insecurities to be reborn, more painful and uglier than ever.

He entered the house and listened for any sign Neera and the baby were home. He hung up his coat and looked around as he waited to hear his wife's voice or his daughter's. Hearing nothing, he slowly walked up the stairs to the bedroom to rest from a long day. As he reached the second floor, he saw the babysitter out of the corner of his eye and turned to face her as she left the nursery.

"Janelle, I didn't know you were scheduled for today."

In fact, he had expressly asked Neera if the babysitter would be there again that day and she had told him no.

The young girl put her finger up to her lips to tell him to lower his voice. "I just put Christina down for a nap. She was exhausted."

In a hushed voice, Varek asked, "Where is Neera?" That he had to find out where his wife was from a sixteen-year-old girl irritated him, but he attempted to keep his tone level to conceal this fact.

Janelle looked at him sheepishly, as if she pitied him because she had the same suspicions as he did. "She said she had to go back to work to finish something."

Distracted, he nodded, said okay, and turned to walk away to the bedroom he shared with Neera.

"Mr. Leale?"

Varek turned around, wishing he could just be finished with the conversation with the female who saw his daughter more than her own mother. Sighing, he said, "Yes, Janelle?"

"Do you need me to stay any longer today?"

Shaking his head, he quietly told her no and turned back toward his original goal. From behind him, Janelle explained that she had given Christina a bottle just an hour earlier and changed her diaper before putting her down for a nap.

"Thanks for everything, Janelle."

Varek had enacted some version of this scene with his daughter's babysitter every weekday for three weeks, with at least a third of the performances a surprise to him. More and more, Neera spent her time at work. He didn't begrudge his wife's return to work six months after Christina's birth. He understood that she was dedicated to her teaching career. It was one of the things about her he found most appealing, but she seemed to never be with the child between day care and Janelle and spent even less time with him.

He removed his work clothes and changed into civilian clothes, carefully hanging his police officer blues as he considered calling Neera. Spying her phone on the night table, he realized he wouldn't be able to talk to her as she was rarely in her office to answer her work phone.

Maybe I should e-mail her. Her students seem to get her that way, he angrily thought to himself.

As he walked out into the hallway, he turned around to look at the phone. He could look at her calls to see if his suspicions were correct. He stood unable to move but staring at the phone. Something in him made him turn around and walk down the hall to his daughter's nursery. Was it fear? Cowardice? He didn't know. But he knew something was wrong between Neera and him.

She had become distant in the months since she'd returned to work. At first, he'd assumed it was just her becoming accustomed to teaching classes, dealing with students, committee meetings, and the other, often arduous tasks that came along with her position. She'd repeatedly denied that there was any problem with work and never seemed to want to discuss what was making her distant to him.

Varek thought about their first years as husband and wife. They had fallen in love and married quickly, a common occurrence for destined ones in the Aeveren world. Marriage wasn't required or even necessary for Aeveren. Finding your destined one was the end in and of itself. But he had proposed to Neera on one knee, knowing she was a traditional romantic, and she had excitedly accepted.

After they were married, they found bliss with one another, but her insecurities began to affect them when he got his job on the force. Convinced he was with another woman because of the hours he was forced to work, she goaded him into jealous fights that often ended up in physical fighting, with him forced to endure her attacks, worried she would hurt herself since at half his size she certainly couldn't hurt him.

Each fight would end with them in bed shortly after, their lovemaking as passionate as their fighting. He finally convinced her that there was no other woman, but her temper caused their marriage to be tumultuous, at best.

When they found out they were going to be blessed with a child, he saw she was as happy as he was, even more so. He watched as she blossomed into an even more beautiful woman, glowing from her pregnancy. Her blond hair seemed to lighten during those months, making the contrast between his jet black hair and hers even more pronounced. He'd lie in bed and look into her beautiful blue-green eyes as she'd go through lists of her *current favorite baby names. She'd complain that he disagreed with each one just to say no, but when he heard the name Christina and finally agreed to it, she smiled happily and teased about it being about time.*

Varek stood in his daughter's doorway watching her sleep. Her skin looked so soft as she scrunched her face while she almost imperceptibly changed positions. She had her mother's coloring, but her eyes had more green and less blue. She made everything he went through—with work, with Neera—worth it. He'd never realized he'd wanted children before Christina had come into their lives. Now he couldn't imagine life without her.

He quietly closed her door and walked to his own bed, tired from a long day but exhausted from his thoughts about Neera. He lay down and felt the coolness of the pillow against his head. Closing his eyes, he fell into a deep sleep.

Two hours later, he awoke to the sound of the front door opening. He checked the baby, who was still fast asleep, and made his way downstairs, hoping that night would be different.

He found Neera in the kitchen, and he padded up behind her to wrap his arms around her waist. Surprised, she spun around and Varek braced himself for the yelling, but none came. Instead, when she recovered from her surprise, she smiled and simply said, "Don't do that. You scared me half to death!"

Encouraged, he bent his head down to kiss her and was met with the kind of kiss they'd shared when they were first dating.

"I missed you. What did you have to do at work?"

He listened as she went through a list of issues she had to deal with that required her return to work, but what caught his attention was the way she spoke more than what she said. She sounded like the woman he'd fallen in love with, had thanked God he'd been blessed with as his destined one.

"How is Christina?" she asked as she squirmed out of his arms to get a glass of water.

"Sleeping. Janelle fed and changed her a few hours ago."

"Are you going up now?"

"No, I'll stay down here with you for a little bit."

"Varek, you look tired. Go to bed. I'll be up in a little while."

He would have liked it if she'd wanted him to stay with her, but the kindness in her voice made him feel better. He went to bed hoping things were beginning to improve.

Before he could fall asleep, she came to bed. He hoped he wasn't pushing his luck and rolled over and kissed her tentatively. Her loving response thrilled him, and for the first time in weeks, they made love. As he drifted off to sleep with her in his arms, he felt happier than he had in weeks. Whatever had been the problem was gone.

The next morning he kissed Christina as Neera fed her and told both of them he loved them. He left for work loving the world and wished the criminals would take a day off to let him enjoy his newfound happiness.

A forgotten key to his work locker brought him back to the house almost an hour later. Afraid to wake the baby, he quietly climbed the stairs to the bedroom where the key sat on his night table. He smelled Neera's perfume, the one he loved her to wear, and breathed in its sweet fragrance deeply.

The door to the bedroom was open slightly, and he thought he heard the television because he'd heard voices. He opened the *door and what he saw stopped him like a brick wall. Neera and another man. In his bed. Fucking. With his infant daughter down the hall.*

Varek stood stunned, but quickly shock turned to blinding rage. What a fool he'd been! Neera hadn't had problems at work. What she had was a lover at work. Varek recognized his face as he watched him have sex with his wife.

He pulled his gun and through tear-filled eyes pointed it at them, his hands shaking. They never heard him behind them. He shot three times, knowing immediately that he'd killed them both.

He slid down the wall and hit the floor as his legs collapsed from underneath him. He watched as Neera left this lifetime, leaving the man behind. He'd killed his wife and her human lover.

Varek sat in the darkness of his room, drunk, but unable to pass out. His mind played cruel tricks on him, replacing the image of Neera and her lover with Callia and Amon.

But somewhere deep in his heart something told him that Callia wasn't doing to him what Neera had. She hadn't made him think she loved him and then betrayed him with another. She wasn't to blame for how he felt. Amon was.

Varek pushed down the despair he felt over Callia and that place in his heart gradually became the source of his strength. She was his destined one, the person he was meant to be with, take care of, and love. She needed him to forget his past and be the man she had fallen in love with. She needed him to be her destined one.

CHAPTER TWENTY-TWO

C ALLIA AWOKE EARLY, BLISSFULLY HAPPY with her arms around Amon. She sleepily recalled how sweet and tender he'd been the night before and wanted to do something to show him how much she loved him. Remembering the antique shop in the village and the urn he'd mentioned the last time they'd strolled past the storefront, she decided to surprise him with it.

Soundlessly, she slid out of his embrace and made her way to the room she'd had as hers when she'd first arrived. After a quick shower, she silently padded down the stairs toward the front door. Gethen was nowhere in sight, so she left quietly, hoping to return with Amon's surprise before he awoke.

As she walked the dirt path toward the village, she scanned the gorgeous countryside all around her. Autumn had arrived fully, and as a brisk wind began swirling over the hill she descended, she was thankful she had worn a sweater.

She ran her hand over the sleeve, noting how expensive the fabric was. When she'd arrived, Amon had sent Gethen to buy her a new wardrobe, and as she relished the softness of the cashmere sweater against her skin, she noted that the servant was a man of excellent taste.

The shop opened just as she arrived, and the elderly woman who owned the shop remembered her from her past visits. Callia explained her wish to surprise Amon with her gift, and the woman smiled and remarked about young love as she packed the urn in a box. Thanking the lady, she stepped out onto the sidewalk.

Varek stared at her, stunned at how she had seemed to appear at his silent request. She held a large box in front of her that began to slip away from her grip.

"I'm sorry, Ca..." He stopped himself before he said her name. Tongue-tied, he stood gaping at her.

"Oh, it's okay. I wasn't paying attention to where I was going." Her voice was like a gentle caress in his ears.

Callia smiled to reassure him she was okay.

Varek's mind screamed to him to keep the conversation going. "You speak English."

Giggling the way she always had, she said, "Yes, I'm American. I'm afraid my Italian isn't very good yet."

"I don't speak it at all."

Callia began to ask if he was American too, but a strange feeling came over her, making her dizzy and lightheaded. She swayed to her right side, and Varek grabbed her arm to keep her from falling.

"Are you okay?"

Unable to speak, she shook her head, frightened. Varek saw the fear in her eyes and put his arm around her. He looked around and saw a table and chairs a few hundred feet away. His room was just two doors down, so he guided her toward it instead as he reassured her she'd be fine.

Once inside his room, Varek took the box from her and helped her to the bed. Callia said nothing, but continued to feel lightheaded and disoriented, like she was coming down with the flu. She closed her eyes and lay still, afraid if she moved the feeling would get worse.

Varek sat on the edge of the bed watching her, desperately wanting to touch her, to run his fingers over her face to soothe her in the way he knew she loved. But he sat motionless, unsure that he should do anything. Minutes went by as he debated if he should simply take her back to their time. There was nothing he wanted to do more in this world than have her back, but how would he explain everything to her? She knew nothing of what Amon had done. She didn't even recognize her destined one as he sat on the bed just inches from her.

She didn't even know the name of the man who remained silently watching her. As she struggled to stay awake, she sensed his hand stroke her forehead and was overcome by a feeling of warmth and security.

This stranger whose name she didn't know was her destined one.

Varek saw her relax as he softly ran the pads of his fingers over her skin. She was the same Callia he'd known. God, he wanted to take her into his arms!

"Who are you?" she asked quietly.

"Varek."

Callia kept her eyes closed and let the sound of his name repeat in her head. Varek. Her destined one. When she opened them, she looked into his deep black eyes. She searched for recognition that he knew she was his destined one.

"I'm Callia," she said softly.

My Callia.

They sat silently in his tiny room, neither one knowing what to say. When she finally spoke, her words sent Varek's heart soaring.

"You are my destined one."

To Varek, he was sure he hadn't heard sweeter words in what seemed like months.

No longer willing to hold himself back, he bent his head down and kissed her softly on the lips. All of his sadness at losing her welled up in him and he pulled away, unable to control his emotions.

Callia felt him move away from her and she lay there confused about what to do now. She couldn't just leave Amon—she loved him. But she couldn't deny the pull Varek had on her as her destined one.

Her head spinning from the realization that she'd finally, after almost seven lifetimes, been given a destined one and now had to figure out what to do with Amon, Callia slowly sat up and spoke to Varek, who remained with his back to her.

"I can't be with you now. I'm sorry."

Varek turned around with a look of pain on his face.

"You don't understand," Callia continued. "I have someone who loves me very much. I can't simply abandon him. I can't hurt him like that."

As he faced her, his thoughts filled with rage. He didn't give a damn about Amon's feelings. But he knew he had to understand this was who Callia was. Hurting someone wasn't something she'd do if she could avoid it. He silently acknowledged that no matter how much it hurt him, he'd have to let Callia handle Amon in her way.

"What will you do? You can't deny our biology." Knowing this was only a partial truth, he hoped she wouldn't act like he had when he'd realized she was his destined one. *Please don't let her think of free will.*

"He's been very good to me. He deserves my respect and the truth."

Varek saw a look of sadness come over her face, and he was stung by jealousy. He hated the idea that she would feel bad for Amon or miss him, knowing what he'd done. And the idea of her telling him the truth sounded like a very bad idea.

"Do you really think telling him that your destined one has come is a good plan?"

Callia slowly stood up from the bed and faced Varek. "He deserves the truth." She reached for the box with Amon's surprise and Varek placed his hand on hers.

"I need to know you're okay. I can't let you go if I think you might be in danger." He thought of what Amon's reaction to the news would be.

"I'll be fine. He's Aeveren and knows that I'm not his. This is part of who we are."

Varek was thrilled that she seemed to accept him so easily.

"But I love him and want to handle this my way."

Instantly disheartened, Varek sat down on the bed, saddened by the realization that she didn't love him. He remembered how she looked at him that first night at the orphanage and wished she looked like that now.

Callia sat down beside him and turned toward him. "I'm sorry. I guess this isn't what you'd hoped for with your destined one. I just need you to know this is who I am."

Varek nodded. He hesitated, and then asked the question he needed the answer to. "Do you feel anything for me?"

"I knew as soon as you touched me who you were. We are meant for each other. I feel the pull of your heart on mine as we sit here. It's just that there's another who must be considered."

Callia kissed him and instantly realized that Varek possessed that special something she'd never found in any other man.

Unwilling to let her go, Varek held her hand as she started for the door.

"When will we be together?"

Callia squeezed his hand and smiled. "I don't know, but I will come to you when I can."

Varek watched her leave, concerned that Amon would harm her. He prayed to God that she would be safe.

"But I'll kill him if he does anything to her."

As she walked away from Varek, Callia felt her feelings for

him blossom. She had waited so long for her destined one and felt her attachment to him already. But her feelings for Amon remained, and she was saddened by what she knew was the end of her time with him.

Callia arrived back at the villa as Amon walked out the front door. She wondered if he sensed the difference in her now.

Amon strode toward her wearing just pants and a shirt. The chilly wind bit his skin, but the worry he'd felt when he found her gone pushed everything else out of his mind.

"Where were you?" His tone was sharp and unlike any she'd ever heard from him toward her.

"Amon, it's too cold out here. Let's go in."

Callia led him into the house and handed him the box. "I wanted to get you a surprise."

As she watched him open the box and take out the urn, she felt a pang of sadness at the end of them. She had left the villa that morning on a quest to find a gift to express her love for him, and now as she watched the broad smile light up his beautiful face, she realized she would have to tell him that Aeveren biology had brought an end to their time together.

He looked at her lovingly and walked to her. "It's beautiful." He placed the urn on a nearby table and kissed her sweetly. "I was worried about you."

Amon studied Callia's face carefully. Had he worried needlessly? Or had Varek spoken to her and now biology was his enemy also? Nothing in her expression told him that Varek had triumphed. For now, Amon wanted to believe that life was what he had made it and Callia was still his.

Knowing she had to confront him but unable to, Callia kissed him on the cheek and begged off spending time with him, retreating upstairs instead. She needed time to think, to figure out how she would tell Amon that being Aeveren had cut their time short.

She thought about how cruel life could be. She'd waited lifetimes for a destined one, but Amon had given her everything she'd ever wanted in a relationship...well, almost everything. What he couldn't give was beyond his control. No matter what he bought her or where they traveled to, he could never be the one destined for her.

And now that she'd met the one meant for her, she understood what had been missing for all her lifetimes. Even though she'd just met Varek and knew so little about him— what was his last name? how old was he?—Callia knew that the indescribable feeling deep inside her that made her feel warm and safe was what her destined one gave her.

She looked out the balcony doors at the beautiful countryside. Sadness crept into her heart as she realized she couldn't avoid Amon any longer. He deserved to know. He deserved at least that.

Callia turned away from the beauty outside to find Amon behind her, a pained look on his face. Her sadness once again physically affecting him, he looked as if some invisible attacker stabbed at him. Sure that her feelings were the cause of his pain, as they had been when they first arrived in Italy, she quickly worked to alter her mood to spare him further unhappiness.

As she forced a tiny smile, she repeated to herself that she was thankful for having such a person in her life. But her words were joined by others, words that spoke of things other than thankfulness. Confused, Callia forced her mind to remain quiet and listened for the foreign words that invaded her thoughts.

Varek...New Hope...Elan...Nil...

Amon's mind raced as the pain receded in his body. Callia's expression looked like a mixture of concern and concentration. What was she thinking? Had Varek gotten to her? Had he told her everything about what had happened before time had changed?

Callia's mind was bombarded with Amon's thoughts, and she struggled to adjust not only to her new ability but also to the thoughts she clearly read in his mind.

He knew Varek's name! How could he know her destined one's name? And why were his thoughts full of references to times the three of them had shared when she had just met Varek?

Frightened, she stepped back away from him. The ideas she heard from him made her feel like she was standing in front of a stranger. His thoughts tumbled into her mind, building a reality that Callia couldn't ignore. Things weren't as she'd thought they were. Something was wrong.

Amon watched her back away from him, her face twisted as if she'd just come to some horrible conclusion. He instinctively reached out for her and was stunned when she recoiled from him. Feeling his world begin to slip through his fingers, he scrambled to control himself as the pain of her emotions surged once again into him.

He let out a strangled cry. "Callia? What's wrong?"

Her mind raced to put together the pieces of his thoughts that continued to flood her mind. As they threatened to overwhelm her, she let them explode out of her.

"How do you know Varek? How could we have all been together when I just met him today? What does all this mean?"

Amon heard her panicked voice as he clutched at his gut, a stabbing pain shooting through him. What was worse was Varek's name on Callia's lips. He had gotten to her and told her everything! And she believed him!

He lurched toward her, stiff from the agony her emotions inflicted on him. "What did he tell you?" he yelled.

Callia looked into Amon's eyes, now much deeper blue. His expression signaled he was out of control.

"What did he tell you?" he repeated in a voice full of anguish.

Callia's mind raced to answer a question that seemed to make no sense. Did Varek know what Amon knew? Did they all know one another?

"Nothing! He told me nothing!" As she spoke, she continued to move away from him and he continued to follow.

She had to be lying. How else would she know?

Amon grabbed Callia's arm and held her at his side, his fingers painfully pressing into the flesh of her upper arm. He looked down into her frightened face with a menacing stare.

"I want to know what he told you!"

Callia tried to pull away from him, but his large hand squeezed her arm tighter, bringing tears to her eyes. Desperately, she looked up into those eyes for any sign that the man she loved still existed in Amon but saw only the face of someone whose deceptions had come back to haunt him.

"He said nothing! *You* told me!"

Amon's expression softened as he processed what she'd said. "You lie!"

Wrenching her arm from his grip, Callia began to cry, causing him to double over in pain. As waves of pain rolled through him, he struggled to understand her explanation.

"I heard your thoughts. I heard everything. But I don't understand! How can you know my destined one? And why do your thoughts say we've all spent time together?" Callia sobbed as she sank down in a heap on the bed.

Amon remained doubled over in pain but transfixed on her words. She was able to read minds and hear others' thoughts. Had she always had this ability? His mind frantically searched for the answer, recalling that she hadn't been able to know his thoughts when the three of them had been together.

Callia understood his thoughts and took the memory he analyzed into her mind. Amon and Varek had been in her life before. His memory played out in her mind. Snow on the ground. Varek driving her car. Amon sitting in the backseat watching her, but he looked different.

She turned to look at him, horrified. Painfully, she expressed the realization his memories had shown.

"Amon, what did you do to me?"

Sure that if he had to endure any more of her emotions he wouldn't survive, he turned and careened his body toward the door to escape. He locked the door from the outside and braced himself against it as he caught his breath.

He met Gethen on the stairs and frantically ordered the servant to keep Callia in the house or else. Gethen stood stunned as his master took the steps by two and stormed out of the house.

Callia sat slumped over on the bed, exhausted from what had happened. Amon's thoughts had shown her a life she'd enjoyed with Varek, not Amon. But how had she met Amon instead?

Suddenly, terror seized her. Amon knew Varek was in the village! Callia ran to the bedroom door and hysterically jerked the doorknob left and right. She was a prisoner. She dashed to the balcony doors and threw them open. Outside she looked over the edge to the ground two stories below and understood the frightening truth. She was trapped, and Varek was waiting for her, not knowing that Amon knew everything.

IN THE VILLAGE IN HIS tiny room, Varek sat on the bed thinking of his days with Callia before Amon had changed time. He let his thoughts drift back to her lying in his arms as she told him she loved him for the first time.

Silently, he prayed they would soon be lying in bed telling one another they loved each other like before everything happened. Then, for a moment, he remembered sadly that she had no memory of all those times they'd shared. None of those moments so special to him existed for her. He swallowed hard, pushing the lump in his throat down, and reminded himself that she was his, a gift he'd been given, and they'd have lifetimes to create new memories.

His thoughts turned to Amon and his hands balled into fists. He'd take that bastard to Nil and enjoy every moment of it. He thought of Callia at his house at that very second and worried she might be in danger. Pledging to see that she was safe if he didn't hear from her soon, he was focused on one idea.

I don't care what the Council wants. I'll kill him if he hurts her.

CHAPTER TWENTY-THREE

A MON PACED LIKE A CAGED animal outside in the chill. Thoughts came and fled at such speed that his head spun. Callia had met Varek. She knew he was her destined one. She had somehow been granted the power to know others' thoughts. She knew he'd manipulated her to get her there. It was all slipping away, just as it had with his destined one when she learned of his use of his powers on her.

No! I won't lose her!

He could simply leave this place and time with Callia, and Varek would never find them. He knew this. But Callia would know. He didn't have the ability to erase her memory.

Amon raced to find a solution. As he paced, the cold autumn air stung his skin, but he didn't care. He frantically sought the answer that would fix the situation so he and Callia could return to the happiness of the past few months.

Fucking Varek!

But it wasn't just Varek. It was Markku. And Frederika. And the goddamned Council. And Callia.

For the first time, Amon blamed his unhappiness on

Callia. As the thought jumped through his mind and settled in a spot close to his rage-filled thoughts of the rest of them, he felt disappointed. Just like his destined one, she would reject him because of his powers.

A voice inside him told him she was different. This time was different. He wouldn't be judged for who he was. She would understand he did it all for her.

He knew what he had to do. She'd understand, and everything would return to how it had been before Varek arrived. She loved *him*.

Amon walked back into the villa focused on what he had to do. He moved past Gethen, ignoring his questions about Callia and his well-being, and walked to the desk in his study where he kept his gun.

VAREK SAT RESTLESSLY IN HIS room, getting up from his bed every few minutes to open the door and look for Callia. Each time he didn't see her he grew more concerned. She hadn't given him any particular time she'd be back, but his gut told him something was wrong. Something had happened.

Throwing on his coat, he stepped out onto the sidewalk and slammed the door shut. From his doorstep, he saw Amon's villa on the hillside, like a beacon to guide him to her.

As he walked, he patted his jeans' pocket that contained the talisman the Council had given him. He didn't know if he'd need it to get Amon to Nil—they'd told him all he'd need to do to get back was focus on returning to the Council chambers—but he wasn't taking any chances.

Today he'd get Callia back and take that bastard to Nil, whatever it took.

He quickly made his way up the dirt path that wound up the hillside, and as he got closer to the villa, he saw Amon through one of the windows. He was walking up the stairs that led to the second floor and looked like a man possessed.

Varek prayed he wasn't too late. A careless mistake by a man preoccupied meant he found an unlocked door at the back of the house, and he entered to hear noises upstairs.

Callia banged on the bedroom door to be released, hoping Gethen would free her. The doorknob moved and she stepped back, waiting for the person on the other side of the door to appear. Hope and fear mingled inside her frantically.

The door flung open and Callia stood facing Amon, his blue eyes flashing so darkly she took another step back, frightened. Staring at him, she noticed the gun in his right hand.

"Amon, please let me out. We can talk."

For a brief moment as his eyes met hers, he looked like the man she'd fallen in love with just a few short months before. His eyes were once again a beautiful ocean blue, and strands of his pale blond hair had fallen onto his forehead. His face looked almost angelic.

But as quickly as he seemed to revert to the man she knew, he changed into one she barely recognized. Trying to diffuse the situation, she tentatively extended her hand and gently touched his arm.

"Please, Amon. Don't do this."

He looked down at her and cupped her face with his left hand. He began to tenderly stroke her cheek with the back of his hand as he stared intently into her eyes.

"I would never hurt you, Callia. You know that, don't you?" His voice sounded far away and frightened her.

"Amon. We can talk, I promise. Please just put the gun away. You're scaring me."

Shaking his head, he pulled her to him and wrapped his left arm around her, holding her tightly to him.

"There's no need to be scared, carina. The gun isn't for you."

Callia's mind raced to figure out who the gun was for. Was he so distraught that he intended to kill himself? Or did he plan to kill Varek?

"Amon, please! I love you. Don't do this!"

He gently pushed Callia away from his body and placed his hands on her shoulders. The gun rested against the back of her right shoulder and the hardness of the metal made her stiffen her back.

"I love you, carina. I never meant to hurt you."

One thought lodged in her mind. *Oh my God! He's lost his mind and he's going to kill me too!*

As Callia prayed he wouldn't kill her, they heard a voice call Amon's name. He roughly grabbed her by the hand and dragged her behind him down the hall. As she reached the stairs, Callia saw Varek standing in the living room below.

Varek looked up to see Callia cowering behind Amon, a

look of terror in her eyes.

"Let her go, Amon!"

Amon shook his head and pulled Callia in front of him. For a moment, she thought he would release her, but that wish faded when he began to guide her down the stairs. He held her close to him, and she realized he was never going to let her go.

When they reached the main floor, Amon positioned her in front of his body and draped his arms over her, the gun still in his left hand when it came to rest near her collarbone. Callia's eyes pleaded with Varek to save her.

The two men stared one another down, Amon's eyes full of desperation and Varek's full of vengeance as he stood face to face with the man who had taken away the most important person in his life.

Callia felt the deep rise and fall of Amon's chest against her back as he held her tightly to him.

"How's my favorite prisoner from Nil?"

As he spoke, the hollow sound of Amon's voice resonated within her. *Varek was a prisoner in Nil?* Her destined one was a criminal? Confused, she looked at Varek hoping for an answer.

"He's right, Callia. I'm a prisoner in Nil. I have been for almost three lifetimes." Varek stopped his confession abruptly but then continued, hoping she would be as understanding as when they'd first met. "I murdered two people—my first destined one and her human lover."

After he was done, Varek searched her eyes for the acceptance she'd always given him, but whatever she might have been feeling about the truth of his existence was hidden by the fear of the man looming behind her.

"Nice, Varek. A murderer," Amon seethed.

"Amon, let her go. This is between us."

"There's nothing between us. You're a fucking murderer. What would I have to do with the likes of you?" Amon's voice nearly hissed in disgust as he spoke.

"No, you know that's a lie. You know Callia and I found you to help us find the murderer in New Hope."

As Varek spoke, Callia struggled to face Amon. None of what he was saying made any sense, but she knew from Amon's thoughts that he believed it. She wrestled out of his hold and faced him.

"What is he talking about, Amon?"

Before he could answer her question, Varek continued his story. "He manipulated time, Callia. We were in love. We met in February, and I was sent to New Hope by the Council to find the person who was murdering Aeveren parents."

Callia looked at Varek and shook her head. "I don't know what you're talking about. I didn't meet you in February, and there's no murderer in New Hope. Why are you saying this?"

"He's not just upset that your destined one is here, Callia. He doesn't want you to know what he did."

Callia turned to Amon. "What does he mean 'what you did?'"

"Carina, he's a criminal who's served time in Nil for murder. You can't trust him."

As she stood between the two men, she turned left and

right, desperately searching for answers.

Varek's mind raced to think of something to convince her of their life together. He softly spoke her name to get her attention. "There once was a boy you cared about who you never told your feelings to. You told me about him the first time you told me you loved me."

Callia searched his mind and found his thoughts of the first time they made love when she told him the story of Marco. She closed her eyes and allowed herself to experience all the memories he had of their life together. As she did, her fear turned to sadness, and she turned to Amon with tears in her eyes.

"What did you do to me?" she cried.

Amon said nothing, but his hands began to shake as the pain of her emotions rolled over him. Her sadness was so complete, so obvious in her eyes, that he fell to the floor, writhing in pain.

Varek stood stunned at what was happening before his eyes. He grabbed Callia and pulled her away from Amon.

"What's happening?"

"I don't know. He can't seem to stand when I'm sad," she told him through her sobbing.

Varek noticed at that moment that Amon was trying to aim the gun and lunged to take it from him. But Amon squeezed the trigger before Varek reached him.

Callia screamed. "Varek!"

The bullet whizzed past him and lodged in a wall. Before Amon could get off another shot, Varek jumped on him to pin him to the ground, but he suddenly seemed to have regained his strength and took Varek to the floor.

Amon hovered above him. "No more talking. Time for you to go."

Callia watched in terror as Amon pointed the gun at Varek's head. She couldn't let this happen!

"No! Don't!"

She ran up behind Amon and tried to push him, which gave Varek the opportunity to throw him off. The gun bounced out of his hand as it hit the floor and then skidded across the room.

Now as he hovered over Amon, Varek fought the urge to strangle him for all he'd done. But he knew he needed to get Amon to Nil and Callia back home to New Hope as quickly as possible.

Behind him, he heard Callia weeping and felt Amon's strength drain out of his arms. He dragged him to a chair and taking advantage of his weakened state, yanked a cord out of the wall and tied him before he searched his pocket for the talisman.

Wishing he could go to her and comfort her, Varek kept his hand on Amon's arm just in case he tried to teleport. If Amon thought he was going anywhere, he was going with him. But Varek noticed he seemed to once again be in tremendous pain as Callia cried nearby.

As she sat on the floor, her head in her hands, Callia asked Amon the questions Varek knew would haunt him during his time in Nil.

"How could you do this to me?"

The question hung in the air unanswered. Desperate to understand, she asked again and then asked the question whose answer she feared most.

"Was none of it real?"

Callia felt utter sadness as she thought of the love she had believed they shared. With tears rolling down her cheeks, she walked over to Amon and stood staring down into his face.

Amon said nothing as her emotions sent another surge of pain through his body. He hung his head and squeezed his eyes shut as he tried to block out each question she asked.

"Did you ever care for me at all? Or was this all some kind of cruel game?"

Even through the bone-crushing pain, the question of if he'd ever loved her sent a stab of hurt to his heart. He had cared for her as much as he'd ever been able to care for another in all his lifetimes. But she'd never believe him if he told her this, so he remained with his head hung in so much pain, it took his breath away.

"I never meant anything to you." Callia waited for Amon to tell her she was wrong, that it wasn't like Varek had said, to say anything, but he sat motionless with his eyes closed and his head hung.

Varek's heart broke watching his destined one ask another man these questions. He knew he had to accept the reality Amon's actions had created for them.

Amon moved slightly, and Varek shook himself out of his thoughts. "Callia, I'm going to have to leave you for a little bit."

Still sobbing, she looked away from Amon and focused tear-filled eyes on Varek. "What do you mean you're leaving? Where are you going?"

"I have to take Amon to the Council in Nil."

Amon's head snapped up, and he began to fight against the restraints.

"No fucking way! I'm not going anywhere with you."

Varek struggled to calm Amon but seemed to be no match for the tempuster's strength. Callia knew she had to help or he'd overcome Varek and get free. She focused on his mind and found his thoughts of her. Her eyes closed, she moved from thought to thought, experiencing the feelings he had for her, the loneliness he'd lived with for lifetimes, the loss of his destined one.

"I was wrong, Amon. You did care for me. After all those years of loneliness—lifetimes—you finally thought you'd found someone to replace your destined one who refused you. Someone to fill the void left by Sevine's absence."

Callia's own sadness waned, but she took on Amon's sadness, which was even greater than hers. Her voice trembled as she expressed his thoughts, each one worse than the last.

Amon's attempts to free himself stopped as Callia's words cut at him like razors. He lifted his head, and his eyes met hers as her emotions pummeled him once again.

"Sevine left you after lifetimes as your destined one because of what you did to her, Amon. You broke her heart too."

Callia stepped closer to him, and when she began to speak, her voice was filled with so much grief, Amon thought he would die.

"She loved you as I did, but you betrayed both of us, used both of us, manipulated us."

As she spoke, tears ran down her face from the thoughts she found in his mind. He would be tortured for the rest of his lifetimes, no matter where they would be spent.

"Callia, I have to go. As soon as I get back, I'll take you home. Keep the gun with you in case anyone comes, and wait for me."

Varek waited for her to respond and then used the talisman to take Amon to Nil. Callia watched in sadness as he left and fell into a crumpled heap on the leather couch.

Her brain attempted to process everything that had happened. She'd been happily in love with Varek, and Amon had manipulated time to be with her. She knew from reading his thoughts that he'd been drawn to her because she reminded him of his destined one who had forced him to release her from a life with him. And now he was gone to Nil.

But Callia wondered about what would happen to Varek and her. He was a convicted murderer. Had she been able to accept his past before, or had she struggled with it?

She thought about all the times she'd asked her grandmother about Aeveren biology and who her destined one would be, and how her grandmother had always told her that their biology doesn't make mistakes. Varek had been sent to her to care for her as destined ones were. She knew very little about him, but he had been kind and understanding when she had told him about Amon. Maybe Aeveren biology didn't make mistakes.

Callia walked around the place she'd called home for months. It felt empty now, like a movie set discarded after filming has wrapped. None of it—not the life with Amon— had been real. But her feelings for him had been. She'd loved him, and she knew, even though he'd refused to answer her questions, that he'd loved her too.

Sometimes love isn't enough.

SECONDS AFTER LEAVING AMON'S VILLA in the Italian countryside, the two men appeared in the Council chambers in Nil. Varek had hoped the Council had understood his thoughts when he'd let them know he was arriving with Amon. As he adjusted to the new surroundings, he remembered to keep his hold on Amon and grabbed his shoulders tightly. The effort was unnecessary, as Varek realized when he looked down at Amon's hands secured by shackles at the wrists. His eyes dropped lower and saw the familiar leg irons. Amon was now a prisoner in Nil.

Quickly, Varek examined his own arms and legs. No restraints held him. He lifted his head and saw the chamber filled to capacity with some even standing around the edges of the room. His gaze traveled over the faces of the people looking down at Amon and him. Some looked surprised, their eyes wide in disbelief, while others looked pleased at the presence of one of their race's most powerful captured and standing in front of them.

Amon stood, stunned to be where he was, unable to understand that he was under the Council's control. As his mind attempted to sort out the details, the head of the Council leaned forward in his seat and trained his eyes on Varek.

"Mr. Leale, we meet once again, and I may say under pleasantly surprising circumstances." As the man spoke, a smile broke out across his face.

Varek said nothing, unsure of exactly how he should respond to the statement that the Council was surprised he'd succeeded in the task they had assigned him. And he knew he wasn't who they wanted to hear from anyway.

Shifting his attention to Amon, the councilman spoke again, his voice flat and deep. "Welcome to Nil, Amon Kalins."

CHAPTER TWENTY-FOUR

A MON THRASHED AROUND LIKE WILD animal trapped in a cage against the restraints that had instantly appeared on his body when he arrived with Varek in the Council's chambers in Nil. Varek watched him struggle against leg irons and shackles that held him fast to the spot on which he stood. He sounded like a wounded creature whose mind frantically searched for a way out of a desperate situation. A tiny lick of pity touched Varek's heart, but he pushed it away, reminding himself of the harm Amon had caused Callia and him.

Whatever he gets, he deserves.

Varek looked from the desperate scene with Amon to the Council, which sat transfixed on the tempuster's every move. Behind the Council members stood the sorcerers, ready to impose additional magickal punishments on Nil's newest prisoner at a moment's notice.

"I'd like to go. I want to get back to Callia," Varek said to the Council in general.

Only Amon seemed to hear him. He turned to look at Varek and his eyes flashed a rage that made Varek thankful

Amon was restrained. The Council seemed oblivious to his request, so Varek repeated it.

"Mr. Leale, you'll go when we allow it. For now, you'll stay." The tone of the head councilman's voice made Varek think that any more requests would be met with leg irons and shackles of his own.

The head of the Council spoke, this time to Amon, his voice bellowing and triumphant like an emperor addressing a vanquished foe. "This has been a long time coming, Mr. Kalins."

Amon looked up at the man taunting him and hissed in anger. The relaxed, confident man who had infuriated Varek was gone, and in his place was an emotional being on the verge of spinning out of control.

"Fuck you! You won't keep me here!"

"Silence, or I'll have one of these men behind me make you silent."

"Fuck you!"

With a wave of his hand, the head of the Council instructed the sorcerer to the left of him to perform the required task and the man began chanting something in a deep voice.

"Now, Mr. Kalins, we will continue."

Amon opened his mouth to speak, but only strangled noises came out. The Council had complete control over one of the most powerful members of their race. Now he would be powerless, as so many others had been to him.

But forty-seven lifetimes of control wouldn't be erased

with the wave of a hand, and Amon struggled even more now, his chains making a haunting clanging sound as he flailed his arms in an attempt to at least free his hands.

"Remain still or I will make sure you're completely immobilized."

Varek watched Amon struggle for a few seconds more and then stop, his face and body showing only frustration. Varek saw the satisfaction on the councilman's face when Amon looked up at him and knew that he was enjoying his weakness.

"Mr. Kalins, you are in Nil because of your actions. Unlike others who have appeared before us, you have committed several offenses that you must answer for. If we can be assured you would respect these proceedings, we will allow you to answer the charges of this Council."

Amon made no movement but then ever so slightly dropped his head and slowly lifted it again, a sign of his acquiescence. Another easy wave of the head councilman's hand set the sorcerer's mouth in motion once again and moments later, the spell was revoked. Varek waited for the stream of anger to begin flowing from Amon's mouth, but there was nothing. Amon stood silently, his eyes alone expressing his contempt for the assembly in front of him.

He stood straight, his head lowered to avoid looking up at the Council that would stand in judgment of him. His wrists shackled, his shoulders remained back, a sign that, like many who had stood there before him, he wasn't broken yet.

"We will begin then, Mr. Kalins. We will move from the past to the present addressing your crimes in the order they occurred, not as to their severity. Do you have anything you'd like to say before we begin?"

Silent, Amon's expression remained unchanged, except for an almost imperceptible arch of one eyebrow. His body remained still, as if to show the men and women seated above him that they had no effect on him.

"Then we'll begin."

The Council began with the seemingly minor crime of his reversing time as a teenage boy in his first life to escape punishment for not working when he'd been ordered to. Amon looked amused as the details were read aloud, as if he was enjoying this walk through his early history.

As the next of his crimes were reported, he continued to smile. When the head councilman's adjutant was finished, Amon raised his eyes to the Council above.

"Is this to be my punishment—forced to listen to ridiculous exaggerations of the harmless pranks of a youth?"

"Patience, Mr. Kalins."

Minor behaviors continued to be discussed in grave tones, giving the proceeding a comical tone. But as the description of the crimes of his tenth lifetime were reported, the tone abruptly seemed far more appropriate to the subject.

"Do you remember the circumstances described, Mr. Kalins?"

Varek watched as Amon's petulance evaporated, replaced by what seemed like pain. His back bent slightly, and he grimaced as the Council stared down at him.

"I do."

"Then in your own words, please tell this Council of the events leading to the first murder of an Aeveren by your hands."

Amon's face stilled and the painful grimace ebbed away. As he began to speak, his voice wavered slightly. Varek stood riveted at the sight of Amon explaining why he'd killed a fellow Aeveren to keep his abilities a secret from others. The murder was premeditated and cold-hearted, with Amon stabbing his childhood friend of his tenth lifetime as the young man begged to be spared and repeatedly professed his love and friendship for him.

When Amon finished, a councilman asked him, "Did you feel any remorse for this heinous crime, Mr. Kalins?"

Amon stared straight ahead and said nothing. He knew what they wanted to hear. They wanted to hear him say he was sorry, that he wished it hadn't happened, that he didn't know what he was doing.

But none of that would be true. He wasn't sorry. He had no feelings about it whatsoever. And he'd known exactly what he was doing.

He knew his silence would hurt him, but he had no intention of apologizing for doing what he needed to do to survive.

The Council interpreted his unwillingness to speak for exactly what it was and continued on to his next crime. As each manipulation and crime at his hands was detailed, Varek listened in rapt attention, realizing he had vastly underestimated Amon Kalins. His thoughts turned to Callia, and he thanked God Amon had cared for her, considering the catalogue of atrocities he stood listening to now.

"Mr. Kalins, we now turn to the death of a loved one of your third destined one."

Amon felt sick as the words were spoken. He'd known this crime would be examined more in depth because it had caused him to lose his destined one, and he'd dreaded it. Memories of Sevine flooded his brain and for the first time in his inquisition, Amon felt guilty. His responsibility for the death of her friend had haunted him since the moment he'd realized it was the one thing for which she couldn't forgive him.

As the details of the man's death were relayed, Amon stood passively, his eyes closed, listening to the events that had resulted in his lifetimes alone. Unlike with so many of the descriptions of his crimes, he was unable to coolly refuse to accept blame now.

"And why did you do what you did that caused this human's death?"

In a voice that betrayed the emotions he felt three lifetimes later, he explained. "I thought he was going to take Sev...Frederika from me." For one of the few times during his hearing, Amon's words sounded full of regret.

Varek listened to him speak about losing the woman he loved to another and found himself thinking of his own crime that had sent him to Nil. He was surprised to admit that he understood Amon's jealousies and insecurities.

The chamber fell silent at Amon's humble admission. The Council members seemed to understand his behavior as one instance when the results of his actions truly affected him. He had already paid for this crime with the loss of his destined one and lifetimes of solitude.

Amon stood with his shoulders dropped, exhausted after the discussion of this crime. But at least from this point on, he knew there would only be two more major offenses he'd have to answer for: his association with the Soren and his crime against Callia and Varek.

As he thought about this, he turned to see Varek still standing at his side. He'd have to admit his crime toward him and Callia in front of him.

That's why they kept him here. Judge and jury for my last crime. Maybe if the Council is lucky, they'll get to see Varek beat the hell out of me.

Amon readied himself for what was to come. He would easily get through the interrogation about the Soren since he'd only dealt with them through intermediaries. And then the issue of Callia would have to be explained. Amon's stomach tightened at the thought of her still back in his villa, her heart full of sadness and hatred for him.

Looking up toward the Council, Varek saw on their faces that some of their bloodlust against Amon had been satisfied. They'd successfully humbled him into what every other person who'd stood in his place had been—a criminal worthy of their sentence to Nil. He waited and watched the scene around him, almost afraid of the next crime to be introduced.

The head of the Council called a brief recess, and after the members filed out, Varek was left only with Amon and the guards that stood behind them. More than anything, he wanted to be with Callia. He didn't care what they did to Amon now. This interrogation had shown him that he was much worse than anything he'd conjured up in his mind about him. He didn't need to hear the details of what he'd done to him or Callia. He just hoped he could repair the damage and get back to the life he'd had before Amon Kalins.

For Amon, it didn't matter what they brought up next. Nothing would ever be as bad as what he'd done to lose Sevine. The anguish he'd spent lifetimes denying, burying his guilt deep inside him, was all over him now. He deserved to be in Nil.

When the Council reconvened, he stood knowing that the end was near.

"Mr. Kalins, your part in the rebel group the Soren is another problem."

Amon didn't know if he had anything left in him, but he decided he would defend himself against this one charge. "I have had very few dealings with the Soren and on all occasions, I've only dealt with one man."

"What can you tell us about the group?"

"Very little. I know they want domination over humans and use dark magick to get it. Other than that, I know nothing else."

"And have you participated in any of their dark magick for any reason?"

Amon knew there had to be at least one person in the chamber who could know his thoughts, so he decided not to bother lying. Anyway, nothing he'd ever done with magick was even remotely dark.

"No. My interest in magick has always been of the light kind."

"You said you have only dealt with one person from this group. What is his name?"

Now Amon would get to repay Markku for his treachery. "Markku Dunning."

"And what was your relationship with Mr. Dunning?"

"He performed magick for me."

"Such as? Can you give us examples?"

"Markku is particularly adept at binding spells." Amon knew the Council would frown upon his use of binding spells, but at least they weren't technically dark magick.

"And when was your most recent association with Mr. Dunning?"

Amon turned to look at Varek and saw his face grow stern at the thought that he'd used a spell on Callia and him. Turning back to the Council, he said sheepishly, "I had Markku bind Varek so he wouldn't be able to travel through time, no matter what help you gave him."

The head of the Council spoke up and asked the question that was on Varek's mind too. "Then how did Mr. Leale apprehend you?"

"I don't know, but I can guess. Varek appeared right after an argument I had with Markku when I threatened his life. I assume he revoked the binding spell to retaliate against me."

The head councilman grinned and in a low voice

remarked, "There is no honor among thieves."

Amon knew Varek was angry, but worse was yet to come. Now he'd have to answer for his crimes against Callia. The examination about his relationship with Markku and the Soren had been just a brief respite.

"Mr. Kalins. Now we come to what you've done to Mr. Leale and his destined one."

Amon braced himself for this final interrogation.

"This is not the first time you've disregarded Aeveren biology because you wanted another man's destined one, is it?"

Victoria.

Amon had been so busy reliving the pain of losing Sevine that he had forgotten what he'd done to Victoria Adams and her family.

"No."

"And what happened when you chose to take Mrs. Adams from her husband and child, Mr. Kalins?"

Amon closed his eyes as the memory of Victoria Adams replayed in his mind. She'd loved him and in some ways, he'd loved her, but she was a victim of his manipulation as much as Callia.

"I wanted Victoria for my own. She was married to her destined one, but left him for me."

"Tell this Council what happened when she left her destined one for you."

Amon cringed as he began to answer. "I left her a short time after."

"And what happened to Mrs. Adams?"

As Amon stood not knowing the answer, the councilman said, "Perhaps you don't know, Mr. Kalins. Victoria Adams committed suicide after you left her alone without a thought of her welfare and without her husband or child."

His eyes closed again, and Amon felt a sense of regret that filled him with sorrow. Victoria's death was as much his fault as any other he was guilty of, even more so despite being at her hand.

The councilman turned his attention to Varek. "Mr. Leale, this Council would like to hear your impressions of Mr. Kalins's behavior toward you and your destined one."

Varek turned toward Amon and wondered which of the thousands of things he'd wanted to say to him should be first. Nothing he could say would make his sentence any worse. Varek knew Amon was going to be in Nil for a long time for all that he'd done. But he hesitated, and the head of the Council addressed him.

"Mr. Leale, that was not a request."

After a deep breath, Varek began. "Amon wanted Callia from the moment he met her. I believe he planned his manipulation of her from the very beginning. He saw me as disposable, an obstacle easily removed through the use of his powers."

Varek knew they may have wanted more, and he could have said more, but what Amon had done made him feel foolish and powerless. The truth was the deck was always stacked in Amon's favor and there was nothing he could do about that. But, damnit, he hated the feeling of weakness it caused in him.

"Mr. Leale, how is your destined one?"

This Varek would say more about. The sight of Callia despondent over what Amon had done to her had filled him with rage, and he wanted Amon to pay for what he'd done to her.

"Callia is devastated. While it hurts me to admit this, she loved him. She entered into her relationship with him honestly and continued to want to be honest with him when she realized I was her destined one. Now she realizes she was just a pawn to him."

Varek couldn't look at the man next to him without wanting to attack him, but he'd have to content himself with the fact that his future would be in Nil, and Varek knew all too well what that would be like.

"Mr. Leale, this Council sincerely hopes your relationship with your destined one can be repaired. We owe you a debt of gratitude for your help in bringing Mr. Kalins to justice. For this, your sentence is commuted. We also want to inform you that according to Aeveren law, we do this only with the agreement of your first destined one. As the victim of your crime, her approval was necessary for any of this to occur. As she can forgive, this Council feels justified in allowing your release. Return to your current destined one knowing your future is once again yours."

Varek's heart leapt in joy, but the reality that Callia was still in Italy months earlier stopped his celebration.

"Callia's still in the past. How do I get her back to the

present?"

"The talisman we gave you will work one last time to return to any point in the past and then back to the present."

Varek smiled and expressed his deep thanks, but he stopped suddenly when he realized they had offered him a chance to go back to any time in the past. Memories of Christina flashed through his mind. Maybe he could change what happened.

"Mr. Leale, you may leave."

Maybe they'd give him two chances to go back in time. He had to ask.

"Is there any way the talisman can be used twice?"

"No, Mr. Leale. We each have choices to make in our lives. This is one you must make."

Varek's stomach dropped. He couldn't leave Callia alone in Italy. But what about Christina? The choice was heartbreaking. Wherever Christina was, he prayed that she was loved and cared for. Promising himself he'd find his little girl, he set his mind on where and when Callia was and disappeared from the Council chambers in Nil.

Amon stood alone, looking up at the Council and steeled himself for his sentence. Varek's words reverberated in his head and for the first time he understood he wasn't leaving Nil any time soon. Now it was just a matter of for how long.

"Mr. Kalins, it is the judgment of this Council that you will spend the remainder of your lives serving out your sentence in Nil. At the end of your fiftieth lifetime, you will be permitted to move on to the resolution of your time on Earth."

Amon stood silently, unable to grasp the enormity of his sentence. As the room emptied, guards took possession of him and led one of the most powerful Aeveren to his home for the rest of his existence.

VAREK FOUND CALLIA SLEEPING ON Amon's couch, her hands tucked up under her head and her legs drawn up toward her chest. He stood watching her sleep and wished when she woke up that everything would be back to the way it was. Gently, he nudged her shoulder to wake her, and she opened her eyes to look at him.

"Varek?"

"I'm back, honey. Everything's going to be okay."

"And Amon?"

Varek wondered how much he should tell her and decided less was better.

"Nil."

As she sat up, Varek extended his hand, and Callia put her arms around him. As she let her body mold to his, she whispered the question she feared the answer to most. "What about you?"

"I'm free," he said as he wrapped his arms around her. "My future—our future—is our own."

Callia backed away from him and looked up into his eyes. "Our future" sounded wonderful, but as she looked at him with his deep black eyes, thick black hair, and beautiful mouth, she was unsure of everything but how much she was attracted to him.

Varek bent his head down and kissed her as if it had been years since he'd tasted her lips. His tongue eagerly explored her mouth, and when she reciprocated passionately, he pulled her to him so their bodies touched from head to foot.

She felt so incredible pressed up against him that all the uncertainty about their future slowly began to fade away.

"Callia, I know you don't remember us, but I love you with all my heart. I told you the day I lost you, I need you. I don't want a life without you."

He cradled her face in his hands and hoped she'd someday be as in love with him as he was with her.

Callia smiled. "What did I say to you when you said that to me?"

"You told me there was no life for you without me and that you loved me."

Unsure of what to say but sure he was the man she was meant to be with, she answered softly, "Let's go home, Varek."

Varek took her in his arms and smiled. "First thing we have to do is take you to see Tia. I promised her I'd bring you home."

"You know Tia?" Callia asked, surprised to hear the little girl's name.

Maybe Aeveren biology might have gotten things right after all.

CHAPTER TWENTY-FIVE

ROOM 14 AT THE NEW Hope Inn looked just like Varek remembered. The same drab interior. The same makeshift kitchen area. The same full-size bed. As he settled down on the lumpy mattress, he thought about how wonderful it had felt that first night away from Nil. Now it just felt like a shitty bed in a cheap motel.

He missed his bed at Callia's.

Varek pressed his thumb on the remote and a white dot appeared in the center of the television and slowly spread across the screen. As it warmed up, Varek tried to get comfortable for the night. Shirtless and barefoot, he still wore jeans and he unbuttoned them. As *CSI Miami* came into focus, he closed his eyes.

Nights in Room 14 were still difficult, but he knew he had to give Callia time. He remembered what they'd been, but it was all new to her. He just had to be patient, he kept reminding himself. She hadn't asked him to move out of her house, and there was nothing he wanted to do less in this world, but Varek knew she had to come around on her own.

They saw each other every day, and each time he felt her heart open up more to him. It was odd to be in the demoted position of new boyfriend after what he'd been before everything happened, though.

After an hour daydreaming about Callia, Varek watched the credits of *CSI* scroll and fell into a light sleep. The next thing he heard was a soft knock at the door, and he rolled out of bed, groggy and disoriented. As he made his way to the door, he ran his hand through his hair and sleepily made a mental note that he should get a haircut as the hair fell back down onto his face.

He opened the door and was shocked to see Callia standing there. Even through sleep-filled eyes, she looked beautiful in a pink sweater and jeans.

"Hi. Can I come in?" she asked.

Varek nodded and stepped aside as she walked into his room. Callia stood in the middle of the room looking around as if she was inspecting where he spent his time away from her. Suppressing the urge to put his arms around her waist and draw her to him, he offered her a seat at the table and stood next to the wall.

Callia watched Varek as he stood in front of her. She had never seen him without a shirt and saw now that, other than the marks from his time in Nil, his torso was perfect. Her eyes drifted over his broad chest and chiseled abs until they reached the top of his pants that flapped open at the button. The blood rushed to her cheeks and her face became hot.

Varek saw her gaze rest on his waist and quickly

remembered that his jeans were opened. He fumbled to button them.

"Is everything okay, Callia?" he asked nervously as he maneuvered his hands to cover what she'd been looking at.

Callia wished he hadn't adjusted his jeans. She liked the idea that he saw her as a sexual creature. Since they'd gotten back, he'd been wonderful to her but hadn't shown any interest in moving toward being really together. She was his destined one, and she hoped he would begin to see her like that, but so far nothing. She had made her mind up to go to his room at the Town Inn to show him that she was ready to be truly his, and as she sat looking at his striking body, she congratulated herself for being so lucky to be given such a gorgeous man for her destined one.

"Everything's fine. I just wanted to see you...see where you stay."

She felt the heat rush to her face again as her eyes met his. He looked into hers with eyes that seemed oddly menacing among his appealing features.

Varek was relieved to hear her say she was okay. Since everything with Amon, he worried that at any time he could lose her. He knew this was irrational and hated himself every time the thought crossed his mind, but it was there, nonetheless.

But if she was fine, why was she in his room now?

He silently scolded himself for having no food or anything to drink to offer her, but Room 14 at the Town Inn wasn't a home. It was a place to stay until his life came back to him.

Not knowing what to say, he sat down on the side of the bed facing the table and waited for her to speak.

Callia sensed the awkwardness in the room and wondered if she'd made a mistake coming to see him. Maybe he didn't want her that way. Maybe everything that had happened with Amon was too much for him to forget. But now that she was there, she took a deep breath and forged ahead with her plan to seduce him. She silenced the worries bouncing through her mind fretfully and listened for what he was thinking. She knew she shouldn't, but anything that could help her understand him was welcome. She hadn't had any success using her new ability with him since returning from Italy, however. Unlike Amon, Varek was now impossible to read, it seemed.

After an uncomfortable silence and no clear indication of what he was thinking, Callia steeled herself and stood up.

"This is nice here. Do you like it?"

As she spoke, she slowly moved over to in front of where he sat, just inches away from his legs. Looking down at him, she gently touched his hair and ran her forefinger along the strands that hung on the side of his face.

Varek heard her ask him something but was unable to remember seconds later what she'd said as she touched him. He hoped to God she hadn't asked anything important, but this quickly receded as he struggled to manage the emotion she was bringing out in him now. She was so close.

Callia watched what seemed like pain cross his face, and her heart felt like a fist had tightened around it. He didn't want her. He couldn't forgive or forget what had happened.

She slowly dropped to her knees in front of him and looked up into his face. Her seduction plan in ruins, she knew she had to try to reach his heart.

"Varek, I'm so sorry. I spoke to my Aunt Jean today. She told me everything—how heartbroken you were when you visited her, how you promised to bring me back. I didn't know. She helped me see what I think I've known since we got back. I love you. Please, do you think we can ever be what we were?"

Varek listened as she spoke the words he'd waited for, prayed for since he'd found her in that Italian village. She stared up at him, her eyes wide with hope that her words were touching him, and suddenly it was too much for him. Filled with the kind of happiness he'd only felt when Neera had agreed to marry him and when his daughter was born, he closed his eyes.

As she waited silently for him to respond to her plea, sadness washed over her. He wouldn't even look at her!

She rose and quickly moved toward the door, anxious to escape the rejection she had so desperately feared would greet her. She couldn't blame him, but it still broke her heart to know she'd finally been blessed with a destined one and now she'd lost him.

Varek's eyes flew open when he heard her go to leave. He lunged off the bed to grab her arm. He couldn't let her go! Why was she leaving?

"Callia! Don't leave!"

One stride brought him to her, and he turned her toward

him. Her face was wet with tears.

"I understand, Varek. It's just too much to forgive," she said sadly.

Brushing a tear from her cheek, he shook his head. "There's nothing to forgive. You didn't do anything wrong. Someone did something to us, and we'll have to get past it. Together."

Callia's tear-filled eyes grew bigger, and she threw her arms around him. As she held him tightly, her head resting over his heart, the sadness and fear flowed out in her tears.

He reveled in the feel of her pressed against him. Stroking her long brown hair, he closed his eyes again and let every thought but how much he loved her leave his mind. Slowly, he become aware that she was quietly crying and felt her tears wet his skin. Tenderly, he pushed her from him and looked down into her beautiful, tear-stained face.

"Don't cry. No more crying."

Callia nodded while he wiped the tears from under her eyes with his knuckle.

"The past doesn't matter now. This is a fresh start for us."

"Okay." Callia hesitated but then continued with the question she'd wanted to ask since they'd returned to New Hope. "What were we like before? Was it love at first sight?"

Varek grinned and laughed. "Not exactly."

A look of confusion came across her face. She couldn't imagine not falling head over heels for him.

"I was the problem, Callia. I didn't know if I could handle another try at a destined one after almost three lifetimes in Nil.

But it didn't take long for me to realize I was crazy in love with you, especially after seeing you date other men."

"Why did I do that? That's awful!"

"No, you had every right to see other men since I'd told you I wasn't what you wanted. That's on me. And it showed me how much I loved you."

Callia looked at the man standing in front of her—her destined one. Was it possible she had been fortunate enough to get a man who was caring, understanding, strong, and unbelievably sexy? Concerning his sexiness, she had no doubt. The proof was right in front of her in his stunning face and beautiful body—his beautiful, half-naked body.

"How did I get so lucky to get such an understanding man?"

Varek threw his head back and laughed.

"What's so funny?"

"Do you want to know what you used to call me? Cro-Magnon."

Callia looked at the smile on his face and couldn't imagine why she'd ever refer to him as a caveman.

"Why?"

A glint appeared in Varek's eyes, and his expression changed from lighthearted to dark and sexy. He pulled her to him, his strong hand on her lower back, and bent his head to hers, positioning his mouth close to hers. A rush of heat flooded her body, and she began to breathe raggedly as this entirely different Varek looked into her eyes.

His eyes stared deeply into hers, and he groaned low and

deep as his right hand lightly tugged her head back.

It seemed like an eternity passed as she waited in anticipation for him to kiss her. His lips were so close and the gentle pull of his hand in her hair sent waves of sensations down her neck. When he finally pressed his lips to hers, his kiss was powerful and demanding.

Varek didn't want to hold back anymore. Weeks of waiting for her had created a need desperate in him that demanded to be filled. He eagerly let his tongue explore her mouth, mingling with her tongue and playfully flicking at its tip.

He wanted to possess her, make her his and his alone. Each time he tugged her hair, she moaned, exciting him more. His mouth left hers and moved to her ear to nip it with his teeth.

Callia felt excited by his power and knew she must have loved him when he took control before. He was exactly what she wanted, a commanding lover to satisfy her every need.

He slid his hands under her sweater and peeled it off her body. He made quick work of her bra, and in seconds his mouth began its sensuous pull on a nipple. His jet black hair hung down, covering much of his face, so all she could see when she looked down to watch was his mouth on her skin and his hand cupping under her breast.

Her skin felt so good as his tongue traveled from one breast to the other. He nibbled tenderly, bringing the nipple to a sharp peak he flicked with his tongue. She pulled his hair off his face and then gave it a not-so-gentle tug to get his attention. A moan escaped from him, and he looked up at her to see her eyes closed, her expression one of desire.

Varek knew what she wanted, even if she didn't remember exactly why. He slid his hands to her jeans and pulled them down quickly, wanting the taste of what they concealed on his tongue. His mouth found what it desired through her damp panties, and seconds later, his eyes found her in full view after he tore the fabric from her body.

He looked up and saw a mixture of fear and excitement. Varek licked his lips and opened her up to him with his thumbs. He felt her shudder at the touch of his fingers on her sex, and he moaned as his mouth met her skin.

She stood on unsteady legs as he brought her to the edge and then pulled back over and over. Her hands pushed on the back of his head, wanting more, but he was stronger and controlled the sensations that came so close to release.

"Please…Varek…please…" she moaned, her voice trailing off.

There was no sound like a woman you love begging you to make her come, but Varek waited a few moments before returning for the final delicious assault that would send her crashing over the edge. When he felt her close to her climax, he pushed two fingers into her and she shattered into a million pieces, her legs unable to hold her weight anymore.

Varek caught her as her legs buckled and swept her up in his arms. He laid her gently on the bed and bent over her to sweetly kiss her but was pleasantly surprised when she tugged at the button on his jeans and began pulling his pants off him.

"I thought you liked me in control," he said in a lazy drawl as he slid out of his pants.

Almost panting, Callia looked at him through half-closed eyes. "I do, but I need you. Now." As she spoke, her hand wrapped around his stiff cock and stroked.

The effect of her hand on his excited skin was exquisite, and as Varek let her caress him, his head fell back on his shoulders in ecstasy. But this wasn't how he wanted to come. Not the first time with her.

Varek positioned himself above her and kissed her deeply. Then he entered her for the first time again, thrusting slowly at first but then faster as she writhed under him, guiding him into her with her hands pushing on his buttocks. Her short nails ran up and down his back, exciting him even more, and glided softly over his hips where his brands were.

Callia wrapped her arms tightly around him and came, her body milking his cock to climax. As they lay in each other's arms, exhausted, Varek told her again that there was no life for him without her. But she sensed a sadness in his voice.

"What's wrong?"

He kissed the top of her head and squeezed him to her. Nothing was wrong with them now, but there was still something he needed to do.

"I promised myself I'd find my daughter, but so far, I haven't found out anything."

The sound of his voice broke her heart. She wanted to take it away and bring him the happiness that he brought her.

Stroking his cheek, she said in a quiet voice, "Don't worry.

We'll find her."

Varek smiled at the pronoun she used. We. We'll find her. His Callia was back.

THE NEXT DAY HE MOVED back into Callia's house, but with one significant difference. He wasn't going to be in the spare bedroom anymore. As he moved his belongings back home, Callia left to run an errand, kissing him on the tip of his nose as she stood on her toes and told him she loved him.

A few hours later, she returned, looking like she held the world's biggest secret. Varek had made dinner and was sitting on the couch as the meal cooked.

"Varek, I went to see my great-aunt today."

"That's good. Am I still a cutie to her?" he joked.

"We need to talk." Her tone was serious and instantly made him anxious.

He sat up straight and felt his stomach drop. Ancient Aeveren, in his experience, rarely added anything to his life other than calamity.

"Callia, what's wrong?"

"I hope you don't mind, but I told my Aunt Jean about Christina in the hopes that she could help us find her. She knows a lot of very important people in our world."

Varek braced himself for bad news. Something had happened to his baby girl after he was sent to Nil. He sat waiting for Callia to continue, his stomach in knots from guilt.

"Varek, she found her! She found Christina! She's right

here in New Hope!"

The sound of her voice sounded less ominous than before, so Varek took a chance and asked the only question he needed an answer for.

"Is she okay?"

Callia smiled and took his hand in hers.

"Varek, it's Tia."

EPILOGUE

Three months later...

ALLIA AND VAREK STOOD ON the sidewalk looking at the house for sale at 704 Sunset Street. A typical small-town home, it was just big enough for a young couple starting a family.

"Honey, are you sure about this? I don't want you to feel like we have to buy a home right now. The baby isn't due for six months."

Smiling, Varek patted Callia's tiny baby bump. "Callia, we'll need the room even more than we already do by then. I don't want to have to worry about moving when you're ready to have this baby."

"But what about the price?"

"I have a good feeling about my job at Titan. They like me because I have experience as a cop, and they're a growing security company. We can handle the mortgage."

Callia kissed him and smiled. "I guess I should have said something about this before now, but it never came up. I was left a pretty large sum of money when my parents died."

Curious, he asked, "How much?"

"Well, I haven't spoken to the accountant or lawyer recently, but the last time I did, I could buy a handful of houses just like this one. So I think we can afford the mortgage. I just want to make sure you're as happy with the house as I am."

Varek looked into his wife's beautiful eyes and smiled. "As long as we're together, I'm happy. It doesn't matter where."

"Maybe we should ask Tia then."

Callia looked around for her adopted daughter and saw her sitting in a sandbox on the side of the house.

"Tia! Come here, sweetie!"

Varek watched as her long strawberry blond hair flew behind his daughter as she ran toward them. His heart swelled as she stood in front of Callia and called her "Mommy." Three lifetimes in Nil when he was sure he'd never see the outside again, much less be reunited with his daughter or get another destined one, and now he stood looking at a house with both of them and a new baby on the way. This time was different.

"Honey, Tia and I agree. We love it. Now it's up to you."

Tia looked up at her father and gave him her biggest pretty-please eyes.

Varek looked down at his little girl's face and knew he couldn't deny her just as he couldn't deny Callia. "If this is what my girls want, then that's it. We'll buy it."

Callia kissed him and took his hand. On his other side, Tia wrapped her little hand around his forefinger and skipped along as her parents walked hand in hand toward her great-grandmother's house to tell her the good news.

THE END

Keep reading for an excerpt from Destiny Redeemed, the second half of the Destined Ones Duology.

DESTINY REDEEMED
CHAPTER ONE

T HE USUALLY QUIET MAIN STREET of Cochecton, New York hummed with the excited squeals of miniature devils, witches, and ghosts along with a variety of cartoon and movie characters. Stopping at each house with the hope for more treats than tricks, children scurried here and there as parents dutifully followed behind. The small town's downtown was lit up as bright as day, but behind a building two streets over, there were no costumed children or candy but a scheduled meeting of people who had finally ended their wait. It would happen tonight.

A solitary man walked nervously through the hoard of masked children and doting parents, looking for the first opportunity to move into the shadows. To be caught now would mean not only Nil for him but the end of him afterward. They'd never let him live another life if he failed this night.

A quick left off Main Street into the natural darkness of night forced him to adjust his eyes and for a moment he ceased his hasty march to his destination. His vision focused, he began his journey again, careful as always to make sure no one was following him. He listened for footsteps, the crackling sound of a shoe crushing the swirling dried leaves he'd just passed, but heard nothing. He was alone in the dark alley.

Up ahead he saw the flicker of lights and checked his watch. 7:56. The crisp October breeze hit him and forced him to stuff his hands into his pockets as he walked, and he picked up his pace.

What a difference a year makes, he thought to himself. One year earlier, he'd celebrated Samhain with a few dark Sidhe who had deliciously reinforced his love of their kind and brought in the New Year believing things were going to get better for him. How wrong he'd been! Not two weeks later one foolish mistake—of the many he'd made in his lifetimes—had brought the wrath of the Council into his life and made him enough enemies in the circles he traveled in to make him persona non grata in many of his favorite places. It certainly had been one hell of a year.

That would all change tonight. Tonight, he'd perform the most important magick of all his lifetimes. And when he succeeded, he'd get his life back. No more being shunned. No more being without the protection of the Soren. No more living in constant fear of the Council. Tonight would be the beginning of better times for him.

The meeting place was an old abandoned tailor shop accessed only by the alley he was now on. He hadn't chosen it and had no idea what to expect. He'd simply been given orders to be there at eight o'clock with the implied threat in the man's voice that if he didn't, he'd never find acceptance in the Soren again. Since he'd prayed for any chance to fix what he'd done, no threat was necessary. He would've moved heaven and Earth to get back what he'd had before. Instead he'd move Nil.

As he walked down the side of the building, he looked up to see the quarter moon above peaking through ominous dark clouds and then glanced down at his watch. 7:59.

Showtime.

He turned right around the corner of the building and saw just one person.

Was he early?

"Where's everyone else?"

The man he spoke to stood stiffly, looking back at him as sternly as he always had. Dressed in all black underneath a black overcoat, only his deep green eyes disrupted his funereal appearance.

"There is no one else. It's just us."

"Why? Has everything been called off?" he asked, his voice verging on frantic at the thought that his one chance at salvation had been ripped away at the last moment. Before the other man could answer, he continued, his hands punctuating his words.

"What happened? Why would they do this to us?"

"Markku," Gethen said icily, "nothing has happened. There was no need for more people to be involved, so I told them so. The plan remains the same."

"No need for more people? We're breaking the big man

out of Nil, and you don't think we need anyone else? Have you lost your fucking mind, old man?"

GETHEN WATCHED AS MARKKU PACED back and forth past him in the small area they stood in, his progression halted by walls of discarded pallets on three sides of them. As was often the case when he was around the excitable Markku, Gethen felt heartburn stab at him just below his sternum. He was sure the man was something far more than just a magickian by the way he made both him and his master feel ill whenever he was around.

Sure he needed Markku to calm down, if not to help his heartburn then to complete the Herculean task they had ahead of them, Gethen put his arm out on one of Markku's passes by him and stopped him.

"Enough. We need to get going. Collect yourself now because if this doesn't work because you couldn't focus…"

Markku didn't let him finish the statement. Gethen knew no matter how much he found him irritating, the magickian understood how much was riding on what he did or didn't do tonight.

Putting his hand up to stop him, Markku interrupted. "Yeah, yeah. I know."

Gethen watched the man shake out his arms and then his legs as if he were getting ready to perform some feat of physical strength. Already disgusted in the short time he'd spent with him, he leveled his gaze on him as he gyrated like a man having a seizure and in a voice that he hoped signaled his irritation asked, "Are you done? May we leave now?"

"No problem, Gethen. Lead the way. Home, James."

Not appreciating his allusion to him being a chauffer, Gethen squinted his eyes into angry slits and mumbled, "Just follow me and get ready."

Gethen led Markku to a clearing on the mountaintop outside of town. As he stood waiting for the man, the chill of the wind cut at him, intensifying the feeling of dread that had resided in him for almost a year.

For every day his master had been imprisoned in Nil, he'd worked to find a way to bring him back. Each day the foreboding feeling that told him that Amon was suffering grew worse and ate at him, magnified by his failure to solve the puzzle of how to free him from his hell. But now, finally, he'd do what he must to return him to his life.

Markku set out his supplies and looked up at Gethen, who watched him closely. "I don't understand what you need me for if you can travel between worlds."

"Only I can travel between them. Amon is Aeveren, so he's why you're here. The spell is to protect him, not me."

Nervously, Markku fingered his knife. "What do you mean?"

Gethen glared down at him angrily. "What I mean is that you need to protect him or he could be harmed and then I may never get him out. So get moving and finish whatever you have to do to ensure he won't be injured when I bring him back."

Markku began to chant and the wind grew stronger,

whipping over them. Gethen prepared himself for the journey to Nil, focusing on his master's soul for direction. He'd never been to Nil before, but he knew all he had to do was find Amon and take him out of there.

Looking up at Gethen, Markku nodded. "It's finished. He should be safe to bring back."

He better be.

Closing his eyes, Gethen became mist and the wind took him away as Markku looked on in stunned silence. Moments later, he rematerialized in Amon's cell and as his eyes refocused, he saw the horror he'd feared all those months.

Falling to his knees, he knelt next to his master and watched in fear and sadness for a sign of his breathing to ensure he was still alive. He wanted to reach out to touch him, to give any comfort to the one he loyally served, but hesitated out of fear of causing him further pain, his hand frozen in midair over a bruised and broken Amon.

His eyes catalogued the pain Amon had suffered in his time in Nil, from the scarred wounds on his back, to the cuts and bruises on his face, chest, and arms. In sadness, Gethen realized he barely recognized the soul that sat slumped over on the floor next to him, a man he'd known and served for lifetimes.

Swallowing hard, he pushed his emotions down to deal with the task at hand. He leaned in close to Amon's ear and whispered quietly, "Master?"

TINY TRAILS OF MOISTURE TRICKLED down the wall to the grey cement floor. The prisoner in cell 801 felt one touch his shoulder as it was stopped on its journey, and he shivered at the feel of it as it touched his tender skin. The dampness of his cell, the chill, reflected what the place had done to him. Underground, in the bowels of the Earth, he did little more than exist in this place, like a creature unwelcome in the light of the sun and home only in the cold darkness of Nil. Beneath him, the cold floor made the painful areas on his legs ache, and a dull throbbing throughout his body reminded him of the countless punishments in his time there.

The nighttime noises of Nil stabbed at him, and as they had every night for the past year, they become the terrifying soundtrack to the worst part of Amon's time in Nil. The screams of the weak reverberated through his body, a reminder of the horrors he'd endured on so many nights there. Not that he needed to be reminded. The pain that ran over every square inch of his skin, tactile terrors chasing after one another in a constant game of sadistic tag, never let him forget what he'd suffered through and what lie ahead in his future.

His mind drifted back to the night just after he'd arrived when the guards not only looked the other way to allow the other inmates to perform their initiation ritual on him but also told them who he'd been before being sent to Nil, as if they'd needed any encouragement for their bloodlust. Nothing in forty-seven lifetimes had been as terrifying as the hungry look in the eyes of the men who pushed him down face first on the cold, damp concrete floor while the one with the knife loomed over him. He hadn't seen his eyes, but he'd heard his hollow laugh right before the sound of the vicious click of the blade coming out of its home made him stiffen in sheer terror.

How many nights since then had he lay on the hard floor listening to the screams of the most recent victim of the initiation into Nil? How many times had he heard the click of the knife and the tortured moments of silence just before the first cut?

Amon ran his fingertips over the scars on his right shoulder, evidence of his welcome to this place. If that had been all they'd done, he could know he'd survived and not be laid out on the floor of his cell praying for death to at least escape this lifetime, his mind unable to imagine the three future lifetimes ahead of him in this Hell.

He'd changed in his time in Nil. Naturally lean, he now rippled with muscle, a result of the only activity he was allowed other than work. The prisoners were encouraged to be bigger and stronger to survive, but years and lifetimes of experience and rage easily overwhelmed his newer, muscular body. In time, he'd rise to the higher ranks of the prisoners, but for now, just a year into his sentence, Amon remained at the very bottom, vulnerable to attack at any time.

And the attacks came often. Mostly at night, after hours of backbreaking labor when he'd give anything for just a few moments of rest and peace. Fists that pummeled his ribs and tore his muscles, trying to break him.

As he struggled to sit up, he had no idea what had been damaged that night. His right leg may have been broken. He didn't know. All he felt was blinding pain just below his knee. Blood slowly trickled into his mouth from beneath his left eye, and he tasted the familiar tang of it on his tongue. The eye continued to swell so that now he only saw clearly with the right one.

The only thought that stayed in his mind was the one he had each night when he was finally alone.

God, let me pass out and never wake again.

"MASTER? PLEASE ANSWER," A VOICE said plaintively.

Amon heard a voice he was sure couldn't be near and cursed his mind for playing tricks on him. Struggling to open his left eye, he slowly lifted his head toward the sound of his servant's voice. To his left Gethen stared in fear at him.

Barely able to speak, Amon hoarsely whispered, "Gethen? Are you here?"

"I'm here, master," he answered, his voice full of emotion.

Amon's eyes filled with tears at the knowledge that he wasn't alone. He couldn't remember feeling more joy at the sight of another ever in all his lifetimes.

Gethen gently ran his hand over his head, and Amon saw by the sadness on his face that he remembered how he'd looked before being sent to this place. With his hands on the sides of Amon's face, he wiped away the blood that ran from the gash under his eye with his thumb, staying away from the swelling that had closed the eye completely.

Amon savored the warmth of Gethen's skin on his and leaned his cheek into his right palm, thankful for a touch of kindness after so long. If he died now, at least the last moments of this lifetime had been spent with one who cared for him. Closing his eyes, he began to slip into unconsciousness, happy to have Gethen with him once again at the end of a lifetime.

"Master, please don't leave me! I'm here to take you home!"

Amon struggled to remain alert, his eyelids fluttering as he tried to focus.

Home?

"Master...Amon, put your arms around me so we can leave."

He moved to crouch between Amon's legs as he tried to lift his arms but failed. "I can't do this if you aren't touching me." Gingerly, he took his hands and placed one hand and then the other around his waist.

"I need you to stand up. Can you do that?"

Slowly shaking his head, Amon's gaze traveled to his right leg. Gethen reached out and gently ran his palm over the pant leg, causing Amon to wince and softly cry out in pain.

"Okay. Just hold on to me and don't let go."

Amon kept his hands around his servant's waist and rested his head on his chest. He felt Gethen's hand lightly stroke the back of his head, and the rhythmic sound of his heartbeat in his ear lulled him.

"Stay with me, Amon. I'm going to get you out of here."

His eyes closed, he heard his servant whisper, "Please, let this work."

The sound of a guard's footsteps coming down the hallway made Amon stiffen, and he lifted his head off Gethen's chest, knowing that if they caught his servant, they'd kill him.

"Gethen, go! I can't let them find you here."

He began to release his hands from around his waist, but Gethen grabbed them and held them fast to him. "Don't let go! The only way I leave here is with you!"

Fully conscious and working on adrenaline, Amon wrapped his arms tightly around Gethen. If they killed him, he still had three more lifetimes he'd willingly give up, but Gethen wasn't Aeveren and his death would be final. He had to make sure he escaped.

The noise drew closer, and slowly Gethen began to change to mist as he reminded Amon to hold on to him, no matter what. As they left Nil, Amon breathed a sigh of relief and felt himself begin to slip away.

MOMENTS LATER, GETHEN REAPPEARED SAFELY on the mountaintop, but he looked down in horror at the body of the man in his arms. Amon, unconscious, slid out of his grasp to the ground below him. Gethen fell to the ground next to him, devastated what he'd feared had happened. Because he was Aeveren, the journey between worlds had been too much for Amon.

"Markku! Give me your coat!"

"What happened?" he asked frantically. "I swear I did everything right, Gethen."

Gethen draped the coat over Amon's shirtless body. "Coming from Nil to this world was too much for him. We need to get him to the house. And when we get there, I need you to do another spell to make sure no one can find him there."

Markku nodded and helped Gethen to his feet.

"Can you carry him? I'm too weak," Gethen said as he looked down sadly at Amon.

Bending down, Markku lifted Amon and quickly began to make his way to the house. As he walked, Amon opened his eyes and mumbled Gethen's name before fading out again.

"Don't worry, big guy. The old man got back A-OK."

As Markku approached Amon's house, Gethen stopped him and took his master's body into his arms. Turning to Markku, he nodded in the direction of the town. "After you do whatever you need to do so he'll be hid, I need you to find a healer."

"I don't know where any are, though."

Gethen glared over the still body in his arms, forcing Markku to step back.

"Okay. I get it. Find one!"

Gethen left Markku outside performing his spell and took Amon to his bedroom on the second floor. Carefully, he removed Markku's coat and laid Amon on the bed. He remained unconscious, and in the light of the room, Gethen once again studied the effects of Nil evident on his body. The former beauty of his master was absent, replaced with muscle, scars, and fresh injuries.

Weakened by the rescue himself and now nauseous from the evidence of the violence he saw Amon had suffered, he stumbled back into a chair beside the bed and rested comfortably for the first time in almost a year, hoping that his weakness was merely overexertion and not something more.

Hours later, he awoke to find Amon still unconscious and no sign of Markku. His immediate reaction was to threaten the missing man, but Gethen stopped himself. Markku had successfully protected Amon on the trip back from Nil; he wasn't still unconscious because of any failure of Markku's. Gethen knew the journey from one world to the other might hurt him, but there was no true safeguard against that. Amon was Aeveren, unlike him, and they didn't move between worlds easily.

Markku would return with the healer soon. Literally, his future happiness depended on it. Still exhausted, Gethen settled back into the chair and with heavy eyes watched his master sleep. He'd done it. He'd saved Amon as he'd done for him so many years ago.

But would Amon ever be the same after what had happened to him in Nil?

CONTINUE THE DESTINED ONES DUOLOGY WITH
DESTINY REDEEMED TODAY!
AVAILABLE AT ALL MAJOR RETAILERS

ABOUT THE AUTHOR

K.M. Scott writes contemporary romance stories of sexy, intense, and unforgettable love. A New York Times and USA Today bestselling author, she's been in love with romance since reading her first romance novel in junior high (she was a very curious girl!). She lives in Pennsylvania with her teenage son and a herd of animals and when she's not writing can be found reading or feeding her TV addiction.

Be sure to visit K.M.'s Facebook page at facebook.com/kmscottauthor for all the latest on her books, along with giveaways and other goodies! And to hear all the news on K.M. Scott books first, sign up for her newsletter today and be sure to visit her website at www.kmscottbooks.com.

BOOKS BY K.M. SCOTT:

Crash Into Me (Heart of Stone #1)

Fall Into Me (Heart of Stone #2)

Give In To Me (Heart of Stone #3)

The Heart of Stone Trilogy Box Set

Ever After (Heart of Stone #4)

A Heart of Stone Christmas (Heart of Stone #5)

Unforgettable (Heart of Stone #6)

Temptation (Club X #1)

Surrender (Club X #2)

Possession (Club X #3)

Satisfaction (Club X #4)

Silk (Volume One)

Silk (Volume Two)

Silk (Volume Three)

Silk (Volume Four)

SILK Box Set

K.M.'S BOOKS ARE IN AUDIOBOOK TOO!

BOOKS BY GABRIELLE BISSET:

Vampire Dreams Revamped (A Sons of Navarus Prequel)

Blood Avenged (Sons of Navarus #1)

Blood Betrayed (Sons of Navarus #2)

Longing (A Sons of Navarus Short Story)

Blood Spirit (Sons of Navarus #3)

The Deepest Cut (A Sons of Navarus Short Story)

Blood Prophecy (Sons of Navarus #4)

The Sons of Navarus Box Set #1

The Sons of Navarus Box Set #2

Blood Craving (Sons of Navarus #5)

Stolen Destiny (Destined Ones Duology #1)

Destiny Redeemed (Destined Ones Duology #2)

Love's Master

Masquerade

The Victorian Erotic Romance Trilogy